Winding Back the Clock

Winding Back the Clock

by Ian Laurence

AuthorHouse™
1663 Liberty Drive
Bloomington, IN 47403
www.authorhouse.com
Phone: 1-800-839-8640

This is a work of fiction. All of the characters, names, incidents, organizations, and dialogue in this novel are either the products of the author's imagination or are used fictitiously.

© 2012 by Ian Laurence. All rights reserved.

No part of this book may be reproduced, stored in a retrieval system, or transmitted by any means without the written permission of the author.

Published by AuthorHouse   09/11/2012

ISBN: 978-1-4772-2982-8 (sc)
ISBN: 978-1-4772-2983-5 (hc)
ISBN: 978-1-4772-2984-2 (e)

Any people depicted in stock imagery provided by Thinkstock are models, and such images are being used for illustrative purposes only.
Certain stock imagery © Thinkstock.

This book is printed on acid-free paper.

Because of the dynamic nature of the Internet, any web addresses or links contained in this book may have changed since publication and may no longer be valid. The views expressed in this work are solely those of the author and do not necessarily reflect the views of the publisher, and the publisher hereby disclaims any responsibility for them.

PROLOGUE

Silesia is a region of Central Europe, at the present time located for the most part in Poland, with small areas in Germany and the Czech Republic. Over the past one thousand years, the borders of Silesia and its rulers have changed many times. Most recently, Silesia was conquered by Prussia in 1742 and remained under German rule until the end of the first world war, when the eastern portion of Upper Silesia was ceded to Poland.

In 1939, this area of Upper Silesia was the first to be invaded by the Germans and the Poles repatriated. After the second world war, the reverse occurred. Virtually the whole of Silesia was ceded to Poland and all ethnic Germans evicted.

The historical capital of Silesia is Wroclaw, known to the Germans as Breslau, and one of the main land-owning dynasties in this area was the Schimonsky family, the most famous member of which being Emanuel von Schimonsky, who became Prince-Bishop in 1824.

The Schimonsky family was evicted from its lands after the implementation of the decisions of the Potsdam Conference in 1945 and one branch of the family was resettled in Weimar in the state of Thuringia. Two brothers, Oskar and Stefan, became prominent members of the STASI, the secret police of the newly formed East German State, the DDR. The brothers were determined that their homeland should be returned to Germany and the Schimonsky lands reclaimed.

CHAPTER 1

Katie Talbot sat on the low, grey stone wall that was rough and uneven and mostly overgrown with moss and lichen and wandering strands of bindweed and ivy. This solitary wall was all that remained standing of her ancestral home. Below Katie's feet was the exposed labyrinth of the cellars, which corresponded in area to the plan of the house. But, tragically, what was also revealed was the secret extension to the cellars in the furthermost corner, where the accumulated treasures of generations had been hidden before the onset of the Second World War.

Katie sighed and lifted her gaze to scan the vast acres of the old family estate, which from this vantage point stretched in every direction as far as the eye could see. The house was perched high on the *Kreiderfelsen*, the chalk cliffs that dominate the east coast of the island of Rügen. Katie shielded her eyes from the sun as she looked away to her right, to a place that had special significance for the family. At this point of the coastline the cliffs had an interlude, where a narrow spit of land called the Schaabe separated the inland waters of the Bodden from the bay. It was from this bay that her parents had made their escape in a small boat as the Russians approached. It was the end of an era and a dynasty.

The cliffs then continued to end at Kap Arkona, the north-eastern corner of the island, and Katie could make out the two lighthouses; the squat, short, original light and the modern, thinner, much taller one. Beyond the land the waters of the Baltic Sea shimmered in the afternoon sun, calm and uncharacteristically benign. The next point of land was Sweden, which the boat had reached safely. From Sweden the young couple then went to the United States where, fifty years ago, Katie had been born. If it had not been for Hitler and the Third Reich, this would have been her home. She would have grown up in this outpost of Germany, living the life of the wealthy, landed gentry.

With another long sigh, Katie got up from the wall and walked away from the ruin and down a narrow country lane, lined with blackthorn and honeysuckle and alive with the hum of insects. The lane wound down the hill and led to a pretty little house with a thatched roof and stone walls that were covered with climbing roses in full bloom; pink and white and obscuring most of the windows. It had formerly been a tied cottage, belonging to the family estate.

A frail old woman leaning on a stick stood in the open doorway that faced up the lane and Katie had been aware of the old woman, watching and waiting, as she approached.

Katie stepped through the garden gate that was secured open on a latch and advanced to offer the old woman her hand. The woman was wearing a cotton dress in a faded print and despite the warmth of the day had covered her shoulders with a white shawl, crocheted in a loose weave and with a tasselled border.

'*Guten Tag,* Frau Weber,' Katie said formally.

The old woman offered her a limp hand and her lined face cracked into a half smile of welcome. '*Guten Tag,* Gräfin von Arnitz.' The old woman made a slight deferential bob in honour of the family, her former employers and benefactors that had ruled the estate for three centuries.

'I saw you up by the *Schloss,*' said Frau Weber in a high-pitched, quavering voice. 'I would recognize your hair anywhere. Please come in. I have just made tea. And perhaps you would like a piece of *Pflaumenkuchen.* I made it myself this morning. The plums have been exceptionally good this year.'

'That would be most kind.'

Katie was ushered into a small living room that seemed very dark after the bright sunshine outside. The windows were small with heavy curtains and the size of the room was diminished by what the Germans call *massiv Möbel*. There were large dark oak chairs with chintz fabric upholstery and a refectory table stood in the centre of the room.

'Please make yourself comfortable while I get the tea.' Frau Weber disappeared into the kitchen and Katie looked around the room with a lump in her throat. There were framed photographs everywhere; on the walls and on every available surface. The photographs were mostly in black and white and many were cracked and faded with age. Katie knew that several of the photographs were of her immediate family; her parents and grandparents and their relations and the army of retainers, including a very young Frau Weber. Katie's parents had managed to flee, but the majority of the rest had perished, during and after the conflict.

Frau Weber came back into the room, carrying a tray of tea and two portions of cake. 'You found it necessary to return?' This was phrased as a question, rather than a statement. 'To reflect? After all these years?'

'Yes, I suppose it must be a long time. Because my previous visit was shortly after the *Wende*. But I came to visit you. Not to have melancholy and be depressed about the house.'

Frau Weber looked at her in surprise. 'Why would you want to visit me?'

Katie reached inside the cotton bag she had brought with her and took out a manila folder. From the folder she extracted a photograph. 'Do you recognize this man?'

Frau Weber fetched her spectacles from the top of the dresser. She then squinted at the photograph with a puzzled expression. It was a portrait of a middle-aged man, smiling seductively at the camera. He had a full head of black, shiny hair and his face had the square jaw that is typical of eastern Europeans. Above the photograph was the heading of a dating agency called Happy Days, wording that was lost on Frau Weber.

'He's vaguely familiar,' Frau Weber said at first, but then her face took on a look of astonishment and loathing. '*Mein Gott!* It can't be. Yes, he looks so much older, but it must be. It must be the Stefan.' Frau Weber handed the photograph back to Katie with a trembling hand.

Katie nodded. 'Stefan Schimonsky. That's who I thought it was. You told me about him on my last visit. Thank you for confirming his identity. Now tell me if you recognize anything else.'

Frau Weber took the photograph again. Suddenly she stiffened. 'Oh, *Mein Gott im Himmel!* The ring! It is the von Arnnitz ring!' The man was sitting at a desk with his hands clasped in front of him. '*Was eine Frechheit!* How dare he wear the family ring!'

'I agree. The impertinence makes me very angry.' Katie went to the mantelpiece and took down a photograph of a young couple; her mother and father. Katie's father was standing behind her mother with his hand on her shoulder. Together the two women compared the ring on the fingers of Katie's father and the man in the photograph. The gold ring was wide and heavy and the seal of the family crest was quite visible.

'It is the same.' Frau Weber was still trembling with indignation.

'I agree. It is the same ring. And I know that this ring was part of the family valuables left in the secret cellar. My parents had not dared to take anything of value with them. They were supposed to be poor people out fishing.'

'Then this really is the Stefan.' Frau Weber's voice was full of loathing. 'I was hoping never to see, or hear of him again.'

'I came upon him purely by chance.' Katie put away the photograph. 'His present name is Steven Jackson. He must have changed his name when he moved to England.'

'So where is he now?' Frau Weber asked.

'He is a ship-broker and property developer in the city of London. I got to know of him through an agency that introduces single people to each other. But his biography from the agency says nothing about his early life. Only since he arrived in England in 1990.'

'That Stefan was a dreadful fellow.' Frau Weber took off her spectacles and sat on a chair opposite Katie. 'I knew he was up to no good as soon as I saw him. Those small piggy eyes and that shiny hair. And his brother, Oskar, always so smooth talking and condescending. The Schimonsky brothers.' Frau Weber shivered and fished a handkerchief from her apron pocket to wipe away a tear. 'They tortured and killed my husband.'

'They took you away as well, didn't they?' Katie said softly.

Frau Weber nodded sadly. 'After the DDR was established, the STASI took over the *Schloss* as their headquarters. But it wasn't a problem. They didn't bother with us. That is, until the Schimonsky brothers arrived.'

'When was that? In the 80s?'

'It was the first of July 1986. The date is etched in my memory. They started throwing their weight around almost immediately. Interrogating people. And then they took me and Artur to the prison in Stralsund.'

'That must have been terrible,' said Katie. Somehow, somewhere, the Schimonsky brothers must have got wind of the treasures. 'But you survived?'

'They only kept me for a week. Never interrogated me. I expect they got what they wanted from Artur.' Frau Weber snivelled into her handkerchief. 'Sent me back.'

'And you never saw your husband again?' Katie felt it was not necessary, or appropriate, to state the obvious. That Artur had divulged the whereabouts of the cellar.

'No. And they wouldn't give me any information.'

'Not even the return of his body?'

'No. And after the *Wende* it was the same. They destroyed all the records.'

'Very unsatisfactory,' said Katie. 'You have my every sympathy.'

Frau Weber sighed. 'So what happens next? What are you going to do?'

'I'm going to find out from Stefan where the treasures have gone and get them back.' Katie paused. 'Isn't it strange? After all this time, suddenly, some clues are appearing.' Katie then reached inside her bag again to produce a glossy magazine. 'This is a catalogue of paintings to be offered for sale by Sotheby's. A big New York auction house.' Katie opened the catalogue at one of the pages and passed it to Frau Weber. 'Do you recognize this?'

This time Frau Weber nodded immediately. 'Of course. It's the Titian. It hung in the main staircase of the house. I remember it being taken down to be hidden in the cellars.'

'I thought you would be able to confirm it.' Katie took a clutch of old photographs from her bag and selected one. She showed it to Frau Weber. 'This is the photograph of the painting that my father took before he left.'

Frau Weber nodded. 'It is the same.' She then looked at the photograph more closely and her face cracked into a smile. 'You can still see where the painting had to be repaired. I was in the house when your grandfather's gun went off by accident and the bullet went through the painting in that top left hand corner.'

Katie smiled too. 'I remember my father telling me about that. So, I'm glad that you agree that this is the same painting.' Katie closed the catalogue and sat back in her chair. 'I have been looking out for our treasures coming up for sale ever since I came with my parents, that day soon after the fall of the communist state.' Katie paused, suddenly overcome with emotion. 'I will never forget my parents' faces when they saw the house destroyed and the treasures gone.'

This time it was Frau Weber who put a hand on Katie's arm to console her.

Katie took out a tissue and blew her nose hard. 'But, let us be thankful. At last something has happened. And now we have two leads.'

'Do we know who is selling the painting?' Frau Weber enquired.

Katie looked at the blurb. 'The catalogue has no mention of the identity of the vendor.' Katie smiled. 'I should like to see what they offer as the provenance.'

'Can you make a claim of ownership?' Frau Weber asked.

'I am certainly going to make a claim. But I have no documentary evidence and so it would probably have to be decided by the courts. You are the only living witness and so I hope you would be willing to testify if it comes to that.'

'Of course I would be willing to do that. That's no problem. But it's that man that I would be worried about.' Frau Weber shivered again. 'If that man really is Stefan Schimonsky, you must be terribly careful.'

Katie smiled grimly. 'Don't worry. I will be. But now is the time for action.'

#

The trip had been worthwhile. With Frau Weber's confirmation, the two leads now had more substance and Katie was already deciding on the follow-up. She crossed over the Rügenbrücke into Stralsund and stopped to fill up her rental car. Back in 1990, when she had visited with her parents, a full tank had been essential, as at that time there were no petrol stations between the coast and Berlin. And now it was autobahn all the way, instead of the narrow and twisty coast road between the Hanseatic cities of Rostock and Stralsund that had taken for ever to drive along. But thinking of these changes was, in a way, depressing, as it brought awareness of the passage of time.

She could now pin-point the disappearance of the treasures to 1986. After all these years, was it hopeless? The Titian had turned up in New York. And the rest? All over the world? As she drove into the sunset, these thoughts just emphasized the size of her task.

#

After Katie had departed, Frau Weber went outside to call in her son who had been working in one of the outbuildings and to tell him all that she had discussed with Katie.

'The countess is convinced that this Steven Jackson is one of the Schimonsky brothers. The STASI men who killed your father.' Frau Weber's voice had a catch. 'You must do your best to try and find him. This man must be destroyed. Maybe he will lead us to his brother and we can destroy him as well. And if we gain some of the family treasure along the way, we will have deserved it. We have suffered enough.'

Detlef Weber went back to his workshop deep in thought. So, after all this time, the countess had discovered the identity of one of the Schimonsky brothers. The countess was only concerned with recovering the family treasures, but the information for Detlef had an entirely different meaning.

Ever since the fall of communism and the disappearance of the STASI agents from the estate, Detlef had been determined to find the men who had tortured and murdered his father.

He had firstly gone to Berlin, to visit the STASI headquarters in the Normannenstrasse, to see what information he could find, as citizens had been given the right to examine the files. But as far as discovering information about the Schimonsky brothers, this had been disappointing. Detlef was able to examine his own file, the existence of which he was absolutely certain, as the vast majority of the population of the DDR had had a file with the STASI. The file mainly documented his exploits as an athlete, but there were also an unbelievable number of pages detailing trivia about his private life. The fact that he had never married and whether he was a homosexual was commented upon several times The only interesting information he had gleaned was that he now knew who had informed on him. This included his old schoolteacher and the local postman. So what, thought Detlef. There was no point holding a grudge against them. That was how things had been in the DDR. So many people were frightened and felt they had to conform to the system.

But there was no way of getting information about the STASI hierarchy and the agents who ran Rügen. Detlef presumed that, in any case, all documentation relating to important officials had been shredded as the regime fell in 1989. Hundreds of sacks containing shredded documents had been found in the cellars of the STASI headquarters and these documents were being reconstituted in Nuremburg. A new computer programme was speeding up the task, but Detlef doubted that anything would ever come of it.

But now, at last, he had a lead. He needed some help and advice and he knew where to find it.

CHAPTER 2

Katie alighted from the bus at Lehniner Platz and walked the short distance to the Markgraf Albrecht Strasse, a side street off the Kurfürstendamm, the main thoroughfare of West Berlin. The narrow street was lined with mature lime trees, which, because of the continuous good weather without rain, had left everywhere with a coating of gum. The cars that had been parked for some time had lost their shine and the pavement felt sticky underfoot.

Professor Manfred Ahrens answered the front door of the apartment block himself, instead of just pressing the release button.

'Good afternoon, countess.' The professor made a little bow as he shook hands. 'How pleased I am to see you. I live on the first floor, what we used to call the *belle étage*. I suggest we take the stairs. There is an elevator, but I never use it. It is the original and is very unreliable. This building dates from 1911. Almost every week someone gets stuck in the elevator and Herr Gersonde, who lives in the ground floor apartment, has to crank the elevator car down again. Very tiresome.'

Katie followed the professor through the wide, wood-panelled hallway and up the stairs. The professor had to rest at the first landing.

'Not as young as I was,' he apologized. 'I am waiting for a hip replacement.'

Katie knew that the professor had been retired for some years and he looked his age. He was short and of slight build with sharp features and a full head of white hair. Despite his lack of mobility, he looked in good health, although his skin was very pink and flaky, a common problem with old men, requiring him to stay out of the direct sun at all times.

'I love the apartment,' said Katie, looking around her as she was ushered into one of the reception rooms.

'Mostly original,' said the professor proudly, supporting himself on the back of an armchair. 'Typical of the *art nouveau* period. Just one ceiling was damaged in the war. The other decorated ceilings are original, as are the mouldings and the architraves and the stained glass panels in the doors.'

'Impressive.' Katie meant the architecture, not the artwork on the walls that she found disconcerting. Every single painting, print and photograph depicted naked female figures, some in very erotic and revealing poses.

Katie took a seat on a sofa as the professor sat opposite her. 'Thank you for agreeing to see me, professor.'

'The pleasure is all mine, countess. It is an honour to entertain a member of our aristocracy.'

Katie smiled 'We do not have the status that we used to have.'

Professor Ahrens also smiled. 'Nevertheless. And you speak such perfect German. For an American. And with such a wonderful upper class Prussian accent.'

'My parents only spoke German at home. So German was my mother tongue until I went to school in Boston at the age of six.'

'So that explains it. How interesting. Now. To business. You were recommended to see me by Fred Nightingale in London. He is also an authority on sixteenth century art.'

'He seemed to be very knowledgeable, but he said you know more about Titian than anybody else.'

'I have indeed made the work of Tiziano Vecelli a speciality of mine,' said the professor proudly. 'So, tell me. What do you know about the great man?'

'That he was a Venetian and was born at the end of the fifteenth century. And, of course, most of his paintings have a religious theme.'

'Quite so. Have you ever been to Venice?'

Katie shook her head. 'No. But I would very much like to.'

'If you get the chance, you must take it. It is such a beautiful city. But a visit these days can be ruined by there being so many other tourists. May is probably the best month. The weather is kind and it is before the summer vacation period. If you go, you must see my very favourite painting by Titian. It is a painting of the Assumption on the high altar of the church of Santa Maria dei Frari. It is magnificent.'

'I know that it is one of his most famous paintings,' said Katie. 'And very large.'

'It is, believe it or not, about seven metres tall,' said the professor. 'And took over two years to complete. It is what we call a landmark painting. By that, I mean that the artist is showing his subjects in ways that were quite new. Here, Titian is portraying the virgin not just as a human being, but one destined for the presence of God. It combines the earthly with the heavenly. The virgin is being launched from the darkness of her tomb into a blaze of light.'

'I hope to see it some day,' Katie smiled. 'But I came to see you today to discuss another of his paintings.'

'Indeed.' Professor Ahrens picked up a catalogue, the same one that Katie had shown Frau Weber. 'The Death of St Peter Martyr. In 1867 it was supposed to have been destroyed by the fire in the Cappella del Rosario,' the professor had a dry laugh,

'but it was in Vienna all along. My, my. I wonder how many other supposedly lost paintings are reposing in private collections?'

'Quite,' said Katie with a grim expression.

'I mentioned the Assumption just now, because The Death of St Peter Martyr has also been called a landmark painting. It was painted in 1530, fourteen years later, and Titian has moved on. With these trees blowing in the wind,' the professor pointed to the picture, 'Titian is introducing a sense of *movement* and it is as if the trees are being involved with the murderer and his accomplice in the enormity of the occasion. And, in fact, it was the first time that such an act of violence had been seen in an altarpiece.' The professor frowned. 'I agree with the criticism at the time. The subject is not something I think of as being appropriate in such a location.'

'I hadn't realized that this painting was so important,' said Katie.

'Indeed it is. So, this is a remarkable example of Titian's work.' The professor put down the catalogue to give Katie a wry smile. 'And it is so seldom that these paintings come up for sale. Most of Titian's paintings are in museums and national galleries and churches and so this is a rare treat indeed. And, of course, its value is immense, almost without price. At auction, my estimate would be at least fifty million dollars. Which means it will probably go to the Getty Museum, the Clark Institute, or some other wealthy American foundation.'

'As you know, professor, I believe this painting belonged to my family and was looted from the ancestral home on Rügen.' Katie reached in her bag to produce the faded black and white photograph. 'My father took this photograph when the painting was hidden with the rest of our treasures before he and my mother escaped to America.'

Professor Ahrens took the photograph and went over to the window to see it more clearly. Then he examined it closely with a magnifying glass. 'It is the same painting, no doubt. But this photograph does not prove your ownership.' He smiled. 'Anyone could have taken it at any time and it does not show the location.'

'This painting was given to my great-grandmother by the Empress Elizabeth of Austria in 1897. Just before the empress was assassinated. My great-grandparents were frequent visitors to the Imperial court in Vienna.'

'Ah poor Sissi. That was a tragedy And then her cousin was also assassinated. Do you ever wonder how life would have been if those events had not taken place? And the first world war had never happened? A world war that set the pattern for the next?'

'In my opinion, the first world war would have happened anyway,' Katie countered. 'It was the Kaiser that was the problem. He was determined to exert German dominance. Especially over the British. And strange, as he was a grandson of Queen Victoria.'

'I know that view is becoming more accepted,' said the professor, with a frown. 'It was expounded very forcefully in the film that was part of the recent exhibition 'Vicky and the Kaiser'. But I must say that I was not convinced.'

'I think it also stems from his birth in England,' said Katie. 'It was difficult and resulted in him having a withered arm. Maybe that is what made him hate England.'

'Yes. Yes. Maybe,' said the professor.

'But, of course, you are right.' said Katie. 'I would have been brought up on Rügen, instead of in America. I often think of that period in our history.'

'So do I,' professor Ahrens sighed. 'So do I. Now, I understand that you have no proof that the empress gave this painting to your great-grandmother?'

'No.'

'That is a shame and the crux of this claim of yours. It could be, of course, that the transfer of ownership was officially recorded by the palace and the documentation was lost in the war. Which is very probably the case. And very bad luck. If we had that official documentation, it would obviously give your claim more credence.'

'Professor Ahrens, I really need some advice as to what to do next. I was hoping that this photograph and the corroboration of an ex-housemaid, who remembers the painting hanging in the hallway of our house up to the outbreak of war, would constitute a claim.'

'Hmm.' The professor scratched his chin thoughtfully. 'I am afraid, countess, that this evidence may not be enough. An old woman's memory may not be thought to be reliable after such a long period of time. Documentation is everything.'

'So I suppose the question is whether I consider legal action,' said Katie. 'There have been several cases recently where the courts have decided on ownership, particularly concerning works of art stolen by the Nazis.'

'Indeed,' agreed the professor,' but in these cases there was good documentary evidence as to whom the original owners were.'

'Then I will have to consult lawyers in New York,' said Katie. 'and get their opinion.'

'And you had better make the auction house aware of your claim to ownership,' said the professor.

'Do you know who is selling this painting?'

'I have only recently received my catalogue and so I have not had time to find out any details. The auction house will give you all the information you need.'

'Might I suggest that any provenance provided after the dates we have mentioned would be a forgery?'

'From your point of view, yes, it would be,' said the professor.

'And I could, of course, examine this provenance?'

'Most certainly. Sotheby's are obliged to give you full details of the history of the painting available to them and the name of the present owner.'

'I will ask,' said Katie, 'and I shall do as much research as I can into the provenance they supply.'

'One thing has struck me,' said the professor. 'The painting is in remarkably good condition. Seeing that it is five hundred years old. I would have thought that if it had been in a cellar for forty of those years it might have shown some deterioration. This fact might contradict your claim.'

'My family packed it very securely. And the house was high on the chalk cliffs. The cellars were always bone dry. And my grandfather made some ventilation shafts into the cellar.'

'Then all I can say, countess, is that I hope your claim is successful.'

#

The man knew that the caller to his apartment in New York would be German. The number of this telephone was only known to colleagues in Germany.

'*Ja?*' he said softly.

'It is as I suspected. The countess came to see me today. She will probably contest the provenance of the Titian.'

'Does she have a case?'

'I am not sure. She has a photograph that her father took. This photograph could have been taken anywhere at any time. What is more worrying is the testimony of an old retainer. She remembers the painting being in the house and being stored in the cellar just before the war. But the quality of her memory after seventy years when she was a young servant must be questionable.'

'And you found no records in Vienna?'

'No. Most of the records of the palaces in Vienna were lost or destroyed in the war. There is no record of the Titian being given to the von Arnitz family.'

'But that is not a problem. We acknowledge that the painting was owned by the von Arnitz family.'

'Correct,' said the professor. 'But the question may arise as to whether Count von Arnitz had the authority to sell the painting.'

'I see your point.'

'But may I remind you, that this public sale was totally unnecessary. The painting could have been placed privately with no attention being drawn to it. As we have done before. The countess would never have known.'

'I decided to take a chance because I will get significantly more at an auction. Every million extra will help me to finance my current project. Placing this painting at auction will achieve at least twice as much as a private placing. Lord Halifax is asking 65 million dollars for Portrait of a Young Man by Titian, which is at present on loan to the National Gallery in London. The Getty Museum paid 38 million dollars for a Titian in early 2005. I cannot afford to sell this painting cheaply.'

'I still say,' said the professor tetchily, 'as I did previously, that this public sale is much too risky. And the countess will now be able to learn your identity. I fear the worst.'

CHAPTER 3

'Katie, are you sure you know what you're doing?' Angela Johnson poured out two more glasses of wine. The two women, friends since college days at Yale, were having lunch in the restaurant on the top floor of Harvey Nichols department store in London's West End. 'If you go to the south of France with this guy, well, you're, you know, dammit Katie, you're more or less agreeing to have sex.'

'I know.' Katie bit her lip and frowned.

'Are you comfortable with that fact?'

'I think so.'

'Dammit Katie,' said Angela again, 'think so isn't good enough. You have to be sure.'

'Yes. OK. I'm sure.'

However, Katie was definitely not sure. She knew that she was being stupid and reckless. And that was why she had decided that she could not tell Angela the reason she was going to sacrifice herself. Sacrifice was probably the right word and she could only hope it would be worth it and she would find some of the treasures.

Steven Jackson was not the type of man to whom Katie would normally have been attracted, either physically or mentally. Steven was a big man, an inch or so over six feet and with heavy features and eyes set a little too close together. Also, he was not an intellectual. He had no interest in music, theatre or the arts and conversation was sometimes difficult. In fact, Katie knew that she and Steven had absolutely nothing in common whatsoever.

Katie could not imagine herself and Steven being compatible in bed. Katie had not had sex with a man since being divorced from her husband about a year ago. Nigel was of the same height as Steven, but slight of build and with delicate features. He was a very accomplished pianist and his thin sensitive fingers knew exactly how much pressure to bring to her erogenous zones, engaging in as much passion as he would if playing a Beethoven sonata. Katie imagined that with Steven it would be much more blunt and basic.

Bearing in mind Steven's past with the STASI, Katie knew that she was engaging in a high-risk strategy. But the DDR was a long time ago and Steven appeared to have become fully Westernised, even Anglicised. His CV listed him as being an enthusiast for cricket and he had been opening bat for a well-known amateur London side. But could Steven have changed that much? Katie knew she would have to be very, very careful.

Katie had spent a lot of time thinking about her friendship with Steven and if she was going to get any information from him there seemed to be no alternative but to continue the relationship. Steven was one of the links to the stolen treasures and this link had to be pursued. Every time she met Steven she was aware of her father's ring on his finger, a constant reminder of her quest, but she dare not mention it yet and any casual probing of Steven's past had proved useless. And Steven's reticence had been reciprocated. All Steven knew about Katie was that she was an American lawyer recently divorced from her English husband.

Steven had a beautiful apartment in Beaufort Gardens, a side street off the Brompton Road, close to Harrods department store. Katie had been there once; only briefly, but long enough to see that there were none of the family treasures on display. Steven also had a house in the south of France to which Katie had been invited for a long weekend. She just had to see if any of the treasures were there.

'Then are you sure that you're,' Angela paused and looked at Katie directly, 'up for it?' Then to add emphasis, she said, 'you were fifty last birthday.'

'I'm on HRT,' said Katie simply, by way of explanation.

'So what?' Angela snorted. 'You might still need some extra help. Could be embarrassing.'

'Angela, I'm sure I'll be fine.'

'I mean, what do you know about this guy? Do you know enough about him to trust him for a long weekend? He might be violent.'

Katie shrugged her shoulders. 'So far he's been absolutely charming. We have been on four dates so far. Twice to the theatre and twice to a restaurant for dinner. We had drinks at his apartment on one of those occasions. All that has happened so far is a goodnight kiss.'

'He's just grooming you. I still say he will be expecting full sex,' said Angela dismissively.

'I feel confidant I can deal with it,' said Katie firmly.

'I still don't know why to went to that dating agency,' Angela's tone was still disapproving. 'I'm convinced all the men on their books are perverts. They are just looking for easy sex. Once this guy gets his evil way with you, he will soon tire of you and dump you. Mark my words.'

'You still have a husband,' Katie retorted. 'I felt I needed some companionship.'

'Huh,' said Angela, as if that was not sufficient reason. Katie often wondered how much companionship Angela got from her husband. Hugo was a professor in Semitic languages at London University. He spent long periods away in Middle Eastern countries and even in term time was often away lecturing. But then Angela seemed to spend long hours in her office at the literary agency that she had started from scratch.

'Couldn't you have found someone at work?' Angela continued. 'Yours is a top law firm. Surely you could have found someone suitable there? And you must have made lots of contacts.'

'I'm afraid my age is against me.' Katie's voice had a tinge of sadness. 'All the unattached men, and the attached ones for that matter, want somebody younger. Forty seems to be the cut-off age.'

'Well, I don't understand it,' said Angela. 'You are slim, pretty, intelligent and very good company and you have such a wonderful asset with your gorgeous red hair. Men should be lining up at your door.'

Katie had always thought that Angela aspired to her physical characteristics. But Angela's genes were against her. Angela was a clone of her mother; small and dumpy and short-sighted. Her large spectacles with thick black rims did nothing for her appearance, neither did her mousy brown hair with the ever-present Alice band. 'Angela, it's just that men want younger women. It's a sex thing.'

'Like your husband Nigel,' said Angela with a curl of the lip. 'Running off with that little tramp. I must say, Katie, I never really liked him.'

Katie shrugged her shoulders again. 'We were very happy. While it lasted. At least he waited until the boys were grown up.'

'You hadn't thought of going back to Boston? You don't have to marry another Englishman. You might meet a nice American guy looking for someone as charming as yourself.'

'I had thought about that, but all my friends and family are here now. After my parents died I have no family in Boston.'

'Katie, all I can say is that I think you should not do this. It's far too risky. I am turning matchmaker. I am going to scour the whole of London to find you a mate.'

Katie smiled. 'Well, I appreciate that.'

'Then you can forget this whole south of France thing?'

Katie shook her head. 'It's just something I have to go through with. If it doesn't work out, I'll come back to you.'

CHAPTER 4

Detlef Weber had lived all his life on the island of Rügen, but he had visited Berlin many times. The train deposited him at the station for Zoologischer Garten in the centre of West Berlin, from where he could take the underground railway.

Throughout the journey, other travellers could not help but take notice of Detlef. He commanded a presence, for he was a big man, standing over six feet tall, broad and muscular. He was a carpenter by trade, but in his youth he had been an ironman, competing in triathlon at the standard distances, which were a 1.5km swim, a 40km bicycle ride and a 10km run. He achieved to such a level that he made the national squad and had taken part in the Olympics of 1984 at Los Angeles, although he had not won a medal. Detlef had also competed in biathlon, another demanding sport, involving cross-country skiing and rifle shooting. Now in his fifties, these days were long gone and his main exercise was hunting on foot for wild boar.

Detlef left the U Bahn at Strausberger Platz and emerged on to the Karl-Marx-Allee. This broad street, lined with trees and flanked by eight-story buildings, each one with a facing of white ceramic tiles, was a showpiece of reconstruction created by the government of the DDR in the 1950s. The street was originally named Stalinallee and gained notoriety on the 17th of June, 1953, when a worker uprising was put down by Russian tanks. And later it was used for the Mayday parades, demonstrating the military strength of the DDR.

Detlef found Marco's bar in a nearby side street and as soon as he entered he recognized Rainer Sampels, who hopped down from his stool to greet Detlef warmly with a hug and lots of back-slapping. Rainer was the fellow Olympian that Detlef had contacted. Rainer edited a newsletter for ex-Olympians of the DDR and had said that with his network of contacts he was sure that he could help Detlef in his quest.

In stature, Rainer was the opposite to Detlef, for he was short and thin, with close-cropped ginger hair and wire-framed glasses with circular lenses. He had been a gymnast and had won a gold medal at the Games in Los Angeles.

'Detlef! Large Kindl?'

'Thank you very much. My favourite.'

'OK. Let's find a corner.' Rainer picked up a *Krug* of beer in each hand and led the way to a secluded table. 'So. Sorry to hear about your mother. It must have been a great shock. And made quite a change in your life.'

'Totally,' said Detlef, with a sniff, fumbling for his handkerchief. 'As you know, my mother was everything to me.'

'Couldn't go on for ever, though, could it?' said Rainer, looking at Detlef nervously. 'She was, what, 94?'

'Right,' Detlef nodded. 'Doesn't make it any easier, though.'

'You found her?'

'I'd been out for the day. Came into the house and there she was. Middle of the kitchen floor. The doctor said it was a heart attack.'

'So. Natural causes,' said Rainer.

24

'Well,' Detlef paused. 'On the face of it. But I'm not hundred percent sure. OK, yes, she was 94 and very frail. However, she was in good health and good spirits on the morning of the day it happened.'

'Hmm,' mused Rainer. 'I get your drift. You think it was too much of a coincidence after the visit of the countess?'

'Rainer, I just don't know. Yes, maybe. My mother had agreed to testify about the painting.'

'You said that the countess was going to contest ownership?'

'Yes, and she said she was going to make enquiries straight away as the sale was already scheduled. The painting is expected to make a vast amount of money. The seller certainly would not want any problems of ownership.'

'And your mother was the last surviving witness?'

'She was the last surviving member of the staff.'

'I must say that it does seem a bit of a coincidence. Very timely and very suspicious,' said Rainer.

'I asked around,' said Detlef. 'We're a small community. We do get a lot of tourists, particularly visiting the *Kaiserstuhl* and the fishing village. But none of the neighbours had noticed any strangers, or anybody hanging around the house.'

'Very difficult to investigate, then.'

'Impossible,' agreed Detlef. 'OK, I know it may well have been natural causes, but I imagine it might be possible to induce a heart attack in a very old person. Like somehow giving them a severe shock.'

'We'll never know,' said Rainer. 'So, I suppose this means that the countess has nobody to back up her claim.'

'That's right. The painting is being sold in America fairly soon. I don't know what she will do now.'

'Legal action,' said Rainer. 'It always seems to come to that these days.'

'Probably,' Detlef agreed.

'The countess may have lost out, but she has led us to Stefan.'

'And you've found him?'

'I have,' said Rainer triumphantly. 'Having his new name and knowing that he lived in London made it easy. You remember Norbert Fischer? We used to call him Bert.'

'Of course I remember Bert. He won an Olympic silver at biathlon.'

'Bert now lives in London. He works in the City, not sure what he does, but it something to do with finance. Anyway, I asked Bert if he could help and he tells me that he has found out where Stefan lives.'

'Well, that's very good news,' said Detlef.

'I will give you Bert's address and phone number. Now, any ideas about dealing with Stefan?'

'No. It will depend on what I find. But I have been getting in some shooting practice.'

'Very good. Let's hope you can get a shot at him.'

'And if I do, I'm not going to miss.'

Rainer smiled. 'I'm sure you won't. You will have Bert to help if required. I wish you the best of luck.'

'Thank you. So how have you been, Rainer? You said life had been up and down.'

'Don't like to talk about it. I had a short spell in prison.'

'So what happened?'

'I was a salesman. Got mixed up with the wrong guys. We were selling investments, turned out that it was really a pyramid scheme. Fraud. Got a two year sentence.'

Detlef could not find a reply.

'Still, that's in the past. OK now. Things are much better. I have my own taxi firm. Wife and two kids.'

'Well, I'm pleased for you,' said Detlef. 'Do you hear anything of the other guys in our squad?'

Eventually the reminiscences dried up and Delef departed to retrace his journey as Rainer ordered another beer. Then, with a thoughtful expression, Rainer took out his telephone to make a local call.

'It's Rainer. I've just had a very good idea.'

CHAPTER 5

The Lear jet landed at Toulon at 3pm local time, having taken only two hours to fly the length of France from Farnborough. By the end of the flight, Katie had decided on her plan of action. And it stemmed from the first vital decision that she had made. There was no way she was going to have sexual relations of any kind with Steven. Her feelings had progressed from maybe to maybe not to definitely not.

Steven had become very drunk very quickly. The stewardess had served an excellent lunch of lobster salad, but the meal had been preceded and accompanied by champagne and Steven had consumed glass after glass. As the flight progressed, Steven had become more and more obnoxious, loudly bragging about his business exploits and any attempts that Katie made to change the subject had been in vain.

But what had really annoyed Katie had been Steven's persistent attempts at physical contact. It was as if it had already been agreed that sexual relations were going to take place and preliminaries could begin. At first there had been a hand on her shoulder, then an arm round her waist and then a hand on her knee and thigh. Katie had handled all these approaches with tact, either moving away or removing Steven's hand with polite firmness. It was Steven's clumsy attempt to fondle her breasts that had finally moved Katie's emotions to repulsion. Steven, she decided, was the most unpleasant man she had ever met.

So. The decision had been made. She would have a good look round the house and then leave, telling Steven that she never wanted to see him again. Whether or not there were any treasures in the house made no difference to this decision. She had brought all her credit cards and had quite enough money to make her own way back to London.

#

Henri, the local taxi driver from Grimaud, was waiting at the airport to greet them and load the bags into an ancient Peugeot. Steven was effusive in his welcome to Henri, a welcome that was reciprocated with a dour and resigned expression. It was obvious to Katie that Henri had experienced Steven before.

'So. Let me tell you about the house.' Steven had removed his jacket and tie, but was still sweating profusely. The old car had no air conditioning and the weather was typically provençal: a brilliant blue sky and the temperature in the thirties. Steven's hand was now glued to Katie's left knee and all attempts to remove it were in vain.

'Grimaud is a medieval hill village.' Steven found a handkerchief to mop his brow. 'Not to be confused with Port Grimaud, which is a fairly recent development on the coast. Built round canals for people with boats.'

'I have been down here before,' said Katie through thin lips.

'Of course, yes, of course.' Steven had started to sober up and sensed Katie's antagonism. He removed his hand from her knee. 'Well, yes, the house. Also medieval. It dates from sometime in the sixteenth century. I thought it too small and so I bought the place next door and knocked the two together. You'll like it.'

For the rest of the short journey Steven attempted to converse with Henri in very inadequate French until they climbed the hill and entered the narrow streets of the village, which in some places were only just wide enough for the car. Henri stopped outside a terraced house, completely blocking the street to other traffic. Katie got out the car and stood back to look at the house, which was built of the local stone, with wrought iron balconies and a vine covering much of the façade.

'Good view of the chateau,' said Steven. Opposite the house Katie could see the ruined chateau on top of the hill that dominated the village. 'Very picturesque,' Steven continued. 'We have *son et lumiere* performances throughout the summer.'

The overnight bags were carried into the house and Henri was paid off. Steven then took Katie on a tour of the house. All the rooms were small and with low ceilings. The staircases, one at either end of the converted house, were narrow, with stone steps in a tight spiral and with virtually no handrail. They looked very treacherous. Katie was impressed with the house and said so. Everything was immaculate and furnished in very good taste, but the whole house smelled a bit musty, which was not surprising if it was shut up for long periods.

'You've furnished it all very nicely,' said Katie, as they stood in the drawing room. 'Particularly in here, with the colour co-ordinated carpet and curtains.'

'I have to confess. I employed an interior designer.' Steven took her hand. 'What the house really needs from now on is a woman's touch. Someone who calls it home.'

'Quite.' Katie released her hand and made to leave the room, wishing she could say 'You'll be lucky'.

They continued their tour of the house, but Katie was again disappointed. There was nothing on display that was part of the treasures taken from Rügen. The whole trip had been a waste of time. And now she had the problem of dealing with Steven.

The tour ended on the second floor. Steven had carried both their overnight bags up the stairs and now deposited them in the main bedroom. Katie had become more and more anxious as the tour had progressed and this final act of Steven's meant that she had to leave right now.

'Steven,' Katie swallowed hard, 'I've changed my mind. I want to go home. I'll make my own way.'

Steven's face registered complete surprise. He stood looking at her for a moment as the words sank in. Then he sat on the bed with his head in his hands. 'Katie, I'm so sorry. I've been a complete bore. I apologize.' Steven looked up at her beseechingly. 'Can you forgive me and we can start over?'

'No. Steven, I'm sorry. My mind is made up.'

Steven remained sitting on the bed, still with his head in his hands. Katie made to pick up her bag and leave the room, but Steven suddenly stood up and barred her way. 'I'm not letting you go, Katie. I want you and I'm going to have you.'

A shiver ran down Katie's spine. She should have imagined this happening. She had been too complacent. She should have secured her exit before making her announcement, even left without Steven knowing. Doing the decent thing had been the wrong decision.

'You cannot stop me leaving, Steven.' Katie was trying to be equally firm, although now she was really frightened. This man had been a top STASI agent, albeit a long time ago, but Katie was now seeing the real Steven for the first time. His whole attitude towards her had changed. Any pretence at being caring and considerate had gone. Katie realized that she had messed up big time. 'I've said I'm sorry. It just isn't going to work out.'

'I'm going to have you, Katie.' This statement was delivered matter of fact. Steven looked at Katie directly, his face registering no emotion. The effects of the alcohol had now worn off and Steven's manner was cold and calculating. 'You can make it easy for yourself and submit. After which you are welcome to leave. Or,' Steven shrugged his shoulders, 'you can do it the hard way.'

'If you touch me, I will scream very loudly.' Katie was desperately trying to think her way out of the situation. How she was going to avoid being raped, because Steven was a big, strong man. A look around the bedroom gave her no inspiration. There was nothing that she could use to defend herself.

'Scream as much as you like.' Steven smiled. 'These walls are two feet thick. And the windows are double-glazed and locked. And don't think you can escape. There is only one door to this house. The one to the street and it is also locked.' Steven reached in his pocket and dangled a bunch of keys.

Katie opened her mouth to scream. She knew that she was in the middle of the village and hopefully somebody would hear her. But before she could utter a sound, Steven had closed the gap between them and put his hand over her mouth.

Katie bit his fingers as hard as she could.

'You bitch.' Steven now pinned Katie against the wall with one arm and then with his other hand ripped her blouse down the front, tearing off all the buttons. He then released his hold on her and with both hands tore off her bra as well. But this allowed Katie to escape from his grip and, now naked to the waist, she could run out of the bedroom and into the wide landing at the top of the stairs.

The landing was, in fact, quite a reasonable sized room, with a chest of drawers and two armchairs and a Persian rug on the tiled floor. Katie again looked round for anything that could be used as a weapon; anything that she could use to defend herself. But there was absolutely nothing she could see for that purpose.

Steven stood in the doorway of the bedroom, breathing hard. 'No escape, Katie.' His gaze now focused on her breasts. 'Katie, they're gorgeous. I knew they would be. Not too big, not too small. Still firm enough to have a bit of shape. And big nipples. I adore big nipples.'

Katie was also breathing hard. She made no attempt to cover herself and her look was one of contempt. 'I'm not giving in. If you want me you will have to kill me.'

'Kill you? Katie, I want to enjoy you alive. I am just going to restrain you. But first of all I want to see the rest of you. I want to see if the colour of your hair matches.'

Steven now made another move towards her, but Katie had been thinking. From way back, it must have been at college, she remembered one thing from talks on self-defence; that it was important to use the opponent's weight in your favour. Looking around the landing, there was a faint possibility that she could save herself.

As Steven approached her, a sadistic smile on his face, Katie made a dash for the stairs. She was wearing flat shoes with rubber soles and could get a grip on the tiled floor. Steven followed, a step or so behind, but then, at the head of the staircase, Katie suddenly stopped and turned around, ducked under Steven's outstretched arm and, pivoting, pushed him in the back with both hands as hard as she could.

This added momentum caused Steven to fall head first down the stone spiral staircase. There was no way he could save himself. There was an agonized yell, a loud thud and then complete silence.

Katie peered down into the gloom, her heart pounding and her bare breasts rising and falling with her deep breathing. All she could see were two motionless feet at the curve of the staircase. Then she suddenly became very weak and shivery and had to sit on one of the landing chairs.

After a minute or two, Katie had recovered some composure after the shock of her ordeal, but her hands were still trembling and her whole body felt weak and drained of energy. Her instinct was to get out the house as fast as she could, as Steven might recover and continue the attack. She went into the bedroom and took a fresh bra and blouse from her case. Speed was of the essence, but she was finding the buttons difficult, her fingers being shaky and fidgety.

Steven was still motionless. What if he was pretending to be injured? And when she examined him, he sat up and grabbed her? Katie gingerly descended the stairs and then took hold of one of Steven's feet and suddenly raised it. The leg was totally without tension. Katie had to conclude that Steven had been knocked unconscious. But then the thought struck her that Steven might have been killed in the fall, which meant that the police would be involved and she would have some explaining to do. It would also mean some unwelcome publicity.

Katie then, now feeling very frightened and with some difficulty and trepidation, manoeuvred herself past the body. To her intense relief, Steven did seem to be breathing and she could determine a pulse. She continued down the stairs to the front door and then realized it was locked, as Steven had boasted.

Back up the stairs and nothing had changed. Katie found the keys in Steven's jacket pocket and went back down to unlock the door. A blast of warm air rushed over her, bringing intense relief. She was free! Katie propped the door open with her case and flopped down onto a nearby chair.

With the knowledge that the ordeal was over, Katie was recovering fast. Her breathing and pulse had improved and her hands were no longer trembling. The question was: what to do next? She couldn't just go away and leave Steven unconscious on the stairs. Sit by the door, or, even better, outside the door, and wait for him to come to?

The minutes ticked by. A woman with two small children passed in the street. '*Bonjour*' the children cried in shrill voices, looking in at the doorway. Katie managed a thin smile and a feeble wave of the hand.

Still no sound from up the stairs. Katie idly turned over Steven's keys in her hand. There were only three. One to the outside door. The front door of the conjoined property had been made into a window and there was no back door, as the house was joined to the one behind it. One key was very small, probably for a drawer, or a cupboard. The third key seemed very similar to one of her own. It was long and double-headed, just like the one to the old safe in her hundred-year-old house in Fulham.

Where might a safe be? She was sitting in a small hallway and the next room was the study. The safe was probably in there. She had already seen that the room itself had no treasures on display, but what might the safe contain? And was there anything else of interest in the room if she delved around? A quick look up the stairs and Steven had not moved. Could she risk it? She might just have enough time to search the room and, most importantly, she had secured her exit.

As an extra precaution, Katie jammed a kitchen chair between the walls at the bottom of the staircase. That would give some early-warning.

Like the rest of the house, the study was neat and immaculately tidy. The bookshelves yielded nothing, neither did the desk. There was a desktop computer, but Katie knew that she did not have enough time to try and extract any information from it, had that been possible. So where was the safe?

It was not on display and so it had to be hidden somewhere. The floor was made of stone flags and there was nothing under the rug in the centre of the room. Katie then looked behind the pictures, the only other possibility. She was right. One of the paintings swung back on a hinge to reveal a wall safe.

The safe was divided into two compartments. On the top shelf were three neat piles of currency notes; euros, sterling and dollars. Katie did not touch the money, but she estimated that there was quite a lot. There were also two extra passports. One was German, the other Russian, and both were in the name of Stefan Schimonsky. Which was final confirmation of Steven's identity.

The lower compartment contained a handgun wrapped in a cloth, a box of ammunition and a manila folder. Katie took out the folder, but was disappointed to see it was only the deeds to the house and the plans for the recent conversion.

Feeling now very depressed that the safe had yielded nothing of interest, Katie was replacing the folder when she noticed a single sheet of paper on the floor of the compartment. She picked it up nonchalantly, but then stiffened in astonishment She could not believe her eyes. On the sheet of paper was printed a list; a list that she recognised immediately. It was a list of the most valuable paintings that had been hidden in the cellar on Rügen, headed by the Martyrdom of St Peter by Titian. It was a list that she had herself. But this list was different. It was annotated. Each item was followed by a series of letters, but these letters made no immediate sense. They would have to be looked at in detail later.

Hardly able to contain her excitement, Katie switched on the photocopier attached to the desktop computer and took a copy. Then she replaced the original and relocked the safe, hoping that she had left everything as she had found it.

Steven was still unconscious, which Katie thought was unusual. And worrying. Katie stood and looked down on Steven and wondered as to whether she should be feeling some remorse. But if she had not acted as she had done, Steven would have certainly raped her and maybe even killed her afterwards. It was legitimate self-defence.

Katie went back downstairs to sit on the chair by the door. Much as she wanted to, she could not leave the house with Steven still unconscious. With a resigned expression, she telephoned the emergency services to request an ambulance. The last thing she did was to remove her father's ring from Steven's finger and transfer it to her own.

#

Katie sat in an armchair in the sitting room, staring into space and unable to think, as the paramedics scurried in and out of the house carrying various items of equipment. Katie had explained to them that she had been in the bathroom when she had heard a noise and found Steven on the stairs. He must have tripped over the rug on the tiled floor.

Katie really did not want to be still in the house. She was feeling claustrophobic and trapped. As she had waited for the ambulance she had expected (and hoped) that the paramedics would just take Steven away to the hospital and she could make her way back to London. She did not feel at all responsible for Steven and wanted to get as far away as possible as fast as she could. But the chief paramedic said she must remain as a witness, for Steven was still unconscious and maybe had a severe, possibly life-threatening, injury.

The chief paramedic seemed very agitated as he paced the floor in the hall, speaking rapidly into his cell phone. Eventually, he came through the open door of the sitting room and spoke to Katie in passable English.

'It is not good. We dare not move him yet. I have requested the duty doctor. He will be here very soon.'

Katie had sensed from the attitude of the paramedics that Steven was badly injured. In fact, she feared the worst and that Steven had broken his neck and was paralysed, deduced from the fact that his leg had been totally without muscle tone when she had tested him immediately after the fall. Katie was starting to feel anxious, for if this was the case there would be questions to be answered and it would depend on what Steven said, if and when he regained consciousness.

'We think he may have fractured his spine,' continued the paramedic. 'That is why we cannot move him yet.'

The duty doctor now arrived, the flashing green light on his car adding to the blue one of the ambulance. These lights were reflecting through the window and off all the shiny surfaces around the sitting room, adding to the drama and increasing Katie's level of anxiety. A policeman had also arrived and was directing traffic away from the blocked street. And, inevitably, a group of neighbours had assembled at the street corner to view the proceedings and gossip in hushed tones.

Katie was becoming more and more restless as time went on and nothing appeared to be happening, but eventually the doctor and the paramedics reappeared, carrying a stretcher with Steven totally encased in an inflated splint.

The doctor came into the room to speak to Katie. 'Not good, although he is now showing signs of regaining consciousness. We suspect that he has fractured his spine in the fall. How badly, we are not sure, but we are taking him to a special clinic in Nice.' The doctor handed Katie a card. 'Give the clinic a call later.'

As the doctor left, another man now came into the room. He was dressed formally in a suit and collar and tie and Katie had not been aware of his presence in the house. He smiled a welcome and, without being invited, sat on a chair opposite Katie.

'Good afternoon, Madame. My name is Inspector Fabre.' The inspector showed Katie his identification and took a notebook from his pocket. 'I am with the police at St. Tropez. They sent me because my English is probably the best.' He smiled apologetically.

A policewoman in uniform now also entered the room and sat on an adjacent chair.

Katie looked from one to the other in dismay. It had been naïve to expect that the police would not be involved.

'I understand that you are Mrs Katherine Talbot?'

'Yes.'

'A man has been seriously injured and is in a coma,' said the inspector. 'The paramedics tell me that it was apparently an accident in that he fell down the stairs. You were in the house. I should like you to tell me what happened.'

Katie swallowed hard. She now realized that this could not be passed off as an accident. That had been her automatic response to the paramedics, not wishing to explain the details of the encounter. The doctor had said that Steven was beginning to regain consciousness. When he did become fully aware of his injury, Steven was certain to blame her. Lawyer training told her that it was important to give a truthful account now, before Steven could accuse her and give another version of events.

'We arrived this afternoon from England to spend the weekend here,' Katie began hesitantly.

'Forgive me for interrupting,' said the inspector, 'but what is your relationship to Mr Jackson? Are you partners? Do you live together in England?'

'No. Up to now we have only had a casual relationship.'

'I have to be blunt. Does that mean a sexual relationship?'

'No.'

'I see,' said the inspector with a frown. 'And yet you agreed to a weekend away together.'

'I had anticipated some intimacy,' said Katie reluctantly.

'Hmm.' The inspector gave her a quizzical look. 'Please continue.'

'Mr Jackson showed me round the house and then I realized that I had made a terrible mistake. I decided I wanted to go home. I said I would make my own way.'

'And Mr Jackson did not take that very kindly,' said the inspector, nodding his head in understanding.

'No. He started to attack me. Firstly, he tore off my blouse.'

'Not the one that you are wearing?'

'No.' Katie opened her case to retrieve the torn garment that she passed to the inspector.

'And then?'

'He tore off my bra.' Katie passed over the underwear with the straps broken.

'This must have left you with some marks on your body,' said the inspector. 'I should like to verify this straight away. If you proceed to the bathroom with Danielle, she will examine you.'

Inspector Fabre gave the policewoman her instructions, after which she accompanied Katie to the bathroom.

When they returned, Danielle gave her observations to the inspector.

'My officer confirms that you have red wheals on your shoulders,' said the inspector. 'And we have the evidence with the photographs she has taken. I would suggest that I keep these items of clothing also. So, let us continue.'

'I knew that I was going to be raped. I also feared for my life. He ran at me and I managed to duck under his arm and push him down the stairs. It was all I could think of to save myself,' she added simply.

'Thank you.' The inspector closed his notebook with a snap. 'I have a very clear picture. But you must have known the risks you were taking if you were not sure you were going to consummate the relationship. By agreeing to a weekend away you were agreeing to a sexual encounter.'

'I know,' said Katie. 'I just changed my mind.'

The inspector declined to comment, but his look was one of disapproval.

'What happens next?' asked Katie.

'The doctor tells me that Mr Jackson is regaining consciousness. I now have to interview him and hear what he has to say. Whether he confirms your story, or has another version of the event.'

Katie could only nod her head and look at the inspector with a glum expression.

'OK. Danielle will take your details and you must surrender your passport. She will then drive you to a hotel. That could be here in Grimaud, but I am suggesting one in Nice, where Mr Jackson is in a clinic. We will be sealing this house until we know the final outcome. I expect to communicate with you further tomorrow morning.'

#

Katie was feeling totally drained of all energy as she sat slumped in a chair on the balcony of her hotel room, watching the sun begin to disappear beneath the waves of the Mediterranean. A cooling breeze had sprung up and the lights were coming on along the length of the Promenade des Anglais. The meal from room service was virtually untouched, but most of the bottle of white wine had been drunk.

Katie could never have imagined how the day would turn out and she was experiencing a whole gamut of emotions.

Firstly, there was Steven. Katie was desperately sorry for what had happened, but she did not see how she could be held responsible. She was not feeling any guilt, because she had feared for her life and had acted in self-defence. She had not intended, or imagined, such a tragic outcome. And she was determined that Steven's condition (she feared the worst) would not be on her conscience in the future. But, what was weighing on her mind most of all, was what Steven would say to the police when he regained consciousness. Would he deny assaulting her and say she had deliberately pushed him down the stairs without provocation?

All this feeling of foreboding was tempered by the elation that she had achieved a measure of success in what she had set out to do; she had acquired a further clue as to the whereabouts of the missing treasures. Katie had studied the list again, but the annotation made no sense. Hopefully she would discover the meaning of these letters in time.

Katie had telephoned the clinic to be told that Steven had regained consciousness. He was undergoing tests and X-rays and would probably also have CTC and MRI scans to determine the extent of his injury.

The sun disappeared over the horizon as an exhausted Katie prepared for a restless night.

#

Inspector Fabre and Danielle appeared at the hotel at eleven o'clock the next morning. The manager's office had been commandeered for the interview.

Katie, looking pale and anxious, was invited to sit in a chair opposite them.

'I have spoken to Mr Jackson,' the inspector began. 'He has regained full consciousness and is aware of his injury. At first, all he could say was 'she pushed me down the stairs'. I then explained the evidence of the assault in our possession and he capitulated.'

'He agreed with my story?' said Katie, surprised and elated.

'With some reluctance and with some emotion.'

'What does that mean now?'

'I have conferred with my superior officer and we shall not be taking any action. As far as you are concerned, you could make a charge of assault and attempted rape, but I would imagine that, in the circumstances, you would not want to do that.'

'Certainly not,' said Katie. 'It's bad enough as it is.'

'As far as Mr Jackson is concerned, although he has admitted to me on record that he agreed with your version of events, he could conceivably make a counter claim at a later date. So, as it stands, the matter is over. However, Mr Jackson did say that he wished to see you before you leave.'

'I couldn't possibly,' said Katie with a shudder. 'I never want to see him again.'

The inspector looked at her with a frown. 'I think it's the least you can do. You may not think you are to blame, as you acted in self-defence, but you have to admit there was some provocation.'

'Yes.' Katie gave out a long sigh. 'You are right.'

'If you can effect some reconciliation, it might avoid future problems. Clever lawyers might still make out a case against you.'

Katie nodded. 'I will go and see him.'

#

Katie alighted from the taxi and stood for a while, gathering her thoughts. The clinique St George specialised in orthopaedics and neurosurgery and was situated on the top of one of the hills that rise steeply behind Nice. The clinic (which strangely also included a gynaecological unit) was surrounded by lawns and colourful flowering shrubs and there was a wonderful view over the town to the blue waters of the Mediterranean.

With a long sigh, Katie entered the clinic and was shown into a small waiting room. Almost immediately, a nurse appeared, carrying a file and a large brown envelope.

'I am afraid it is not good news. He is badly injured.'

'I was afraid of that.' Katie had already sensed this information from the nurse's demeanour.

The nurse switched on an X-ray viewer on the wall and took a film from the envelope. 'Monsieur Jackson has fractured his spine. This is where the fracture is. It is between vertebrae T3 and T4.' The nurse pointed to the place on the film and Katie could see where the bones were now out of alignment. 'The spinal cord has been severed. That means that there is no nervous function below this point. He has the use of his arms, but not his legs.'

'And this is a permanent injury?' Katie asked, knowing full well that it was.

'Yes. I am afraid so.'

Katie stared at the image, finding nothing else to say.

'He asked to see you. He said that it was important what he had to say.'

Katie had a spasm of anxiety, dreading the confrontation.

'I will take you to him.' The nurse led the way out of the waiting room. 'Oh, by the way, Monsieur Jackson says that his ring is missing. You don't know anything about that?'

'No.' Katie shook her head. 'I didn't notice he had a ring.' Katie was, of course, not wearing the ring. It was in a zipped compartment in her purse.

#

Katie entered the room slowly and with much trepidation. Steven was lying in the bed that was raised at the head by a few degrees. The blankets came up to his neck, but Katie could see that Steven was still encased in some sort of a splint.

Steven's eyes followed her as Katie sat on a moulded plastic chair a few feet away. Steven's face was expressionless and Katie fought back the tears.

For a minute or two neither of them spoke, Steven still looking at Katie and Katie looking at the floor.

Eventually Steven said, 'They told you about my injury?'

Katie nodded, still looking at the floor.

'I broke my back. I shall have to spend the rest of my life in a wheelchair.'

Katie nodded again and snuffled into a handkerchief.

'I had to agree with the policeman. About what happened. But I still hold you responsible,' Steven continued.

'I had to defend myself,' Katie retorted, raising her voice. 'It was all I could think of.'

'You deceived me.' Steven's tone was now accusing. 'I thought you felt the same way about me that I felt about you. Especially as you had agreed for us to go away for a weekend together. Did you expect separate bedrooms?'

'No. Well. I just changed my mind, that's all. Women have that prerogative.'

'I had so set my mind on being with you. I had thought of nothing else for days. I just couldn't bear the thought of your leaving.'

'I still say you were expecting too much.' Katie retorted. 'Up to this weekend we had not been intimate in any way.'

'Whatever. You led me on. I thought that you reciprocated my feelings and then you rejected me. I just couldn't accept that.'

'That was still no reason to attack me,' Katie was again on the defensive.

'I couldn't help myself. I wanted you so much.'

There was a pause in the conversation as Katie looked around the room, wondering what else there was to say and whether she should now leave.

'I can't face the rest of my life like this.' Steven's tone had become more animated. 'There is no cure. You will have to finish the job. Katie, you have to kill me. I don't care how or when, but I'm relying on you to do as I ask.'

Katie chose to ignore this last remark. She could imagine that was how someone might feel when suddenly confronted with this catastrophe.

'Steven, I'm going now. I am desperately sorry for what has happened, but I still reject responsibility. I feel no obligation towards you. And I think it best if we never contact each other again.'

'You will comply with my request, Katie,' said Steven. 'You will. I will see to that.'

'Goodbye Steven.'

Katie then abruptly left the room without looking back.

In the lobby she met the nurse. 'What will happen to him now?' Katie's voice had a catch.

'He will stay in the clinic for a period of rehabilitation.'

'How long for?' asked Katie.

'That depends on how well he progresses. Several weeks, maybe months.'

'And then?'

'He will be disadvantaged for the rest of his life.' The nurse's tone was matter-of-fact.

'Must he stay in a special clinic?'

'No. He can live at home, if the house has suitable conversions for his needs. But he may well need additional care.'

'I know that he lives on his own,' said Katie.

'Oh,' said the nurse, 'I thought you were . . .'

'No,' said Katie firmly. 'I'm just a casual acquaintance.'

The nurse gave her a quizzical look. 'I understood that you were . . .' She looked in the file she was carrying. 'In fact, Mr Jackson has named you as next of kin.'

'What!' said Katie, flabbergasted. Then after a moment's thought she added, 'he's no right to do that.'

'I don't suppose it's that important,' said the nurse. 'He is out of danger. We expect Monsieur Jackson to make as good a recovery as possible.'

Katie then bade the nurse farewell, still fuming at Steven's arrogance. Desperately sorry as she was, she was determined that in the future *she was not going to get involved.*

#

'Well. I told you so.' Angela poured out the wine. The women were having lunch at their usual table in the restaurant in the department store.

Katie nodded. 'It was a complete disaster.' Would she ever be able to tell Angela what had really happened?

'So how come?'

'He was obnoxious. Right from the start. In the aeroplane. Kept touching me.'

'And when you got to the house?'

'Same. Only worse.'

'I expect he was like an animal,' Angela hissed. 'All over you. Fondling your boobs and squeezing your butt.'

'Something like that,' Katie agreed.

'And then?'

'I managed to put him off. Said that I was looking forward to being in bed, but I would rather wait until after dinner.'

'And that worked?'

'Yes. We had a few drinks and then went to a restaurant down in the village. Walking wasn't easy. Everywhere is on a slope and the sidewalks are either cobbles or smooth stone.'

'Nice restaurant?'

'Typical Provençal cooking. I was being very charming and frivolous. Flirting. Anyway, halfway through I said I was going to the restroom. I walked straight out the restaurant, got a taxi, collected my luggage from the house and went on to Nice and checked into a hotel. Flew back to London the next morning.'

And that was how it should have been. Even if she had abandoned her overnight bag. Katie had thought it through so many times. If only she had had just a little foresight as to how things might develop, she could have avoided all the trauma. But hindsight is a wonderful thing.

'So you won't be seeing *him* again,' Angela laughed. 'I wonder how long it took him to realize you weren't coming back.'

Katie could only produce a rather wan smile.

'So you won't be going back to the dating agency either?'

'Certainly not.'

'You're going to New York soon. To that art auction. Why don't you stay with my sister in Bayshore? I'm sure she could fix you up with someone.'

'Thank you. I'll think about it.'

CHAPTER 6

'Nice of you to come down to Naples to visit me, Bill.' Grant Henderson turned to look at his companion directly with a half smile on his face. 'But I guess this is not a social call. And I hope you have remembered that I'm supposed to have taken early retirement.'

Bill Katzler returned the smile. 'Grant, you know that with this company, it's a lifetime commitment. You are always on call. This is important. You know I wouldn't involve you in anything trivial.'

The two men continued their way along the beach. Grant had been walking with head down and stooped to pick up a shell. 'Can't resist picking them up,' he said, almost apologetically. 'Even though I've got bowls full of them all around the house. This is a sand dollar. A rare find. Sand dollars are very fragile and the waves break them up. This is quite a good one. Just about perfect.' Grant carefully put the shell in a plastic bag. 'OK. So what's it all about?'

'Remember Marshall Maxwell?'

'Sure do. I spent long enough on his case. Very devious kind of guy. And better-looking than me. I didn't like him.'

'I would agree with you. On both counts,' Bill laughed. 'However, there's been an unexpected development.' Bill's tone became more serious. 'The President has had a call from the German Chancellor. Maxwell has been funding a new political party in eastern Germany, called the NDVP. Apparently he's been involved with it for some time. Their base is in Weimar, in the state of Thüringen. They just had local elections and this party won the majority of the vote. Which means they have outright control over policy in the State.'

'So is that a big deal?'

'It sure is. It's a far right party. The party has the support of the neo-Nazis and other like-minded groups. And, most worryingly, a good proportion of university students. This sort of success by a far right party is unprecedented since world war two. The Government in Berlin is afraid that it may be the 1920s starting all over again.'

'Come on, Bill. We have had all this before. In fact, haven't we had something like this ever since 1945? I seem to remember there is the NPD, the National Democratic Party. They are a far right party, but they have only made limited progress in state elections.'

'Yes, you're right. The NPD was formed in 1964 and it has had some electoral success. The party is represented in two states of the former East Germany; Saxony and Mecklenburg-Vorpommen. I'm told the NPD have recently merged with another party, the German People's Union, but it looks like this new party has eclipsed them and it is getting the support of all right-wing groups.'

'Bill, all this is nonsense. We have a united Germany that is a major partner in the European Union. The whole idea, plus the common currency, was to prevent anything like the Third Reich ever happening again.'

'That's the theory. But there has to be something in this to get the chancellor worried.'

'So are they saying anything different? This new party? Or is it just Maxwell's money that is giving them this success?'

'Apparently the leader of the party is supposed to be special. Guy called Otto Hauswald. Something of an orator. Big buddy of Maxwell's since schooldays.'

'An orator.' Grant frowned. 'So that is why the chancellor is worried. In fact, I would suggest that is the main reason she is worried. You said Maxwell has been funding this party. Can he legally do that?'

'He's got dual nationality. As a German citizen, I suppose he can.'

'I presume the Germans have proof? And why would Maxwell be doing this? It must be to gain influence. Has he got any commercial interests in the region?'

'We made some preliminary enquiries. Maxwell has bought a small engineering company on an industrial estate in Weimar and is expanding it.'

'Nothing wrong in that?'

'No,' Bill admitted. 'Apparently not.'

'But I suppose the Germans are worried there may be some corruption if Maxwell is funding the party to gain favour.'

'That may well be so,' said Bill.

'I wonder if he has an ulterior motive,' said Grant thoughtfully. 'There must be a bigger picture.'

'Exactly,' agreed Bill. 'And that is precisely what we want to find out.'

'I knew he arrived with a German passport,' said Grant, thinking laterally, 'He was born in East Germany. The family was displaced from the east after the war.'

'Correct. The family originated somewhere near Wroclaw, but this was previously a town called Breslau. Part of Germany before the war. Now it is in Poland.'

'Interesting,' said Grant.

The two men continued at a leisurely pace along the line of the tide as Grant digested the situation. There was a stiff breeze from the north, making the day a little cool for summer in Florida, but the sun was warm and glaringly bright as it reflected off the choppy waters of the Gulf of Mexico.

'You can always tell which way the wind is blowing.' Grant pointed to a flock of terns huddled together on the beach. 'They always stand facing directly into the wind.'

'Were you ever aware of Maxwell's interest in politics or foreign affairs?' asked Bill.

Grant shook is head. 'No. Politics never came into it. And foreign affairs were only business matters. Our investigation was only concerned with the viability of his company. Particularly with respect to the pension fund. We were worried about the workforce. We feared it was going to be another Enron. He was siphoning off money, which we thought meant he was going to do a runner. It was all going abroad to a Swiss Bank. Maxwell said the money was being invested. We had to give him the benefit of the doubt. In the end, it turned out OK.'

'The investment worked?'

'Apparently. There was a sudden injection of a large amount of money into the company. It squared the books. The company was solvent and the pension fund restored.'

'No way we can trace those financial transactions?'

'No,' said Grant, picking up another shell, but then rejecting it, flinging it out to sea. 'Not until the Swiss banks accept complete disclosure. We are putting pressure on them, but it hasn't happened yet.'

'If this gets serious, they might get threats as well,' said Bill.

'So what is it you want me to do, Bill? How can I be of help?'

'We need someone with experience. You know a lot about Maxwell. You speak German. You know Germany, as you were with the Embassy in Bonn for five years. OK, you took early retirement, but we have decided that you are the man for the job. Look at the present state of Maxwell's company and its finances. Quiz him about his political ambitions. Assess the situation and give us your opinion.'

Grant shrugged his shoulders. 'OK. But it may be all smoke and mirrors.'

'I'm suggesting that you go to Berlin and maybe Thüringen first. Weimar is the power base and where Hauswald lives. Get the lie of the land. See if there is any substance in the idea that this new political party is a threat. There's an agent in Berlin who is in charge of the case. Apparently she reports directly to the chancellor. I suggest you liaise with her before you confront Maxwell.'

'OK, Bill. I'll do that.'

'What we are after, Grant, firstly, is an assessment of risk.'

CHAPTER 7

Maybe Steven was right. And it was her fault. Katie had thought of little else since returning from France. Angela's assessment had been correct in that it was obvious what Steven was going to expect and that there would be problems if he did not get it. Katie reproached herself for being so naïve. And for so lacking in imagination and anticipation.

So, as a result of these recriminations, did she feel any responsibility? And if so, what could she do about it? Assist in Steven's care? She had done some research into paraplegia and it made for some distressing reading. Maybe there would be a cure sometime in the future, but for now Steven was severely disabled with no hope of recovery.

However, realistically, Katie felt that in no way could she contribute. It had happened and it could not be resolved. Any contact would only lead to conflict. She stood by her decision never to see Steven again.

Katie was now reviewing her quest for the missing treasures, in the light of finding the list in Steven's safe. However, this list was of no immediate help, as the annotation was still totally meaningless. It did not seem to relate to dates, places, or people. She could only hope that it might make sense later as she enquired further.

The next step had to be to investigate the provenance relating to the Titian and to this end she had made an appointment at Sotheby's.

\#

Sotheby's London office was in New Bond Street. Katie was met by an efficient-looking young man in a pinstriped suit with matching tie and handkerchief.

'Please come into my office, countess. I am Donald Hayes, one of the junior partners. Coffee?'

'Yes, please.' Katie was ushered into a small modern office.

'Do take a seat.' Hayes opened a folder that was already on his desk. 'Now. I understand that this concerns the painting by Titian, The Death of St Peter Martyr, which is for sale by us in New York?'

'Yes. I am contesting the ownership of this painting.'

'So I understand.' Hayes's manner was grave. 'I must say that we always take these claims very seriously. It is most important that we are as satisfied as possible that the ownership is watertight. So, tell me the details.' Hayes pulled forward a pad and pencil.

'I believe that this painting was stolen from my family home on the Island of Rügen in north-eastern Germany. Anything of value was hidden by my family in a secret cellar before the start of the second world war. All these treasures, including this painting, were not discovered by the Nazis and were still there when my parents escaped to America as the war ended. My grandparents remained and died that same year.'

'So, as far as you know, everything was still there in 1945,' said Hayes, making notes.

'Yes. When Germany was partitioned after the war, Rügen became part of the DDR. The house was taken over by the STASI as their regional headquarters. They blew up the house in 1989 when the communist state collapsed. However, I suspect the date of the theft was around 1986, because that was the year the estate manager was interned by the STASI. He never returned.'

'He knew where the treasures were hidden?'

'Yes. He was tortured and killed.'

'And divulged the position of the cellar, I presume. So, probably 1986, but definitely before 1989?'

'Yes. Because I visited the house with my parents in 1990. We found the house destroyed and the secret cellar empty.'

'OK,' said Hayes. 'I think I've got all that.'

'So, Mr Hayes,' Katie smiled. 'I am intrigued to know what you are offering as the provenance.'

'Yes. Well, I can certainly show you that.' Hayes opened the file in front of him. 'We have copies of all the relevant documents here in London. This painting is being sold by Mr Marshall Maxwell. He is an American citizen and chairman and CEO of the MarMax Corporation. You may have heard of him and his company, which is a global conglomerate.'

'Yes. I have heard of him,' said Katie, somewhat surprised that she had. But the owner was always likely to be a very wealthy individual.

'The painting was purchased by Mr Maxwell in 2005 from a Mr Otto Hauswald.' Hayes passed a bill of sale across to Katie.

'What do we know about Mr Hauswald?' Katie examined the document.

'Mr Hauswald is a well-known art collector. His main residence is in Weimar, Germany, but he has other homes. Including one in New York, where he has a gallery.'

'And in 2005,' said Katie. Maybe Maxwell had bought the painting in good faith. 'So can we go back further. How did Mr Hauswald obtain the painting?'

Hayes extracted the next piece of paper. 'Mr Hauswald inherited the painting from his father. The painting had been bought by his father in 1932. For the princely sum of two thousand marks.' Hayes smiled. 'I suppose that was a lot of money in those days.'

'And so how did the family acquire the painting?'

Hayes pointed out the name. 'From a Count von Arnnitz. Your grandfather. Here is his signature and his seal.'

Katie looked at what she knew was a complete fabrication. Her grandfather's signature had been forged and the ring that was now in her possession had provided the seal.

'As far as I am concerned, Mr Hayes, this document is a complete forgery.' Katie leant back in her chair. 'As I know that the painting was in the possession of my family up to 1945.'

Hayes frowned. 'Do you have a sample of your grandfather's signature so that we may get an expert to compare?'

'No,' Katie admitted. 'Nothing survived the war.'

'But you acknowledge that the seal is genuine?'

'Yes.' Katie was not going to admit that the seal was in her possession.

'So the question is, have you got any evidence at all?'

Katie reached into her handbag. 'This is a photograph that was taken of the painting in the house before it was hidden.'

Hayes examined the photograph. 'OK. Yes, this is the same painting, but I suppose this photograph could have been taken anywhere and at any time.'

'I agree,' said Katie. 'The only real corroborating evidence I have is that of an old retainer. I visited her recently. She remembers the painting hanging in the hallway before it was hidden away in 1939. She is prepared to testify to this.'

'And the old lady's name?'

'Frau Hildegard Weber. She still lives in a cottage on the old estate.'

'OK,' said Hayes, continuing to make notes. 'Otherwise?'

'Everybody else has died. My parents died ten years ago and I understand that Frau Weber is the last surviving servant.'

Hayes closed his notepad. 'Countess, we will look at this as a matter of urgency, as the sale date is fast approaching. I suggest that we make another appointment for next week.'

'Then thank you very much for your time, Mr Hayes.' Katie stood up to leave. 'I will return next week. In the meantime, could you possibly give me copies of the documents?'

In the taxi on the way home, Katie suddenly realised the significance of Otto Hauswald in the provenance. The letters OH appeared several times on Steven's list. It looked as if Otto Hauswald was involved in selling a lot more of the family paintings than just the Titian.

Katie retrieved the mail from the mat. Two items with foreign stamps immediately caught her eye. The first was from France, which Katie opened with a shaky hand and a sense of foreboding.

> Dearest Katie,
>
> You will not be pleased to hear from me, I'm sure, but I have
> to remind you of my existence and the condition in which
> I find myself.

The clinic is very pleased with my progress, and they expect that I can return to London shortly. As you know, I am paralysed from the waist downwards, which means that I have no control over some essential bodily functions. I am not sparing you the details, so that you are fully aware of what I have to contend with.

I am being educated to control my bowel movements, which may be the least of my worries. I have a catheter that was surgically inserted and urine is collected in a bag that is well concealed. And, of course, I am impotent. You did not know that sex was very important to me. I used to visit an establishment in Mayfair regularly and that is what I miss most of all.

Otherwise, I am building up my upper body strength and hope to lead some sort of meaningful existence when I return to London.

It may be a forlorn hope, but I would appreciate it if you could at least anticipate paying me the courtesy of an occasional visit. And do not forget my final request to you in the clinic. I am still determined that this will come to pass.

You are always in my thoughts. Steven.

Katie tore up the letter and wiped away an angry tear. This problem was not going to go away. She imagined even more attempts at contact when Steven returned to London. All she could do was to ignore them, for she was still determined never to see Steven again.

Katie then turned her attention to the other letter, airmail from the USA. It contained a card that was embossed with a gold crest and flamboyant lettering.

It was with surprise that she read:

Marshall Maxwell requests the pleasure of the company of the Countess Katherine von Arnitz to a dinner to be held at the Cafe des Artistes, One West 67th Street, New York City on Tuesday the 14th of August. The theme is Friends and Foes. Dress Formal.

The RSVP was to the MarMax secretary. Katie then realized that the sale at Sotheby's was the following day.

#

A week later, Donald Hayes ushered Katie into the same office in Bond Street.

'I hope your committee has found the time to look at my case,' smiled Katie.

'Indeed, we have,' said Hayes. 'In fact, the first thing we did was to send our man in Berlin up to Rügen.'

'Oh. Good,' said Katie. 'Frau Weber corroborated my story?'

'I'm afraid that Frau Weber passed away three weeks ago.'

Katie could only look at Hayes, speechless.

'Apparently it was a heart attack. She was 94,' he added.

'I never thought of this happening,' said Katie in despair. 'I suppose I should have got her to sign a statement and have it witnessed.'

'Yes. Too late now,' Hayes agreed. 'So, I am afraid, countess, in the light of this information, the committee have decided that they have no option but to accept the provenance given. As far as we are concerned, we have to accept the evidence that your grandfather sold this painting. Any evidence to the contrary depended entirely upon the memory of the old retainer, which itself might have been questionable.'

Katie nodded and could find nothing to say.

'We acknowledge that the painting belonged to your family, even though there is no evidence that it was a gift from the Austrian Royal Family,' Hayes added. 'We have to accept that the bill of sale in 1932 is genuine. And with both the signatories being deceased, I would imagine it would be very difficult to prove it to be a forgery.'

'But that is now my only hope,' said Katie thoughtfully. 'Could I have access to the original bill of sale for investigation?'

'I don't see why not,' said Hayes. 'Although it would probably have to be done through the courts. And would take time,' he added.

'So am I to conclude that the sale will now go ahead?'

'Yes. The committee have decided. The sale will take place as advertised.'

#

As Katie fumbled for her latchkey, she was approached by a motor-cyclist, encased in black leather and with an opaque helmet.

'Mrs Katie Talbot?'

'Yes,' Katie replied with some apprehension.

The man handed Katie a supermarket plastic carrier bag and without another word, roared away.

Katie entered her house to peer inside the bag, which was quite heavy. What she saw made her feel quite faint as she recognized the cloth in which Steven's handgun had been wrapped in the safe in Grimaud. There was also the box of ammunition and a set of keys.

Katie sat down in despair. Steven was keeping his word. What on earth was she going to do about this problem?

CHAPTER 8

The German Intelligence Services are divided as they are in the United States and the United Kingdom. The foreign intelligence agency is the BND (*Bundesnachrichendienst*), whilst the domestic intelligence agency is the BfV (*Bundesamt fur Verfassungschutz*). The headquarters of the BfV is in Cologne, but Grant's appointment was with an agent on special assignment to the Chancellery in Berlin.

The original Berlin Chancellery in the Wilhelmstrasse was badly damaged in the second world war and was later demolished by the Russians. The new Chancellery, opened in 2001, is adjacent to the Reichstag (parliament building).

Grant had taken the number 200 bus, virtually a sight-seeing bus, as its route passed so many of the important buildings in the city and consequently was always full to capacity with tourists. Grant alighted at the Reichstag and then crossed the wide grassy area in front of the huge building, concentrating on what his line of questioning should be. Assessment of risk. That was his remit. In his experience, he doubted if he would gain enough information from this appointment to make that assessment. What was important was meeting the agent who had the ear of the chancellor.

From Grant's angle of approach, the Chancellery appeared as a rectangular block of concrete with very large windows. Above this block, the next stage of the building was square with a large round window. Berliners are famous for giving nicknames to their important buildings and this window had produced the name of the '*Bundeswaschmachine*', or 'federal washing machine'. Grant's favourite for a Berlin nickname was that given to the television tower, built in1969 on Alexanderplatz, in east Berlin, which was intended to give an impression of communist strength. Unfortunately for the authorities, it was found that when the sun shone on the tower's stainless steel tiled dome, the reflection appeared as a crucifix. This led to the name '*Rache des Papstes*', or 'Pope's revenge'. All attempts by the builders to rectify this phenomenon failed.

The front of the Chancellery presents a very different picture. Smooth concrete columns in the Palladian style support an awning equivalent to the height of six storeys, above which are a further series of columns supporting another awning. Otherwise, the walls appear as sheets of glass. In front of the building is a large metal sculpture by Eduardo Chillida, now a bright orange rust colour (as it was intended). Why did so many important modern buildings need to have a meaningless monstrosity in front of them (probably at great expense), Grant asked himself.

Grant was directed to a side entrance by the commissionaire, where he displayed his credentials to the receptionist, who invited him to wait in the lobby.

The reception lobby was a small room with bare walls painted in lime green and with two lines of black metal upholstered chairs. There were no other visitors. Grant sat on one of the chairs. He was starting to feel anxious and asked himself why. It was like sitting in a dentist's waiting room. And then he wondered if that was exactly what the room was designed to do.

Up to now, Grant had not even spoken to Frau Ebert and did not know what to expect, but was quite taken aback by the sight of the gorgeous young woman who emerged from the elevator to come and shake his hand.

Suzanne Ebert was early thirty-something with long blonde hair in a modern cut. She was wearing a crisp white shirt with enough buttons undone to show a hint of cleavage and her beige knee-length skirt was tight as a drum across her slim hips.

'Good morning, Mr Henderson,' she said brightly. 'We will go to my office. I speak good English, as my mother was from Bristol.'

'Please call me Grant,' said Grant, knowing how formal the Germans usually are.

'And I am Suzanne.' This was said with some reluctance, to Grant's amusement.

Grant followed her taut bottom and superb legs, thinking that this experience alone had made the trip worthwhile. They took the elevator up two floors and along a corridor to an office with a glass-topped desk and black leather chairs. On the white painted walls were several abstract paintings in bright colours that Grant did not care for. From the large picture window the Reichstag was in full view, with the usual long line of people waiting to ascend to the glass dome, the inspiration of the architect Norman Foster.

Suzanne motioned Grant to a chair in front of her desk.

'The President of the United States has asked me to assess if there is any risk posed by the success of this new political party,' said Grant, emphasizing the authority of his position. His attention was now focused on Suzanne's clear blue eyes and her wide mouth that revealed perfect teeth.

'The Chancellor is taking this very seriously,' said Suzanne. 'She has a very good knowledge of German history. She does not want history repeating itself.'

'Quite,' said Grant, thinking that this was what he had expected. Overreaction and typical German *Angst*. 'So how much of a threat is this new political party that has won a local election? To the country as a whole, that is?'

'At the moment, to the country, not very much,' Suzanne admitted. 'Thüringen is a small state. But the NDVP, that stands for *Neue Deutsche Volkspartei,* is in the majority and as such will dictate local politics. The threat is if it extends its influence to the rest of the country. In our opinion, it has the potential to do this.'

'I understand that this is a right of centre party,' said Grant.

'This party is certainly that,' Suzanne confirmed. 'They have taken their name from the DVP, which existed in the days of the Weimar republic and was liberal, rather than conservative in its policies. It was disbanded after a disastrous election result when the Nazis came to power in 1933. So NDVP is really a misnomer, as this new party is much more to the right.'

'Maybe to confuse the electorate?' Grant suggested.

'There may be an element of that,' Suzanne agreed. 'In fact, I have the suspicion that the party is concealing more extreme, fascist ideals.'

'Then I understand your concern,' said Grant. 'But Germany has had very right wing parties before. I mean, since the last war,' he added hastily.

'Correct. But the NDVP has proved to be much more successful than similar parties in the recent past. OK, this election result may just be a one-off. But I doubt it. The question is whether its policies are going to appeal to other states and, later on, to the electorate of the whole country.'

'So are the official policies of the NDVP so very different?' Grant asked.

'From previous right-wing parties, you mean? Not much, but brought up to date. The propaganda they put out lists the advantages of leaving the Eurocurrency zone and also the European Union.'

'And would that be possible?'

WINDING BACK THE CLOCK

'If the NDVP won a national election and formed a government, we could envisage such a scenario.'

'Hmm,' said Grant, showing obvious scepticism. 'But the Union has expanded recently and will probably expand even more. With Germany as the major player. The European Union would seem to be getting bigger and stronger, with many advantages to a country remaining in the system. So I would imagine that scenario to be a little far-fetched.'

'We are seeing more countries joining the Union,' Suzanne agreed. 'But many Germans feel that the deal is too one-sided,'

'The new country gets more benefit and the Germans get less,' Grant suggested.

'Yes. A significant proportion of the population feel that Germany has had a raw deal with the European Union,' said Suzanne. 'We have always supplied the largest amount of money to the budget and ordinary Germans feel that they do not get much advantage from it. Also, they feel that we are subsidising new members joining the Union.'

'I can quite understand that,' said Grant. 'So do you think the union has expanded too fast?' he ventured.

'Yes. Probably.'

'But not all the countries are in the euro zone,' said Grant. 'I find that strange. It's not one Union, but two. It should be all or nothing. I can't image some of the states back home having a different currency.'

'In principal, I agree,' Suzanne admitted. 'Only seventeen have the common currency. But there is concern with some of the countries that are in the euro zone at present. All the countries run their own economies and one could envisage a case where the country could not keep within the rules of the currency and would have to leave. Were several countries obliged to leave, then one could see a break-up of the euro zone and countries returning to their own currencies.'

67

'I was always sceptical of Europe having a common currency,' said Grant. 'The Unites States is similar to Europe in that we have states that are autonomous to a large degree. These states have monetary union, but they also have fiscal and political union as well. You do not have that and I have always thought it would eventually be a problem.'

'We are starting to see some problems already,' said Suzanne. 'Especially as some states have not kept to the guidelines.'

'And not been reprimanded,' Grant pointed out. 'I remember that in 2004, Greece admitted that it had fudged its entry statistics. What was done? Nothing.'

Suzanne could not find an answer.

'So it's all a bit of a mess, really?'

'We are working all the time on ways to improve,' was all Suzanne could find to reply.

'So, let's go forward in time,' said Grant. 'This new party wins a national election and wants to leave the currency and the Union,' said Grant. 'How would that work out?'

'Well, Germany would again be an independent country. The main theme of the NDVP is Germany for the Germans. They argue that Germany would be a stronger and more prosperous country if it were independent of the European Union. And that would mean, at first, a return to the Deutschemark.'

'Maybe that would be an advantage,' said Grant. 'For Germany.'

'It would put the whole structure of Europe at risk,' said Suzanne, not disputing Grant's remark.

'As I understand it,' said Grant, 'the whole idea of the European union was to prevent another war. Free trade and everything else came second.'

'Quite correct,' Suzanne agreed. 'That is why we have to preserve the union. This new party must be prevented from gaining further influence. But it has a very charismatic leader. And that is partly what makes the difference between the NDVP and other similar parties that have existed for some time, such as the NPD, which has had similar policies, but has made no headway in the polls.'

'Tell me about him,' said Grant.

'His name is Otto Hauswald. He lives in Weimar in the state of Thüringen. I must mention at this point that prior to the *Wende* in 1989, we have very limited information on some influential individuals within the DDR. That is because a vast amount of bureaucratic material was destroyed as the state collapsed.'

'You mean that he could have been a government official?' Grant suggested.

'Or, more likely, in the STASI,' said Suzanne. 'Prominent government members we all knew about, such as Honeker and Krenz. But there were other influential people in the secret services behind the scenes, hiding behind the chairman, Erich Mielke.'

'Hauswald being one of them?'

'And his father. The family must have been very favoured. Hauswald occupies what I can only describe as a palace that is full of valuable furniture and objets d'art. Hauswald's father was an art collector and died before the *Wende*. Hauswald has carried on the tradition of being an art collector and has opened a gallery in New York.'

'And he is very popular within the party?'

'Otto Hauswald is a charmer. At some point in his career he was a clergyman and he is an orator. He holds his listeners spellbound. And he tells them what they want to hear.'

'*Deja vu*,' said Grant.

'Exactly,' said Suzanne with a wry smile.

'So how do you see the future?' Grant asked, feeling that he had got the picture.

'I see it as unclear. Germany is a free democracy and the Government cannot be seen to hinder a specific political party. It is up to the other political parties to emphasize the advantages of their policies against those of the NDVP. We have to see if the NDVP gains strength.' Suzanne paused and looked at Grant directly. 'I said that the party's strength has come partly from the stature of Hauswald. What has also made an enormous difference is the amount of money at the NDVP's disposal.'

'From benefactors?'

'Yes. A large percentage of the funding has come from abroad. And from one individual in particular.'

'OK. So we are now talking about Marshall Maxwell,' said Grant.

'Yes, we are,' said Suzanne. 'The amount of money he has given to the NDVP is unprecedented.'

'But given legally,' said Grant.

'Mr Maxwell is a German citizen and, as such, there is legally no limit to the funds he can donate to the party.'

'And if he were a foreigner?' Grant asked.

'He would be limited to one thousand euros.'

'Quite a difference,' said Grant with a smile.

'Exactly. Quite a difference.' Suzanne returned the smile. 'However, all donations over 50.000 euros have to be reported at once to the president of the Bundestag.'

'So that if corruption is suspected, it could be investigated immediately,' Grant concluded.

'Correct,' Suzanne agreed. 'You can promote the message, but you cannot buy the vote.'

'And, as far as you can see, Maxwell is being purely philanthropic?'

'As far as we can see,' Suzanne agreed. 'Maxwell has a small company in Weimar, but that is relatively insignificant. What this does mean, is that because of this electoral success, the party is also able to obtain funding from the state. A party receives 0.5 euro per vote cast at the previous election, be it for local, European or Bundestag elections.'

'Thereby increasing the money at the party's disposal,' Grant concluded. 'A sort of snowball effect.'

'That is what may happen,' Suzanne agreed.

'So is there anything you want from us?' Grant asked, feeling that the meeting had run its course.

'We feel that Mr Maxwell's donations are producing a disproportionate influence on the electorate.' Suzanne's tone had become more official. 'We would like to know what reason Maxwell has for providing this funding. Is he being just a philanthropist, or does he have an ulterior motive?'

'I understand your concern,' said Grant. 'I will speak to Mr Maxwell and see what he has to say. However, we are also a free country and citizens can spend their money as they wish. Legally, of course.'

'I would be most grateful,' said Suzanne, standing up to indicate the meeting was over. 'And I look forward to hearing from you.'

So far so good, thought Grant as he made his way back to Unter den Linden and lunch with a colleague. What he needed now was some local opinion. Weimar was the base of the NDVP and that would seem to be the most appropriate place to get it.

#

Grant took the train to Weimar and a taxi ride took him the short distance to the Hotel Elephant, which overlooked the *Markt,* the main square and focal point of the town.

He checked in and then questioned the bell captain. 'I'm a journalist doing a piece on Weimar. Particularly on local politics. I believe you a local election recently?'

'Indeed we did,' said the bell captain. 'It was a landmark victory for the NDVP.'

'A new party, I understand?'

'Relatively.'

'And their base is here in Weimar?'

'Yes. And the leader is a local man. Otto Hauswald.'

'I wonder if I might get an interview,' said Grant.

'I doubt it,' said the bell captain. 'He's often away.'

'So, nevertheless, could you tell me where Otto Hauswald lives?'

'Certainly,' said the bell captain. 'Diagonally across the square. Schlossgasse. The house with an iron gate. You can't miss it.'

Schlossgasse was a terrace of large houses and there was only one house with a gate, behind which was a gravelled courtyard. Grant stood and surveyed the house, which looked substantial. The gate was made of wrought iron, a good six feet high and a keypad was on the wall to the left. Grant toyed with the idea of ringing the bell. Would Hauswald give him an audience?

'There's nobody at home,' said a voice behind him.

Grant turned to see a woman who had emerged from the house opposite and was about to clean her downstairs windows.

'This is the home of Herr Hauswald?'

'Yes. Father and son. Old Frau Hauswald lives further down the street.'

'I'm a journalist doing a piece on local politics. What's your opinion of the NDVP?'

'I don't know anything about politics.'

'So did you vote in the recent election?'

'No. I didn't. If you want some local opinion, why don't you ask all the folk in the *Markt?*'

'Yes. Thank you. I will.'

Grant went back to the square and surveyed the scene. The bells in the town hall to his right were chiming the hour. Grant looked up to see that the bells were made of porcelain, which he thought was most unusual. In the square, the market was in full swing. There were several stalls selling fruit and vegetables and others with cut-price clothing overflowing the tables. The smell of *bratwurst* was all pervading. Grant wandered between the stalls, which were all doing good business, but then shelved his original idea of canvassing the local shoppers. A much better bet would be to find an habitual drinker in a *Kneipe*.

After dinner in his hotel, Grant ventured back into the centre of town to find a suitable bar. On the corner of Leipzigertrasse he found the perfect place. It was dimly lit, not many customers and at the bar was a lone drinker.

Grant took the stool beside him and ordered a litre of the local brew.

'My name's Grant.' Grant offered the man his hand. 'I'm an American journalist doing a piece on the local culture. Another beer?'

'Many thanks,' said the man. 'My name's Gunter.'

'Pleased to meet you, Gunter,' said Grant, realizing that he would have to concentrate to understand the thick local dialect.

'You'll find us very traditional,' said Gunter, as the barman put another foaming litre in front of him. 'Very kind of you. *Prost!.*'

'*Prost!*' Grant replied, raising his glass. Gunter seemed an affable sort of guy and ready for a chat. He gave the impression of being a typical working man and as such was ideal for an interview. He was dressed in a blue check shirt and jeans, both of which had seen better days.

'Is that your usual evening entertainment?' Grant indicated the television screen.

'*Volks Hitparade*,' said Gunter, with a grin. '*Volksmusik*. What you would call country music. Very popular here. With the young people as well.'

'I noticed some people in *Tracht* today,' said Grant. 'People wearing national costume, and it's not even a Sunday.'

'Traditional values as well,' said Gunter proudly. 'The family is very important. And we take good care of our property. Houses are well maintained with neat gardens. You will still see the housewife mopping the front door step.'

'So, this local election,' said Grant. 'Did you vote for the NDVP?'

'I certainly did.'

'I'm surprised they did so well,' said Grant, feeling pleased that Gunter was being so co-operative. 'Because there have been similar parties in the past, such as the NPD.

And you could say that the NDVP is the opposite to the communists.'

'Look, we in Thüringen have never been communists. Communism was thrust upon us after the war. We became part of the DDR with no say in the matter.'

'But after the wall came down, many people in the East wanted the DDR back,' said Grant. 'The PDS won a large percentage of the vote.'

'That's because they were so mollycoddled by the state,' said Gunter. 'There was full employment. Everybody had somewhere to live. Free schools and healthcare. But it couldn't last. It was totally inefficient and uneconomic.'

'In the West, we knew that,' Grant agreed. 'It was only a matter of time.'

'With the fall of the communist state, suddenly they were in the real world. For many the change was not good, because so many firms were out of date and inefficient and they had to close. Unemployment has been over 25% ever since. And that,' Gunter poked a finger at Grant, 'is why we want to limit immigration. It makes things worse. We want the jobs for Germans, not immigrants.'

'But the immigrants do the menial jobs the Germans don't want,' Grant countered.

'Then we must pay the lower classes more. And, what's more, the immigrants stay and intermarry and dilute our stock. They are a bad influence, A friend of mine in Berlin said his kids come home from school speaking Turkish.'

'So is this guy Hauswald and his party going to make a difference?' Grant asked.

'We think so. He is bringing new industries into the state. There is a big new industrial estate here in Weimar, for example. And we are going to have a theme park. Disneyland Hansel and Gretel. That will bring lots of employment and boost the tourist industry.'

'I've noticed lots of promotions for the tourist industry,' said Grant.

'We have to make more of our history. Weimar in particular. Weimar is at the heart of German culture, From the time of Goethe. Not to mention the aristocracy at the time, which were great benefactors.'

'The NDVP is campaigning in Saxony now,' said Grant. 'Do you think Hauswald has plans to extend the party influence further? To the whole country perhaps?'

'Might be no bad thing,' Gunter shrugged his shoulders. 'If we get central government pursuing the same policies.'

'Hauwald is in favour of leaving the common currency and also the European union. Would you go along with that?'

'If it makes the German people better off, then I'm all for it.'

Very interesting, thought Grant. The next step in the sequence would be extending the borders, but Grant got the feeling that was not a question to be pursued.

#

'So how did it go in Berlin?' asked Bill.

'I suppose as well as could be expected.' Grant took a sip of his coffee. 'Suzanne gave me the low-down on this political party. But I somehow got the impression that she was not all that concerned. Well, not as concerned as I expected her to be, given the sense of urgency that the chancellor seemed to convey. It was as if she was not giving me the complete picture.'

'Yes. There could be more to this,' mused Bill. 'You may well be right. Now, Grant, I asked for an assessment of risk. What do you think?'

'I don't see any need to panic. I think the whole thing is very implausible. I do not see this party extending its influence to the rest of the country. Even if it has this charismatic leader. Guy called Otto Hauswald.'

'Friend of Maxwell's since childhood, I hear,' said Bill.

'Hauswald is supposed to be an orator. Holds the audience spellbound. Tells them what they want to hear.'

'Not surprising that the Germans are worried, then.'

'Thüringen is not your typical German state. I went down to Weimar to get some local colour. It's all very rural and traditional. Almost as if they are living in the past and would like to wind the clock back a hundred years. I can't see the party doing as well in west Germany.'

'Maybe. Maybe,' said Bill. 'But the Germans are upset about Maxwell's financial input?'

'Yes. They say that what is making the difference is this guy Hauswald and the amount of money at the party's disposal.'

'Maxwell is selling one of his paintings at auction very soon. It is expected to fetch a great deal of money.'

'You think it may be destined to go the NDVP?'

'I do. I think you had better go to the art auction,' said Bill. 'See what happens. Arrange an invitation.'

'Yes. OK. I'll do that,' said Grant.

'The question everyone is asking, I suppose, is why is Maxwell doing this?'

'Quite. Maxwell grew up in that part of the world and he may have some philanthropic tendency. But can we seriously believe that? My bet is that Maxwell has some commercial venture in mind and this party funding is all part of the deal.'

'Very plausible and I think I agree, but we have no option but to take this political thing seriously. I want you to talk to Maxwell now, give it to him straight that we are not amused and ask him for a frank explanation of what he is up to. What happens next depends on his attitude and what he has to say.'

'Do I have a threat if he is non-co-operative?'

'Not yet. The main thing is that Maxwell knows that we are aware of the situation.'

'OK. I'll arrange an interview.'

'You'll be seeing him on Thursday anyway.'

'How . . . ,' Grant began, but stopped after seeing Bill's expression. 'Sorry.'

'Is it his birthday?'

'Yes. His theme this time is Friends and Foes.'

'And presumably you are a foe?'

'Definitely.'

'Which brings me to something else,' said Bill. 'German intelligence has been making enquiries about another of our citizens.'

'In connection with Maxwell?'

78

'It has to, but at the moment I don't see it. The subject is a woman, born in Boston, trained as a lawyer at Yale. She now works in London and is divorced from her English husband. She had German parents who escaped from the Russians after the war. She uses her German maiden name and her English married name.'

'Does she work for us?'

'No.'

'So why are the Germans interested?'

'Routine enquiries. That means they aren't telling us. The Brits would have been much more open.'

'So why are you telling me this?'

'The reason, Grant, is that some bright spark here in Langley spotted her name on the list for Maxwell's party.'

'So what's her link to Maxwell?'

'We don't know. We have done a thorough check on her, but nothing has shown up. So, we would love to find out. We have arranged for you to sit next to her at the restaurant.'

Grant was about to say 'how' again, but stopped in time.

'We'll give you a bio. Apparently, she's a bit younger than you and still quite pretty. You might get lucky.'

CHAPTER 9

Dress formal. These days, in New York, what did that mean? For the men, tuxedo. But for the ladies? Long? Short? Pant suit (elegant)? Having accepted the invitation by letter, Katie telephoned the secretary.

'Whatever you wish to wear,' was the answer.

'What will the hostess be wearing?' Katie persisted.

'She hasn't decided yet.'

It would have to be the little black dress. Every woman's standby. And silver jewellery.

Katie still had no idea why she had been invited. How Maxwell even knew of her existence. The invitation had been to her German title. The family name was on the forged sale of the Titian. It must have something to do with that.

Katie had also prepared herself by looking up Marshall Maxwell on the internet. Wikipedia had given her a full biography, but only from when Maxwell arrived as an immigrant, to setting up his first company and then going from strength to strength. A perfect example of the American dream. The owner of the restaurant had a similar history and Katie wondered if they were friends because of this and hence the choice of venue. Katie also learnt that Maxwell had been married and divorced twice and that his current partner was an Italian fashion designer. Hmmph. Probably half his age, thought Katie.

#

The taxi deposited Katie at the entrance to the restaurant exactly at the advertised time. Punctuality had always been important in this city. Katie was just a little apprehensive. She had never met her host and the odds were that she would not know any of the guests either.

Just inside the entrance, a tall, elegant man was greeting the guests as they arrived. Marshall Maxwell was, Katie knew, fifty two years old, but he looked ten years younger. He had a full head of silver hair and his face had the level of suntan that said he had an exotic lifestyle, but did not sit in the sun. His tuxedo looked expensive and was a perfect fit, but Katie's attention was drawn to the woman at his side. As expected, she did not look a day over thirty; tall and slim and with long black hair. Katie was annoyed to see that she was wearing a full-length, off the shoulder, evening gown in black and gold with gold jewellery. Definitely designed to upstage all the guests. However, Katie was relieved to see that many of the other women lining up to be introduced were wearing either a short dress or an evening pant suit.

'Good evening, countess.' Maxwell shook her by the hand and smiled to reveal his perfect, very white dentition.

'Good evening, Mr Maxwell,' Katie replied. 'Now I am even more intrigued. You recognize me, even though we have never met. And I do not understand why I have been invited.'

'Your invitation said that this is a friends and foes party,' Maxwell reminded her, by way of explanation.

'Well, we are certainly not friends, so I must be considered as an enemy,' said Katie, with a wry smile.

'I am sure that after this evening you will be considered as a friend. Now, may I introduce my companion, Elizabeth Baldini.'

'Good evening,' said Katie. 'That is a wonderful dress.'

Elizabeth held out a limp hand to be shaken. 'I thought it a bit OTT. But Marshall always wants me to look my best'

'You have certainly succeeded,' said Katie.

A waiter offered Katie a glass of champagne and directed her to an easel with a table plan. The restaurant had been rearranged from its usual pattern and nearly all the tables were for eight. Katie found her table on the plan and, as she had anticipated, she did not know any of the other guests, although she did recognize some of the other names at other tables to be from big business or film and television.

As she entered the main restaurant a woman asked her name, whereupon she wrote it in large letters on a label that she stuck onto Katie's dress.

Other guests were assembled in the centre of the room. A man on his own approached her. 'Hi, my name is Tom. And you are Katie?'

'Yes,' Katie replied, glad to have someone to talk to.

'Are you from New York?'

'No. Boston'

'You weren't at Harvard, by any chance?'

Katie had noticed the man's bow tie in Harvard colours.

'No. Yale.'

'I forgive you. So what do you do?'

'Property lawyer. And you?'

82

'Also a lawyer. By education, that is. I now represent the Clark Institute. We're not very big, but we have one of the finest collections of art in the United States.'

'Yes. I know. I've heard of it,' said Katie. 'But I've never been.'

'I recommend a visit,' said Tom. 'It's in Williamstown. A beautiful place to visit. Not all that far from Boston, in fact.'

'I expect you know the history of the murals here.' said Katie. 'I've been to the restaurant before and always admired them.'

'Indeed,' said Tom. 'They were painted by Howard Chandler Christy. He was very well known in the 1920s and 30s. They are as fresh today as when they were painted.'

'So you must be a friend of Marshall's,' said Katie. 'With your common interest in art.'

'Indeed,' said Tom. 'But I'm also in New York to bid for one of his paintings. At the auction at Sotheby's tomorrow. The Death of St Peter Martyr by Titian.'

'I shall be there too,' said Katie, deciding not to let on her involvement. 'But as an observer.'

'I'll see you there, then,' said Tom. 'Now, better find our tables.'

Grant Henderson also arrived punctually for the party. And also he was not sure if he would know any of the other guests, but on entering the restaurant he had a pleasant surprise as he spotted a familiar face.

'Hello, Suzanne. How nice to see you.'

Suzanne was looking very beautiful in a long off-the-shoulder gown in bright red (*knall rot* as she described it). 'And nice to see you.' Suzanne offered a hand in a long black glove.

'The enemies are out in force this evening,' said Grant with a grin.

'Maybe in the majority,' said Suzanne.

'I've not had a chance to speak to Marshall yet,' said Grant. 'This evening is not the time, but I will be seeing him soon.'

'Maybe we can have a chat afterwards,' said Suzanne.

'We'll do that,' Grant agreed, wondering if a chat over dinner would be acceptable.

The conversation was interrupted by the maitre d' calling upon everyone to be seated.

Katie and all the other guests at her table introduced themselves, after which they we again called to order by the maitre d', who introduced Maxwell.

Maxwell and his partner had a lone table for two in the centre of the restaurant. The maitre d' handed Maxwell a microphone.

'Ladies and gentlemen,' Maxwell began, smiling at everyone. 'Welcome to Café des Artistes and I hope you will all have a great time. Yes, as some of you know, it is my birthday. I have decided to be forty again.'

There was loud laughter and applause from the guests, who spontaneously sang 'happy birthday'.

Maxwell beamed his thanks around the room. 'Some of you are old friends, some are new friends and there are some of you that I have never met before. But you all have one thing in common. You belong to one of two groups. As the invitation said, you are either a friend or a foe. Each one of you must decide into which group you fit.'

Again there was spontaneous laughter from the guests.

'So, this party is to say thank you to the friends, for their friendship and support, and to hope that the enemies can be converted.

Thank you all for coming and please forgive me if I do not have time to converse with you individually.'

Maxwell sat down to more applause as Katie surveyed her fellow diners.

'I think this friends and enemies thing is just a ploy to give us a starting topic for conversation,' said Grant, seated on Katie's right.

'I'm not so sure,' said Katie. 'I have never met Marshall before, so I am certainly not a friend. What about you?'

'I've known Marshall for some time,' said Grant. 'But only in a business capacity. Never socially.'

'Maybe we are both considered to be enemies,' said Katie with a smile. 'Did you compete? In business?'

'No. I'm in insurance. Our relations were always amicable.'

'Then maybe you are considered a friend after all.'

'I doubt it,' said Grant with a grimace. 'But you must have some connection with Marshall. He must have some reason to invite you.'

Katie thought for a moment, but then did not see any reason why she should not tell Grant about the painting.

'Marshall owns a painting that used to belong to my family. It's for sale at Sotheby's tomorrow. Marshall probably bought it in good faith, but somewhere along the line it was stolen from my family home in Germany.'

'No kidding,' said Grant. 'So is this sale legit? Do you have a claim? And I expect it's big bucks.'

'Minimum of fifty million,' said Katie.

Grant whistled.

'It is a bit confusing.' Katie then told Grant of her meetings at Sotheby's in London.

'So,' Katie concluded. 'I have never even seen this painting. I only have a photograph. And my only witness was an old servant who has recently died. The provenance includes evidence that my grandfather sold the painting in 1932.'

'You think that the sale document is a forgery?'

'It has to be. But proving it will be difficult. I have no other example of my grandfather's signature and I acknowledge the seal is genuine, because it was stolen with the painting.'

'I'm intrigued,' said Grant. 'I have to be at that auction tomorrow.'

'You're welcome,' said Katie. 'But attendance is by ticket only.'

'Don't worry. I can fix it,' said Grant.

'We all seem to be single people at this table,' said Katie. 'Is there a Mrs Grant?'

'I'm afraid not. My wife was killed in a car crash five years ago.'

'I'm very sorry,' said Katie.

'We were on vacation in Barbados. Some idiot drove into our rental car. My wife died instantly and I had several broken bones. Took me six months to recover.'

'How awful,' said Katie. 'And the other driver?'

'He died as well. Turned out he'd been in a rum shop all day.'

'What very bad luck,' said Katie.

'And yourself?' asked Grant.

Katie then gave him a potted biography, most of which Grant already knew. They then compared notes on the pros and cons of living on one's own.

On the other side of the restaurant, Suzanne and Alex had been introduced at the beginning of the evening and were seated on opposite sides of the table. A mutual attraction had developed, but conversation was difficult. As the meal finished, a small dance band assembled and started to play music from the classic shows of yesteryear. It seemed natural for Alex to ask Suzanne to dance.

After about fifteen minutes of very restricted movement on the tiny dance floor, they repaired to the bar.

'So, Suzanne, what brings you to the party?'

'I work in the fashion industry. I am really here as a guest of Marshall's companion, Elizabeth.'

'So you're a designer?'

'No. A model.'

'So what do you model?' Alex grinned at her. 'Lingerie?'

'No,' said Suzanne with mock primness. 'Haute couture. I am what the media call a supermodel. I model at fashion shows all over the world.' She indicated her dress. 'This is by Givenchy. I borrowed it for the evening.'

'It's beautiful,' said Alex, suitably chastened.

'So what do you do?'

'I'm an artist. I paint. Marshall has several of my paintings in his apartment.'

'You must be good.'

'I've not really broken through to the big time. But I'm getting there. I have an exhibition at my father's gallery here in Madison Avenue. Drop in and have a look.'

'I might do that.'

'All the work is for sale,' said Alex hopefully.

Maxwell had been circulating between the guests all evening, and it was only after dessert that he reached Katie's table. After pleasantries with the other diners, he quietly asked Katie if they could have a private chat. With some misgiving, Katie followed him to what seemed to be the manager's office.

Maxwell waved Katie to a chair. 'Countess, you are aware that I am selling an important work of art at Sotheby's tomorrow. And can I assume you are going to be present?'

'Yes. I am,' said Katie, wondering what was coming next.

'I have been informed by Professor Ahrens in Berlin and Sotheby's in London that you have been contesting the provenance of this painting.'

'Correct,' said Katie. 'I believe this painting was stolen from the cellars of my ancestral home on Rügen. Sometime after 1945, when my parents left. Which means that the bill of sale signed by my grandfather is a forgery.'

'So I understand,' said Maxwell. 'I am aware of all the facts. Sotheby's is satisfied with the provenance, as you have absolutely no evidence to back up your claim, especially as the only surviving witness has died. Nevertheless, you have decided to pursue this matter through the courts?'

'Yes.' Katie's mood was defiant. 'I intend to prove the bill of sale, supposedly by my grandfather, is a forgery.'

'That can be a very lengthy and costly business.'

'I know,' said Katie.

'Countess, I do not like uncertainty. This sale is going ahead. A great deal of money is involved and I do not want a cloud hanging over either the sale, or the aftermath.' Maxwell handed Katie a large brown envelope. 'This is a document that offers you five percent of the sale price achieved tomorrow, if you sign away any rights to the ownership of this painting. This is not an admission of defeat on my part. You receive a substantial sum of money and the matter is closed.'

Katie looked at the envelope dumbfounded. This was something she could never have anticipated.

'Take the document with you. Read it carefully. Bring it to the auction tomorrow and if you agree it can be signed and witnessed before the sale.'

Katie took the envelope and Maxwell escorted her back to her table without another word being said.

Grant looked at Katie's grim expression. 'What was that all about?'

'That painting. Maxwell wants to buy me off.'

'He's worried. You must have a case.'

'Not necessarily.'

'Are you going to accept?'

'I have no idea,' said Katie.

CHAPTER 10

'So what have you decided?'

Grant and Katie were having lunch in Peacock Alley in the Waldorf-Astoria.

Katie took a sip of her mineral water. 'Still not sure.'

'My advice is to agree and take the money. You get at least somewhere between two and three million dollars. If you go through the courts it could take for ever and cost you. And the court may not find in your favour.'

'It's not just the money. It's the principle. I'm not going to sign away my rights.'

'Just look at the facts, Katie. The only evidence you have is that old photograph. You have no corroborating evidence now that old woman is dead. All you can do is to prove that bill of sale is a forgery. Very difficult, with none of the participants alive. It's a no-brainer. Admit defeat and take the money. You won't get another chance.'

Katie sighed. 'Hmm. Maybe you're right. But if I agree, it's well, it's well, like letting down the family. Shirking my responsibility. To the heritage.'

'OK. Maybe it is. But I still think you should take the money.'

90

The taxi dropped them off outside the auction house on the Upper East Side. Katie and Grant showed the doorman their tickets and were directed to the second floor, where the auction was due to take place. In the lobby they were offered a glass of champagne and invited to view the paintings that were for sale.

Almost immediately Marshall Maxwell appeared, immaculately dressed in a pin-striped suit and a very brightly coloured tie. He gave Grant a forced smile. 'Katie?' Marshall took Katie's arm and steered her into a corner. 'So. Your decision?'

'I have decided to decline your offer,' said Katie, looking him calmly in the eye.

Marshall assumed an irritated expression. 'I was hoping to have you on board. We would make a good partnership. Why have you decided against?'

'It's not a matter of money. I would be betraying my family if I accepted.'

'OK. So be it. However, I think your sense of altruism is misguided. Are you going to pursue your claim to ownership?'

'Certainly.'

Marshall gave her another exasperated look. 'I will be in touch.'

Grant returned to Katie's side. 'So you said no?'

'Yes.' Katie's voce was thoughtful as she watched Marshall leave the lobby to enter an office.

'He wasn't best pleased.'

The day's auction was Old Masters and as such was a limited affair. There were only ten works for sale, but the collective value was

IAN LAURENCE

staggering. Grant and Katie wandered into an anteroom where the paintings were displayed. They were only able to view at a distance, as a rope and several security guards were in attendance.

'So this is the one,' said Grant, standing in front of the Titian.

'Yes,' said Katie whimsically. 'And to think that it belonged to my family for all those years.'

'Not exactly a Madonna and child. All rather violent.'

'Yes,' Katie agreed. 'It shows Saint Peter Martyr, a Dominican friar, being waylaid by hired assassins.'

'Not what you would expect to see in a church.'

Suddenly Katie stiffened. She went to up one of the security guards. 'Can I take a closer look at this painting please?'

The security guard took the rope off the hook and accompanied Katie, who went right up to the painting to take a hard look at a certain spot. She had come all over gooseflesh and could not really believe her eyes.

'Thank you,' she said, standing back. 'I should like to see whoever is in charge today. I have something important to say about this painting.'

The guard left the room as Grant, somewhat alarmed, said, 'Katie, what's up? You look like you've seen a ghost.'

'Maybe I have,' said Katie, as the guard reappeared.

'This way, madam,' said the guard.

'Come on. I will explain.' said Katie,

92

Grant and Katie followed the guard to the room where Katie had seen Marshall enter. Marshall was still there, talking earnestly to another man as they examined a catalogue on a desk.

'I am Charles Cameron-Smail,' said the other man, coming forward. 'I am the auctioneer in charge today. How can I help you?'

'I am the Countess Katherine von Arnitz,' said Katie. 'The painting by Titian, The Death of St Peter Martyr, being auctioned today, used to belong to my family. I have just looked at the painting and I am convinced it is a forgery.'

'Good grief,' exclaimed Cameron-Smail.

'Don't be ridiculous,' said Marshall. 'That painting has had two independent assessments. From the two leading world experts on the artist.'

'Countess, why are you so sure that this is a forgery?' asked the auctioneer.

'A long time ago there was a firearms accident at my family home in Germany. My grandfather put a bullet through the painting. It was restored, but not very well and the area was still visible. This painting shows no sign of that damage. I have a photograph of the picture to prove it.' Katie took the photograph from her handbag to show to the auctioneer. 'Here, in the top left hand corner. In the sky above the cloud. The painting is much lighter here, as compared to the darkness of the trees on the other side. You can see where the painting was repaired.'

Cameron-Smail examined the photograph and then passed it to Marshall. 'That certainly looks like restoration. But I would imagine that if the original restoration was not very good, it could be repeated. That is very probably what has occurred.' The auctioneer smiled condescendingly at Katie. 'So that now the painting looks pristine. And that does not detract from the value,' he added. 'It is accepted that very old works of art deteriorate and need to be restored.'

'That is what must have happened,' Marshall agreed. 'I know that further restoration work was done.'

'It all looks too perfect to me,' said Katie. 'In that particular area.'

'Of course,' smiled Marshall. 'The restorer was a perfectionist.'

'You must have had X-rays taken before the painting was offered for sale,' Katie persisted. 'What did they show?'

'Evidence of repair,' said Marshall reluctantly.

'In that area?' asked the auctioneer.

Marshall nodded. 'Apparently that was the main focus of the restoration.'

'OK. Let's go take a look.' Holding the photograph, Cameron-Smail led the way back to the anteroom. He examined the area of the painting that Katie had indicated.

'I see no evidence of repair,' he said. 'They did a very good job.'

'Look at the back,' said Katie. 'There would be a tear in the canvas if a bullet had gone through it.'

The auctioneer indicated to the attendants, who took the painting off the wall.

Katie, Grant, Marshall and the auctioneer waited with bated breath as the painting was turned round. The room had gone silent as other guests gathered round, somehow aware of the tension.

Cameron-Smail ran his hand over the back of the canvas, which was unblemished. 'You are right, Countess. There is no evidence of damage in this area.'

Marshall pushed forward. 'Let me see.' He also ran his hand over the back of the canvas.

'I am really so very sorry, Mr Maxwell.' Cameron-Smail's face was grim. 'I fear that the countess is correct.'

'I do not understand.' Marshall was distraught.

'Please remove this painting,' Cameron-Smail said to the guards. 'The sale of this item will not now go ahead.' He then turned to the others. 'Please come back to my office.'

Marshall could only stand dumbfounded, looking at the back of the painting, still in disbelief.

'Oh my God,' said Grant. 'The question is, where's the real one?'

Back in the auctioneer's office, Maxwell could only pace the floor as Cameron-Smail invited everyone to be seated.

'I consider this to be a very grave affair,' said Cameron-Smail. 'Mr Maxwell, you are sure you delivered the real painting to us?'

'Of course.' Maxwell threw his arms out wide. 'But I never thought of looking at the back.' He paused. 'Why should I?'

'Indeed. Indeed,' said the auctioneer thoughtfully. 'The painting could have been substituted at any time. Presumably after the expert's assessment of the authenticity. I must say, the artist was absolutely brilliant. I could never have told it was a fake.'

Maxwell could only expel a snort of anger.

'We will have to call in the police,' said Cameron-Smail, looking round at everyone. 'And hope they can get to the bottom of it.'

#

It was quite some time later that Grant and Katie left the building, Katie having made her statement to the police.

'I booked a table for dinner at Le Cirque this evening,' said Grant. 'I hope that's OK?'

'Lovely,' said Katie.

'Collect you at 6.30?'

#

Between courses, Katie produced her copy of the list she had found in the safe in Grimaud. 'This is a list that was made by the robbers of the most valuable paintings that were in the cellar.'

'So how did you come by this?' asked Grant, taking it from her.

There was no way that Katie was going to tell Grant about Steven and she had already thought of the answer. 'It was found by the housemaid I told you about. She used to clean for the people who took over our old house. She found it just before the house was demolished.'

'I see somebody made notes.'

'Yes. The majority of the items have either OH or ND against them,' said Katie. 'Having seen the provenance of the Titian, OH is obviously Otto Hauswald, who supposedly sold the painting to Marshall.'

Grant looked at her in surprise. 'You're kidding! Otto Hauswald sold that painting to Marshall?'

'You know him?' Now it was Katie's turn to look surprised.

'No. Hearsay.'

'That's what the provenance shows. I have a copy of the bill of sale. Which is a forgery, of course.'

96

'Of course.' Grant examined the list. 'It's obvious to me that these robbers used Otto Hauswald as a fence. Didn't you say that he has a gallery here in New York?'

'Yes, he does. In fact, I have arranged to see him at the gallery tomorrow morning.'

'So are you going to accuse him? Show him this list and ask for an explanation?'

'I think that would be a waste of time. A piece of paper like this is not really evidence.'

'Maybe not. But it would let him know that you are onto him.'

'I don't think that's a good idea,' said Katie. 'I just want to meet him. I said that I wanted to talk about his father's art collection and how he came by the Titian.'

'I'm surprised he agreed to see you.'

'I think he was interested in meeting me.'

'I'm suggesting it will be a waste of time.'

'Probably. But you never know. He might let something slip.'

'I have a flight back to Florida tomorrow morning,' said Grant, 'but if you would like some moral support, I could delay it until later in the day.'

Gallery Hauswald was on Madison Avenue, sandwiched between a jewellers and an antique store. The front window of the gallery was occupied entirely by a huge bronze Buddha, before which Grant and Katie paused in awe.

'I guess that isn't on your list,' said Grant with a grin.

'Sure isn't.' Katie returned the smile.

The street door opened into a room displaying only three very large paintings, all emphasized by spotlights. There was nobody in the room and Grant and Katie had time to examine them at their leisure. Grant raised his eyebrows at Katie and she shook her head. She knew the list off by heart.

A woman attendant appeared to ask if they needed help. Katie informed her of their appointment and she disappeared into the rear of the gallery.

Very shortly a man appeared, dressed in a grey suit and a red tie, who strode purposefully towards them.

'Otto Hauswald,' he said, shaking them both firmly by the hand. Otto Hauswald was a tall man with curly grey hair getting rather thin on the top, compensated by a beard and moustache that were more white than grey. His dark brown eyes darted from one to the other, as if he was scanning and committing to memory.

'Katie von Arnitz,' said Katie, 'and this is Grant Henderson.'

'I saw you at the auction yesterday,' said Otto. 'Amazing. I have never known anything like it. Marshall is distraught.'

'So have you any ideas as to what might have happened?' Katie asked.

'Absolutely none at all,' said Otto. 'I was totally uninvolved. I attended the auction out of interest.'

'The substitution was very cleverly done,' said Grant.

'It certainly was,' Otto agreed. 'Whatever, it is up to the police to come up with an answer. Now, please come to our customer reception area. Nancy will get us some coffee.'

98

Katie and Grant followed Otto to another room, containing more artwork, but also set out with a low table and four upholstered upright chairs in one corner. All the while Otto was pontificating on the state of the art world and the quality of modern art and the proficiency of the artists and Katie realized that Otto was one of that rare breed; a man who never stops talking. It was impossible to get in a word or an opinion and when a break happened, it was too late, as the conversation had moved on.

Katie was already finding Otto very irritating, although she agreed with a lot of what he was saying. His manner was arrogant and it was as if only his opinion mattered.

'I understand that you sold the Titian to Marshall,' said Katie, managing to interject as Otto arranged the chairs.

'Yes. Indeed I did. In 2005, I believe. It had been in my father's collection.' Otto held up his hand as Katie was about to interrupt. 'Yes, I know you have been disputing the provenance. But that was all before my time. I have to say that I took no interest, nor did I have any idea what was in my father's art collection. He had more paintings that he had wall space. Pictures were rotated all the time. It was only after he died that I actually did an inventory.'

'So the Titian was in your possession in 2005?'

'Indeed it was,' said Otto. 'I placed it in the gallery here and Marshall bought it soon afterwards. I know you think the painting was stolen from your family home, but I have to go along with the bill of sale between your grandfather and mine.'

Katie's expression said that she did not believe Otto's story.

'I gather from Marshall that you are going to contest ownership through the courts' said Otto.

'Yes.' Katie gave him a look of defiance. 'I am.'

'OK,' said Otto, taking note of Katie's look. 'You have no first hand knowledge. Only hearsay. And an old photograph taken by your father. The only credible key to your claim was the evidence of the now deceased servant. I am now going to pay devil's advocate. How many paintings were in that cellar?'

'Thirty seven,' said Katie, without hesitation.

'And how many were valuable old masters?'

'Only the one, the Titian, was of great value. There were other paintings of a similar size, perhaps five, but not of the same quality.'

'And the rest?'

'There were at least ten that were quite valuable, including a Monet. The rest were smaller, more modern works. Such as George Gros, Otto Dix, Emile Nolde.'

'OK,' said Otto, standing up and holding the lapels of his jacket, as if in a court of law. 'Let us assume that, what was the maid's name?'

'Hildegard Weber.'

'And she would have been what, twenty two, or thereabouts?'

'Twenty two.'

'Let us assume that Frau Weber is still alive and is testifying in court. Now, Frau Weber, the date is 1939 and war has been declared. That would be seventy two years ago. Correct?'

Otto moved a pace to the side. 'Correct.'

'And your employer decided to hide away all the valuables in the house.' Otto continued to change his position. 'I cannot imagine, as a junior member of the staff, that you were actually present in the hallway and witnessed the removal of this particular painting.'

'No, but all the paintings were removed, so it must have gone.'

'I understand that there were also paintings of a similar size and subject matter in the house.'

'Yes.'

'And were paintings sometimes taken down and moved?'

'Yes, but only when rooms were decorated.'

'Frau Weber, may I suggest that after seventy years you could not ascertain with one hundred percent certainty that the painting by Titian was hanging in the house, in that position, at that time. I suggest that it is possible that it was removed at an earlier date and it was replaced by another very similar painting.'

Otto looked at Katie and Grant in turn. 'In my opinion, the court would not consider Frau Weber's evidence sufficiently convincing to overturn the provenance and ownership of this painting.'

Katie could only look at Otto with a glum expression, knowing that he was probably right.

'What I suggest, countess, to put your mind at rest and,' Otto looked at her with a half smile, 'to prove my innocence in this whole affair, is that you visit my main residence in Weimar and examine my collection. I can assure you that none of your family's paintings are there, but you must see for yourself. You are most welcome to visit anytime.'

Otto escorted Katie and Grant to the door, explaining the artwork on the way. 'On this wall are paintings by my son Alex. He is very gifted and his work is beginning to be recognized. I have another son, Henry, who has no talent in that direction. He manages the gallery in my absence.'

'Lying through his teeth,' said Grant, after they had walked a few paces down the street.

'Everything?' Katie shot him a quick glance.

'Certainly. He and Marshall are in this together. And all that stuff about his father's collection was all baloney.'

'Sure?'

'Absolutely sure. Experience in my job has given me a very good idea of when people are lying. Making false insurance claims,' Grant added hastily.

'I didn't like him at all,' said Katie, with an expression of distaste. 'So sure of himself. And the sinister way he looks at you with those penetrating eyes. But I think I'll still take him up on that offer of looking at his personal collection.'

'I can guarantee that none of your pictures will be there.'

'Probably,' Katie agreed, 'but you never know when clues will appear.'

Katie and Grant walked on down Madison Avenue, each wondering how to take leave of each other. Grant was flying out of La Guardia, whilst Katie was flying back to London the following day.

It was Grant who broke the silence. 'Katie, I've enjoyed your company so much. Can we keep in touch? And see each other again soon? I do have to come to Europe occasionally on business.'

'I'd like that.' Katie smiled at him and took his hand. 'We will contrive a meeting as soon as we can.' She reached into her handbag. 'This is my card and I've written my home number and e-mail address on the back.'

Grant reached in his pocket. 'And I've done exactly the same for you.'

They both laughed as they exchanged cards.

'I have to go,' said Grant. 'I expect you can walk from here. I'll hail a cab.'

'Then I'll see you soon,' said Katie, leaning forward to give him a kiss on the cheek.

'You sure will,' said Grant, as a taxi stopped by him.

#

When Katie returned to her hotel room, the message light was flashing. The message was from Marshall, inviting her to dinner that evening. He would collect her at seven o'clock unless it was not convenient.

Katie tapped her foot with some annoyance at Marshall's presumption that she was free that evening. She was free, but that was not the point. Should she refuse on principle? After a few moments thought she decided to comply. Marshall might have some information about the missing painting.

#

Marshall and a stretch limo duly arrived at seven o'clock. 'I've reserved a table at my club,' said Marshall, as he met Katie in the hotel lobby. Marshall was looking immaculate in a dark grey suit with a blue shirt and a striped tie. Katie had been in the not unusual quandary of not knowing what to wear. In the end, she had settled for what had been her second choice for the party; a blue silk two piece with a white jacket.

'I'm glad you were free this evening,' said Marshall. 'After I left the message I thought I was being a bit presumptuous.'

'It's fortunate I had already decided to stay an extra day,' said Katie as Marshall helped her into the car.

Marshall was a member of a private club on the upper east side that was restricted to prominent men in American big business. It reminded

Katie more of a gentlemen's club in London, with wood panelled walls and large leather chairs and hushed conversation.

It was not until they were seated in a corner of the dining room that Katie broached the subject. 'Any news on the Titian?'

'Absolutely none. The police have come up with nothing.'

'So what's your theory?'

'I'll give you the sequence from the beginning. Firstly, I had the painting delivered to my apartment from the vault.'

'The vault?' said Katie. 'What do you mean? In your cellars?'

'No,' Marshall smiled. 'There is a company here in Manhattan that stores works of art in a very secure environment.'

'Huh,' said Katie. 'What is the point of owning a masterpiece and keeping it in a vault? I suppose just as an investment. Like buying cases of rare wine and never drinking it.'

'Well, something like that,' Marshall admitted. 'I must explain that I have several valuable paintings. Some I do have on display, but one has to realize these days it is almost impossible to get insurance for what a painting is worth. The cost of the insurance is prohibitive.'

'I see your point,' said Katie.

'So what I do, and a lot of other people do as well, and this is rather ironic in these circumstances, is that we have a copy made. I have a van Gogh in a very prominent position in my apartment. Everyone stops to admire it. But it is a copy. The real one is in the vault. If this one was stolen, it would not matter.'

'So there's quite a business in copying paintings?'

'Indeed there is. And several people making a good living from it.'

'So this will be a line of enquiry by the police? Interviewing all the artists that make copies?'

'Yes. And I understand they are doing just that.'

'So let's get back to the Titian. When could someone have copied it?'

'Katie, I am at a loss. The painting was transferred to my apartment. I then had two experts visit me to have the painting authenticated. Sotheby's, as you know, are very thorough and insisted on this. It was then delivered to the auction house in time for the preview.'

'What I don't understand,' said Katie, 'is the time scale. How long would it take to make a perfect copy of that painting?'

'I would guess weeks. Months, even. It would be very painstaking work.'

'It was copied some time in the past,' said Katie. 'Before you bought it.'

'That had occurred to me also.'

'When it was in Mr Hauswald's possession.'

'Well, the Hauswald family,' Marshall agreed. 'I have already discussed this with Otto and he said it must have been done some time ago, when his father was alive.'

'I suppose we'll never know,' said Katie. 'So when was it substituted?'

'It has to be when the painting was transferred from my apartment to Sotheby's. Somewhere along the line. The police have questioned everyone involved, but come up with nothing.'

'Maybe stolen to order,' said Katie. 'Planned over a long time. It's probably hanging in someone's private collection. Anywhere in the world.'

'My conclusion also,' said Marshall ruefully. 'I will probably never see it again.'

It was towards the end of the meal that Marshall announced his surprise. 'Katie, my real reason for inviting you this evening was not just to discuss the Titian. I have a proposal to make.'

Katie looked at him with some trepidation. She might have known Marshall had something extra to spring on her.

'Katie, I need a new PA. Not someone to arrange my calendar,' Marshall added hastily. 'I have a team who does that. I need someone to accompany me to important business events.'

'You have Elizabeth to do that,' said Katie. Her initial reaction being one of irritation. That Marshall should be so arrogant as to assume that she would be his assistant.

'Yes, I do,' said Marshall hurriedly, aware of Katie's negative reaction. 'But Elizabeth's command of English is not good. She has very limited comprehension of business and finance. At events that are important, even vital, for my business interests, her presence does not help. Sometimes even hinders. I need someone who can converse on equal terms. Look, Katie,' Marshall tried to be condescending, 'it would only be very occasionally. And anywhere in the world. Needless to say, a generous salary and expenses.'

Katie's expression said that she was somewhat mollified.

'You would be a great asset to the team,' said Marshall. 'No decision now. Think about it.'

CHAPTER 11

Detlef had been to London before, as a member of an East German athletics team. And he also had a good working knowledge of English. At school in the DDR it was compulsory to learn Russian, but occasionally other language tuition was available, mostly English and Spanish. Detlef had been fortunate to get a good basic education, but thereafter the accent was on vocational training. Very few students progressed to university.

Detlef had arranged to meet Bert at a pub called the Spread Eagle in Peckham Rye, in the East End. He had his instructions and found the pub with no difficulty. The Spread Eagle was very old fashioned, with wood panelled walls that were covered in memorabilia of London from the time the pub was built over a hundred years ago.

Bert was sitting at the bar with a pint of beer at his elbow. He stood up to greet Detlef as Rainer had done, with a hug and much shoulder-slapping.

'Detlef, my old comrade. How good to see you. You must try the local English beer. Mind you, you may not like it. It's an acquired taste.'

'I will try it,' said Detlef. 'I did not like it last time, but maybe it has improved.'

'You may be disappointed,' said Bert. 'Let's find somewhere to talk.'

Bert led the way to a quiet table. 'Not so important, as I would guess nobody in here speaks German. So, Detlef, how have you been keeping?'

It was sometime later that the reminiscences dried up. 'So, let's get to the job in hand,' said Bert. 'Stefan Schimonsky, or Steven Jackson as he now is. I found him quite easily. He was even in the telephone directory. He lives in the West End and I have his address. I have been doing a bit of surveillance and monitoring his routine. But I haven't seen him for a while, so he may be away on holiday, or on a business trip. So, how would you prefer to get rid of him?'

'There is also the question of the location of his brother,' said Detlef. 'Finding and eliminating Stefan is only the half of it. So we need that information also.'

'I didn't know he had a brother,' said Bert. 'At the moment, I don't see how we can do that.'

'We need to burglarise his apartment.'

'Yes. OK,' said Bert thoughtfully. 'That is probably the only way we can find that out. But before or after we assassinate him? Debatable. Before might alert him to the danger he is in. I think after. We will plan to burglarise the apartment immediately after he is killed. Or even at the same time.'

'So what are the options?' asked Detlef.

'A sniper's rifle would be a possibility. I have investigated and we can get access to the roof of the building opposite. No problem to a marksman like you.'

'I had some practice before I set out.'

'Good. And with a laser sight it would be difficult to miss. We would have to draw up a schedule of Stefan's movements and pick the best time. Also, it would have a much greater chance of success if it were performed in daylight, which means there would be other people around and we do not want you to get caught. The location is very close to Harrods department store, where a policewoman was shot some time ago. There are lots of security cameras. So I have another idea. Maybe a bomb under his car would be better. This could be placed in the middle of the night with much less chance of detection.'

'Yes, but I don't want to kill anyone else.'

'Of course not. But that isn't really a problem. Every morning Stefan goes to the gym early. It's a quiet street and I would doubt if anybody else would be around.'

'All very well talking about a car bomb,' said Detlef, 'but the question is, how do we get hold of one?'

'Hopefully, not a problem. When I talked to Rainer about how we were going to get rid of Stefan, Rainer said he could arrange the necessary hardware. A rifle, bomb, whatever. Rainer's time in prison was not wasted. He made some very useful contacts.'

'You said Stefan is away,' said Detlef. 'I suppose we wait until he returns.'

'Not necessarily,' said Bert. 'In fact, it might be in our favour. We plant the bomb and the next time Stefan drives the car, it goes off. The longer the time difference the better.'

'I see what you mean,' Detlef agreed. 'I will be well away by then.'

'Right,' said Bert. 'In the meantime, I'll show you around and we can do a proper reconnoitre of where Stefan lives.'

CHAPTER 12

'Wonderful. You go back to the States and have two new men after your charms,' said Angela, pouring them each another glass of wine. 'And both about your age.' The two women were again having lunch in Harvey Nichols department store. 'So, tell me about them.'

'Well, Marshall, he's the guy who gave the party, is much the better looking. Could be a movie star. Dyes his hair, I'm sure, and works out. Looks very fit.'

'Yes. Very positive. Physically attractive. Rich and powerful. Can you see a permanent relationship?'

'He already has a fiancée.'

'So?' said Angela, with a curl of the lip.

'Angela, the eternal cynic,' said Katie with a smile. 'He took me out for dinner and gave me a big surprise.'

'He propositioned you already? He really is a quick mover.'

'No. He made me a job offer. To be a PA on special occasions. When he has to meet important people, especially internationally.'

'Huh,' Angela sneered. 'Amounts to the same thing. You mark my words. He's grooming you. Did you accept?'

110

'I'm supposed to think about it. But I think I will. Our firm has not been doing too well since the recession started. Residential property in London has been selling with no difficulty, but commercial property has been particularly badly hit. So the extra money would be very useful. Also, it might be exciting. And if this painting reappears, I'll get to know about it.'

'Good point. Now, what about the other guy?'

'Much more homely. Tall. Quite good-looking. Mischievous smile that I find attractive. Hair going grey and a bit overweight.'

'What's he do?'

'He works for an insurance company.'

'Sounds a better bet. More your type. Sympathetic?'

'Yes.'

'Concerned for your well-being?'

'Yes. I suppose so.'

'Tries to make you laugh?'

Katie thought for a moment. 'Yes. Maybe he does.'

'Sounds like you're better off with him,' said Angela.

'I really am rather fond of Grant,' said Katie, wistfully. 'And he e-mails and texts me almost every day.'

'Sounds like he's smitten. So when are you seeing him again?'

'He says he is coming to London soon.'

'Don't forget that both of these guys want to get you into bed. That's their main objective.'

'Angela, here we go again. You always assume that.'

'I'm a realist. I warned you about that other guy, didn't I? When you had to come back from France in a hurry. You were lucky to get out of that one.'

Katie bit her lip as the memories returned. She could not bear to tell anyone about what had really happened in Grimaud, not even Angela.

'You know I'm right,' Angela continued. 'Didn't you see that column in the newspaper the other day? It was by this woman professor. She did research to show that men have a much larger area in the brain concerned with sex than women have. It explains why men think about sex all the time. Young and old alike.'

'No,' said Katie, with a smile. 'I didn't see it.'

'The way to choose between these two guys is to imagine you're in bed with them,' said Angela, in all seriousness. 'Imagine them on top of you. Ask yourself if you really would want that to happen. And if you could go along with it.'

Katie laughed.

'You'll see if I'm right.'

#

That same day, Grant was entertaining Marshall to lunch at his club in mid-town Manhattan.

'I enjoyed the birthday dinner,' said Grant, once they were seated. He smiled. 'I hope everyone ended the evening as your friend.'

Marshall returned the smile. 'I doubt it. But I hope you did. Thank you for your letter.'

'You're welcome. Just my good luck that I was seated next to Katie.'

'Indeed,' said Marshall. 'Quite a coincidence. It appears that you got on famously.'

'We found lots to talk about.'

'Seeing her again?'

'No plans. Three thousand miles is quite a separation.'

'Quite,' said Marshall.

'I couldn't believe what happened with that painting,' said Grant 'Any news?'

'Absolutely none. The police have questioned anybody who could have had access to the picture, however remotely. Not a clue.'

'Very strange,' Grant agreed. 'It must have been stolen to order. Planned for some time.'

'Probably,' said Marshall. 'I have to admit that I was devastated.' Marshall paused and looked Grant in the eye. 'It had occurred to me that your company might have been involved.'

'Crossed my mind also,' said Grant. His reply had been automatic. Why hadn't he thought of that? Especially after the conversation with Bill. 'I enquired. Negative.'

Marshall's expression said that he did not believe him. 'I had already put the money into my financial calculations.'

'No insurance?'

'None of my paintings are insured.'

'I am assuming that some, or all, of this money was going to Germany,' said Grant, 'and this brings me to the reason I wanted to talk to you. The company is concerned about your financial involvement with this new political party in Germany. The NDVP. The president and the chancellor are in close communication over this issue.'

'I understand the concern,' said Marshall smoothly. 'I am a philanthropist. I support good causes. In Germany, as well as in America. Don't forget, Grant, that I have dual nationality. I am a German citizen. As such, I am free to give as much money as I like to a political party.'

'So I understand,' said Grant. 'Marshall, I am not going to beat about the bush. You and I have always done some straight talking. Your claim to be supporting worthy causes seems to me a bit thin. A smokescreen, if you like. If you have an ulterior motive, I would like to hear about it.'

'Grant, I am supporting this political party and my actions are transparent. Although I am an American citizen, this is my homeland. A political vacuum is being created in Germany. All the main parties are in favour of more and more European integration and the majority of the population do not want that. This party is filling that vacuum and telling the people what they want to hear. The NDVP is a radical party and I agree with their policies. Therefore, I am supporting them with money and advice. It is as simple as that.'

'Hmm,' said Grant, with unveiled scepticism. 'I understand you have started a company in Weimar. In the new industrial estate.'

'Correct. We manufacture machine tools. Something the Germans have always been particularly good at. The problem is getting the local workmen accustomed to the western work ethic. In the DDR, working practices were very lax and the companies were very inefficient.'

'And future plans?'

'If the company is successful, we will expand it.'

'OK,' said Grant. 'Don't forget that we shall be keeping an eye on you.'

CHAPTER 13

Detlef and Bert were having a late breakfast on the next day after the car bomb had been successfully planted. Detlef was leaving for the airport later that afternoon.

'Couldn't have been easier,' said Bert. 'Took about ten seconds. That was a very strong magnet. It's not going to fall off before Stefan gets in the car.'

'And absolutely nobody around,' added Detlef.

'I might be wrong,' said Bert, 'but I'm pretty sure that car was parked out of range of a camera. Still, nobody would be able to recognize us.'

They turned on the radio for the news and traffic report and were horrified by what the presenter had to say.

A car bomb has exploded in the West End of London. The only casualty was the driver of the car, a Mr Mohammad Khan, who was a garage employee taking the car for service. The car in question belongs to a Mr Steven Jackson, 53, a wealthy ship broker and property developer, who is at present in hospital in France. Mr Jackson said that he could see no reason why he might have been targeted. The real IRA, in a coded message, has claimed responsibility for the attack, but it appears that this could have been a case of mistaken identity, as a neighbour of Mr Jackson in Beaufort Gardens is Mr Peter Wilson, a former Northern

Ireland minister. The Metropolitan police said that all past serving officials in Northern Ireland would be receiving extra protection.

'Shit,' said Bert. 'How were we to know that Stefan is in hospital and that the car was going for service.'

'We couldn't,' said Detlef. 'But it means that we failed.'

'Just bad luck,' said Bert.

'We need a plan B,' said Detlef. 'We can't try a car bomb again.'

Bert nodded. 'It will have to be a shooting. We will have to decide how.'

'I've been thinking about that,' said Detlef. 'Just supposing that the car bomb didn't work. Not a shooting in the street, but shooting him in his apartment.'

'At night, you mean. When he is in bed?'

'Not necessarily. I would rather confront him. So that he knows why he is to die.'

'OK,' said Bert slowly. 'If that's what you want to do.'

'Then that's it. When he returns from France. I will shoot him in the apartment and then we will take as much material as we can. His computer and whatever else we find. That should give us the information to find his brother.'

'Time to leave for the airport,' said Bert. 'I'll give you a call when Stefan returns from France.'

'I wonder what's wrong with him,' said Detlef, picking up his suitcase. 'Do you think he is going to die?'

'No. It can't be too bad,' said Bert. 'Otherwise they would have said in the radio report.'

Katie, watching the television news that evening, was both horrified and perplexed. She could imagine Steven having enemies from his past, but why now? She was much more inclined to believe the mistaken identity theory. Her next thought was that it was a great pity that Steven was not in the car.

CHAPTER 14

Weimar is not only famous as the seat of the German government in the troublesome period after the first world war. At various times it was the home of Goethe, Schiller, Liszt and Nietzsche. Walter Gropius founded the Bauhaus movement in Weimar in 1919. There are several notable buildings, including the German National Theatre, the Herder church and the Anna Amalia Library. And Weimar was the European city of culture in 1999.

Katie had telephoned the Hauswald residence, to be told by the butler that Dr Hauswald was away in Leipzig and that he was then going on to New York. However, his son Alex would be at home and would be pleased to show Katie round the art collection.

Katie flew to Berlin and took the train to Weimar the next morning. A taxi brought her to the main square, where she checked into the Elephant Hotel. She then found the Hauswald residence in a side street, Schlossgasse, diagonally opposite the hotel across the square. A wrought iron gate in a stone archway led to a gravelled courtyard and an imposing four-storey house, which had rendered walls painted in muted shades of grey and green with the windows framed in yellow. Katie had noticed that many of the houses in the town were similarly painted, predominantly in a bright shade of yellow. To the side of the front door was a gleaming, red, open-topped Ferrari.

Katie pressed the bell push at the side of the gate. Someone must have been watching, because the gate opened before she could speak into the microphone. A man answered the front door of the house. He was dressed in medieval costume, including knickerbocker trousers, long stockings, a velvet coat and a white curly wig.

His appearance took Katie completely by surprise. She could only assume that he was the butler.

'Good morning,' said the butler, with a welcoming smile.

'Countess von Arnitz,' said Katie. 'I have an appointment to see Mr Hauswald.'

'Please come in, countess,' said the butler, bowing stiffly from the waist. 'Mr Hauswald is expecting you.'

Katie was invited to sit in the hall, as the butler disappeared up the staircase. Katie sat on a red plush settee and gazed around the room. An elaborate flower arrangement stood on a large, round mahogany table and the bare stone walls were covered with portraits of men and women in period dress. The staircase was flanked by two large marble statues of what looked like Greek gods.

Very shortly a young man entered the hall. He was dressed in a black T-shirt and jeans and Katie thought she had seen him somewhere before. The thought also registered that he was very good-looking. He had clear-cut handsome features and a ready smile and reminded her of a boyfriend from her high school days. In fact, he had a rather old-fashioned look, wearing his hair longer than was the current fashion and with a parting, typified by the men in preppy magazine advertisements for clothing such as Ralph Lauren.

'Alex Hauswald,' said the young man, extending his hand. 'I remember you from Marshall's birthday party in New York.'

'Of course,' said Katie. 'I thought I recognized you. I'm sorry we were not introduced.'

'Lots of people there,' said Alex. 'You can't get round everybody.'

'Have you any news of the Titian?' asked Katie, as Alex led the way up the staircase.

'None. A complete mystery. Maybe we'll never see it again.'

'Yes,' said Katie. 'I feared as much.'

'This is what we call the drawing room,' said Alex, as they entered a large room at the top of the staircase. 'You came to see father's art collection. Most of the valuable paintings are in this room.'

Katie started to walk round the room, mentally ticking off each painting. She knew her list by heart.

'OK, Katie,' said Alex with a grin. 'I know why you've come. You want to see if any other paintings from your family cellar are here.'

Katie stopped to give Alex an embarrassed look.

'Fair enough,' said Alex. 'Father sold the Titian to Marshall. It could be that more of your family paintings have passed through his hands. I don't blame you wanting to have a look.'

'I don't want to imply that your father was involved in their theft,' said Katie, still with an air of embarrassment.

'No offence taken,' said Alex, with a shrug of the shoulders. 'I expect you would recognize one if you saw one.'

'I have a photograph of each one,' said Katie, reaching her handbag. 'But I do know them by heart.' She handed Alex the photographs. 'They are old and in black and white, but still good enough to make an identification.'

'Right,' said Alex, riffling through the prints. 'Well, I can tell you that none of these are here now.'

'Uh huh,' said Katie, disappointed. 'But can you remember ever seeing any of them before?'

'Can't say I have,' said Alex, handing back the prints. 'But some of those artists painted several paintings with a similar subject matter, so it's difficult to say. And the prints being in black and white doesn't help.'

'It was always a forlorn hope,' said Katie, looking at Alex with a resigned expression.

'Katie, I know that you disputed the bill of sale of the Titian between your grandfather and my great-grandfather. We're never going to know for sure.'

'Well, I'm sure,' Katie retorted. 'Our old housemaid was definite in her memories at the beginning of the war.'

'OK. Maybe. Perhaps the bill of sale was a forgery. Who knows? We are never going to find out how our family bought the painting.'

'If it ever did,' said Katie.

'OK. Point taken,' said Alex.

'Alex, I know there are none of our paintings here now, but I expect your father sold other paintings to Marshall.'

'Indeed he did. But I've no idea if any of them belonged originally to your family.'

'Well, I guess that's it, then,' said Katie with a forlorn expression. 'Thank you for your time.'

'Not so fast,' said Alex. 'You must visit my studio. See what you think of my work.'

'Oh. OK. Thank you,' said Katie. 'I'd be glad to.'

'My studio is at the top of the house.' Alex started to lead her further up the wide staircase.

'What's your favourite medium?' asked Katie.

'Watercolour, I suppose. But I also paint in oil. Pastel. Everything, really.'

At the top of the staircase they turned into a corridor that led to a large, bright room. A typical artist's studio thought Katie. Paintings were stacked against the walls and everywhere was in a state of untidiness. In the centre of the room was an easel and, in front of it, an upholstered chair.

Alex showed Katie several of what he considered to be his best work and then surprised her.

'Tell you what,' said Alex. 'I do portraits. How about sitting for me?'

'Oh. No,' said Katie, embarrassed. 'Come on. I'm too old for that.'

'Nonsense. You have interesting bone structure. You will make an ideal subject.'

'Well, all right,' said Katie after a moment's thought. 'Why not. The rest of my day is free.'

'Terrific. Sit on this chair. My usual chair for portraits. The light is at its best here.'

Katie sat on the chair as Alex prepared his materials.

'OK. I'm ready. Now, face me, but look over my right shoulder. Perfect.' Alex started to draw a rough outline. 'Tell me about yourself. Where you grew up.'

Katie related her childhood and student days in America and then as a lawyer and mother in London.

'Very interesting,' said Alex, but having recounted her life history out loud, Katie was thinking what a boring existence she had led. So conventional. Nothing adventurous or exciting to mention. And she was sure that Alex thought so too, by his lack of comment. But maybe he was just concentrating. He had put down his crayons and was arranging paints on a palette.

'So tell me about yourself,' said Katie.

'I was born in the days of the DDR,' said Alex, selecting his paintbrushes. 'After the war, our family was evicted from Breslau and resettled here in Weimar. Father then moved to Naumburg, because he started life as a clergyman. Naumburg cathedral was his first position as a curate.'

'I didn't know that,' said Katie. She could not imagine Otto as a dedicated man of the church. 'So you were born in Naumburg?'

'Yes. Then we moved back here and after *Abitur* I went to art school in Dresden.' Followed by three years in the US, at the Hoffberger school of painting in Baltimore.'

'You didn't fancy staying in America?'

'I prefer it here. I can concentrate on my work better. But I visit the USA often. In fact, I've just spent a year in New York.'

'Painting?'

'And helping in father's gallery.'

'So your father gave up the church to be an art dealer?'

'Yes. It was when my grandfather died. It must have been around 1987. I was still only a small boy. We moved to this house to be near my grandmother. I suppose it was inheriting all my grandfather's art collection. Father then decided to go into the retail art business.'

'And your mother?'

'She unfortunately died a few years ago. Cancer. But my grandmother is still alive and well and lives not far away. Further down the street, in fact. She will be eighty soon and we are planning a birthday celebration.'

'Does she live on her own?'

'She has a live-in maidservant. Katie, please try and keep your head in the same position.'

'Sorry. And now your father has moved into politics.'

'He has.' Alex's tone was angry. 'And I am totally opposed to his views.'

'I don't know much about his new party,' said Katie. 'Why are you opposed to it?'

'It is far too right-wing. And it is getting the support of all these factions that I consider undesirable.'

'The opposite to how it was before in the days of the DDR,' suggested Katie.

'Exactly. I am not in favour of communism, but I am still a socialist. I think left of centre is more humanitarian.'

'It's very early days,' said Katie. 'The party may not succeed.'

'It may very well succeed,' said Alex. 'That's what I am afraid of. I'm doing my best, but there is very little I can do about it.'

Katie could add nothing more to this argument as Alex continued to work with a concentrated frown on his face.

After another ten or fifteen minutes, Alex put down his brush. 'Enough for now. I've reached a stopping point. So, what about lunch?'

Katie was again taken aback by this unexpected invitation. Before she had time to think or make a reply, Alex said, 'come on. There's a nice little restaurant round the corner. It's warm enough to sit outside.'

#

'Another improvement after reunification,' said Alex. 'We never had Italian restaurants. May I suggest the salmon and spinach ravioli, the house specialty? It comes with a salad. And a bottle of my favourite white wine.'

The conversation was light and trivial, the weather was warm with the hint of a breeze and Katie was beginning to feel light-headed as the wine took effect. She was feeling totally relaxed and flattered to be entertained by this attractive younger man. But then Alex became more serious.

'Katie, I'm sorry your visit has been in vain. That I haven't been able to help you. To be frank, I would not be surprised if some of your paintings had passed through my father's hands. We don't just have arguments over politics. We also argue over the ethics of sales of works of art. Under the counter dealing has always happened and I suppose it always will. I have often suspected that some of father's dealings were, what shall I say, not for public knowledge.'

'You mustn't be disloyal,' said Katie. 'We have no proof. The Titian was the only clue I had, which led me to your father.'

'It's still very unsatisfactory,' said Alex. 'I've been thinking. I'd like to give you some help in your quest for your family paintings and I've only come up with one thought. When I heard my father and Marshall discussing paintings, they mentioned 'the queen' several times.'

'The queen? What does that mean? The name of a person?'

'Search me,' said Alex. 'I've no idea. I asked them once, but they were very evasive. My guess it's the nickname for a dealer, maybe a woman, who deals in the black market for works of art.'

'Could be a man. A homosexual,' said Katie thoughtfully.

'I only mention it in case you also come across the name. It might be a clue that leads you to some missing paintings.'

'Thank you. I'll bear it in mind.'

#

'This is where we are up to,' said Alex.

'It's a very good likeness,' said Katie, impressed.

'I've got a suggestion,' said Alex. 'Instead of painting your clothes, which would be very boring, why don't I paint us as you really are.'

'You mean,' said Katie hesitantly.

'In the nude. Let's do this properly. Come on. You can put your clothes on that chair over there.'

'I couldn't possibly,' said Katie, as the reality of the situation sank in. 'Alex, I'm too old for that. I was fifty last birthday.'

'Rubbish,' said Alex. 'I'm sure you look great. You're not overweight. Look, I paint naked women all the time and most of them are not nearly as good-looking as you.'

'Well,' said Katie. 'No. I couldn't.'

'It won't be for general display. You may have the painting when it is finished. Something for posterity.'

'Well,' Katie hesitated further. The hell. Why not?

'Good girl. Strip off and we can get going.'

#

'Great,' said Alex. 'You look gorgeous. Nice tits. And I'm glad you don't shave your pubic hair. All the girls I meet have no pubic hair. The ugliest part of a woman is between her legs. That's what pubic hair is for. To cover it up.'

'It's the modern swimsuits,' said Katie. 'They're so brief that they only just cover the essential part.'

#

'It's getting really warm in here,' said Alex, some time later. 'It was a good idea to take your clothes off. I'm going to take off my shirt.'

Alex's bare torso tipped Katie over the edge. Sitting naked and slightly drunk in front of this attractive man was just too much. She felt her nipples becoming erect and wondered if Alex had noticed.

Alex had been silent for some time, concentrating on his work. Eventually he said, 'OK. Come and have a look.'

Katie got down from her chair to look at the painting. Her face was virtually finished, as were the important parts of her anatomy. Including erect nipples.

'So. How do you like it?' asked Alex, putting his arm around her waist.

'It's brilliant.' Katie also put her arms round Alex's waist as Alex turned towards her and held her close. He bent down and kissed her tenderly. 'Time for a break,' he said, leading her to a couch at side of the studio.

#

'Oh my God! Katie!' Angela then lowered her voice. 'He painted you in the *nude?*' She poured them each another glass of wine. The two women were having lunch in their usual restaurant in Harvey Nicholls department store.

'He's an artist, Angela. Proper artists paint naked women all the time. It's the classic subject.'

'Yes. Well. And this guy was really good looking?'

'He was even better-looking when he took his shirt off. He lifts weights. What do they call it? Pumping iron?'

'Were you not turned on? I mean. You naked and him half-naked?'

'I was starting to be. And we had drunk a bottle of wine at lunch.'

'Katie, this is awesome. So the point is, was the picture a good likeness?'

'It's not finished, but the important bits are. The rest, and the background can be done later. He hasn't decided if it will be a rural scene, or something classical with nymphs and things.'

'What do you mean by important bits?'

'Well, obviously the face is the most important. That was more or less finished. And then, well . . .'

'Tits?' Angela whispered. 'You always had very nice tits.'

'And legs. Otherwise just an outline.'

'I mean, was it, you know, full frontal?'

'Just about. You could see my,' Katie hesitated.

'Pubic hair?' Angela finished the sentence.

WINDING BACK THE CLOCK

'Uh huh,' aid Katie nonchalantly.

'My God!' said Angela. 'And when he had finished painting?'

'I went to look at the painting. And then, well, I don't know how, but we started kissing. And then, well, . . .'

'You had sex as well?' said Angela in disbelief.

'He was so good-looking,' said Katie wistfully. 'And I was just a bit drunk.'

'And how was it?'

'Wonderful.'

Angela sat back in her chair with a loud sigh. 'All I can say, Katie, is that you're a very lucky girl.'

CHAPTER 15

Katie answered the ring on her doorbell.

'Sister Graham from the Walton Street Group Practice,' said the caller. 'I telephoned earlier.'

'Of course,' said Katie. 'Do come in and have a seat. Can I take your coat?'

Sister Graham gave Katie her coat to reveal her navy blue and white uniform.

'Would you like tea?'

'Oh, yes, please. That would be lovely.'

Sister Graham sat on a chair within earshot of the kitchen. She was short and round and looked to be at least retirement age. 'Very nice little house you have here. I've always liked Fulham. I live in Hounslow, myself.'

'Quite a journey to work, then.'

'Do you live alone?'

'Most of the time,' said Katie, raising her voice above the noise of the kettle. 'My two sons live away from home. My eldest, Paul, finished university last year and works for a bank in Hong Kong. Jonathan has another year to do at Edinburgh University. He's studying law.'

'So I suppose he's here in the vacations?'

'Not really.' Katie put down a tray of tea on the coffee table. 'There's milk and sugar and a biscuit if you'd like one. No, Jonathan has a girl friend in Scotland. And he also spends time with his father.'

'Can be a bit lonely, then?' Sister Graham looked up at Katie over the rim of her teacup. 'I will have a biscuit, thank you.'

'Sometimes,' said Katie defensively. 'I work full-time and I play a lot of bridge.'

'I get lonely too,' said Sister Graham, with a sniff. 'My husband died two years ago. And we never had any children.'

'I'm very sorry,' said Katie.

'Well now, as I mentioned, I've come to discuss Steven Jackson. He has just returned from France.'

'So you said,' said Katie, unsmiling.

'I must firstly say that I have Mr Jackson's full permission to discuss his medical details.'

'Uh huh,' said Katie.

'And you are fully aware of his condition?'

'I am.'

'Mr Jackson is giving us some concern. He has some complications, such as high blood pressure and a persistent kidney infection, but both are responding well to treatment. It is his mental state that we are worried about.'

131

IAN LAURENCE

Katie just nodded, as Sister Graham seemed to struggle to continue.

'He gave your name as someone to be contacted,' said Sister Graham eventually.

'Really?' said Katie, trying to be as unhelpful as possible.

'His carers say that he talks about you all the time. I just wondered that if you paid him a visit it might, well, you know, cheer him up a bit.'

'I'm not so sure that it would.' Katie stood up and paced the floor. 'Mr Jackson and I parted, what shall I say, not very amicably.'

'You were there when he had his accident, I believe?'

'Yes, I was.' Katie was not pleased that Steven seemed to have discussed her and their relationship with all and sundry. But it seemed as if Steven was also conveniently claiming his injury to be an accident 'We only had a casual relationship.'

'Oh. So you were never, er?'

'No,' said Katie, with as much emphasis as she could muster.

'Well. Yes. But he does seem to have a, what shall I say, an obsession about you.'

'All I can say is that I do not think my visiting him would help,' said Katie, now becoming irritated. 'Surely he has other people to visit him? Friends? Work colleagues? Family?'

'He did have one of his colleagues from work visit him yesterday,' said Sister Graham.

'And family? I know that he's an immigrant. What about family from abroad?'

132

'Mr Jackson told me that he has a brother, but there was a family feud over ten years ago,' Sister Graham said sadly. 'He has had no contact with any of his family since then.'

Katie declined to comment.

'It's just that sometimes we feel he may be suicidal,' Sister Graham continued. 'And I can understand that. It must be very miserable for him. Knowing that he will never get better. We felt that if you visited it would give him some interest. Something to think about.'

Katie still did not answer.

'You might just give it some thought, then?' Sister Graham got to her feet. 'We single people all get lonely.' She paused. 'It's not something one gets used to.'

Katie looked at Sister Graham and then, with a frown, looked away again, feeling some pangs of remorse.

'You'll let me know what you decide?'

'OK. I'll think about it,' said Katie grudgingly. 'I'll get your coat.'

After Sister Graham had departed, Katie poured herself another cup of tea. She had tried to stop thinking about Steven, but with no success. When she remembered their final conversation in Nice it was, however, inevitable that he would return and the nightmare would continue. Steven was not going to let go. The problem had returned and she was no nearer to finding a solution.

CHAPTER 16

Katie expected the ring on the doorbell to be the postman. She looked through the peephole to see a man in blue overalls with a clipboard. There was a similarly dressed man standing behind him.

'Yes?' she called.

'Gas Board,' was the reply. 'We have a report of a gas leak. We need to check your meter.' The man held up an identification tag on a ribbon round his neck.

Katie opened the door with the chain still on.

'We don't need to come in,' said the man. 'It depends where your meter is.'

'It's inside this cupboard in the hall,' said Katie. 'You had better come in.'

Katie took off the chain and the two men entered, closing the door behind them.

Then to Katie's horror and disbelief, the first man turned towards her and produced a gun with a silencer.

'Just take a seat Mrs Talbot. Don't be alarmed. We mean you no harm. Now, we need your car keys.'

134

Katie, starting to shake and shiver, sat down on the sofa and pointed to the keys on the dresser.

The second man went to the door with the keys and left, to be replaced by a young woman.

Katie was now becoming really alarmed. Why not just take the keys and go? There looked to be more to this than just stealing her car.

'So, my name is Charlie and this is Ann,' said the man with an encouraging smile.

Katie looked from one to the other. Charlie had the appearance of a young professional rather than a gangster. He had taken off his overalls to reveal a grey suit with collar and tie. Ann was of a similar age and also smartly dressed in a black trouser suit.

'We may be here for some time,' said Charlie. 'Let's have some tea. Or maybe coffee.'

'What's this all about?' asked Katie. She was now becoming more angry than frightened.

'All in good time.' smiled Charlie. 'I'll have tea with milk and two sugars, please.'

'Black coffee for me,' said Ann.

'The kitchen's through there,' said Katie. 'Make your own.'

Katie was now thinking more logically. Her car must have been stolen for a purpose. A criminal purpose. Maybe a getaway car in a robbery. But it was a Land Rover Discovery, a leftover from ferrying large amounts of luggage to and from boarding school. It was hardly the ideal car for a quick getaway. The next question was whether there was the possibility that she could escape and raise the alarm.

Ann went into the kitchen. 'Can I get you anything?'

'Not for now.'

'Let's turn on the television,' said Charlie. 'And I've brought the newspapers.'

The time passed interminably slowly, with Katie finding no way to escape. Charlie and Ann followed her wherever she went in the house and going to the bathroom was no help. The window was too small to climb out of and, in any case, the drop to the street was too far to escape without injury.

Charlie and Ann had brought a hamper with lunch of sandwiches and a bottle of wine that was eaten and drunk in silence. In fact, there was virtually no conversation at all. Any attempt by Katie to elicit information of any kind was ignored.

By the middle of the afternoon Katie began to get more anxious. 'I have an engagement this evening. I have to leave at 6.30. I must make a telephone call to cancel if I am to be kept here longer than that.'

'No problem,' said Charlie. 'I expect this to be over very soon now. You can definitely keep your engagement.'

All day, Charlie had been taking calls on his mobile telephone at regular intervals, but his conversation had been in monosyllables, yielding no information. Sometime after six there was a knock at the door. Charlie answered it, to come back into the room with the car keys, which he placed on the dresser. Charlie and Ann then gathered up their belongings and made a hurried exit. Katie stood at the door, listening to their footsteps as they ran down the street. Her car was parked in its usual space and Katie looked it over, seeing that the car was apparently undamaged.

Back in the house, Katie picked up the telephone. Her first call was to her bridge partner, apologetically cancelling her presence at the club that evening. The next call was to the local police station.

'I have to report that I was held at gunpoint in my house this afternoon.'

'Your name and address?' This was said deadpan. Katie might have been giving a grocery order.

Katie gave him the information, whereupon there was a short pause at the other end of the line. 'Mrs Talbot, could you confirm your vehicle registration?'

Katie gave it to him, immediately realizing the implication. They were on to her. What had her car been used for?

'Mrs Talbot, please stay where you are. Inspector Carter will be with you shortly.'

Katie sat on the sofa with a feeling of dread in the pit of her stomach. The police had been already on their way.

Barely five minutes later, there was a ring at the door.

'Mrs Katherine Talbot?'

Katie nodded.

'I am detective-inspector Carter.' The man showed Katie his authorisation. 'This is DS Evans. Could you firstly identify your vehicle, madam?'

Katie pointed to her car, parked almost outside the house in the residents-only bay.

'Fine. I gather you phoned the station to report that you had been held at gunpoint this afternoon?' Perhaps we could come in and you could tell us all about it?'

'Yes. Please come in, inspector.' With some trepidation and a sense of foreboding Katie led the way into the house. She then related the story of her kidnap, which was assiduously transcribed by Evans.

'I see,' said Carter as she finished. 'At Eastbourne, late this afternoon, someone fortunately noticed a person in a wheelchair on the beach. I say fortunately, because it was almost out of sight behind some rocks and about to be engulfed by the incoming tide. The wheelchair was deep in the sand and could not be moved by the occupant and the water was already up to his chest. The coastguard and the lifeboat services were alerted and the man was rescued in time.'

Oh my God! Katie's face had become ashen and her mouth was dry as she realized who was the occupant of the wheelchair.

Carter paused as he noticed the change in Katie's appearance. 'The man was suffering from exposure and hypothermia and was virtually unconscious. He was not able to say how he got into his predicament.'

Carter raised his eyebrows at Katie to invite a comment, but Katie just looked straight ahead and remained silent.

'However,' Carter continued, 'CCTV footage from the council car park shows that he arrived with a man and a woman in a car. The car answers the description and number plate of your car. The woman's image was not distinct, but has a passing resemblance to yourself. Perhaps you would like to comment?'

Katie shook her head. 'I was not in Eastbourne today. All I have told you is the truth.'

'Do you know a Mr Steven Jackson?'

'Yes, I do,' said Katie, grim-faced.

'Mr Jackson was the occupant of the wheelchair. How do you know Mr Jackson?'

'He's just a friend. That's all.'

'How did you meet?' Carter persisted.

'A dating agency,' said Katie reluctantly.

'So when did you last see him?'

'I can't remember. Months ago.'

'Otherwise, no contact of any kind?'

'No.'

'So, your last meeting. Amicable?'

Katie shrugged. 'So-so. No animosity. I have no reason to do Mr Jackson any harm.'

'Mr Jackson is a paraplegic. Do you know how he came to be in this condition?'

Katie was in despair, feeling that the questioning was going against her. 'He had an accident. He fell down some stairs.'

'I see,' said Carter. 'Were you there at the time?'

'Yes,' said Katie reluctantly. 'It was in France.'

'Whereabouts in France?'

'Grimaud. I was in the house. I found him on the stairs. He must have slipped and fallen.' There was no way she was going to tell the police what had really happened. Not at this stage, anyway. And later, only if she really had to.

Carter looked at Katie with a frown.

'Don't look at me like that!' said Katie sharply. The shock of being interviewed and the negative thoughts that it had produced were being replaced by some resolve. She felt that she had to somehow be on the offensive. 'I have no wish to do Mr Jackson harm. And I am standing by my account of what happened to me today. Would I have incriminated myself by using my own car if I were doing this? Might I state the obvious, inspector, that this is what you call a 'set-up'?'

Carter appeared to be convinced by Katie's spirited outburst. 'Mrs Talbot, I am treating this as a serious case of attempted murder. Another ten minutes and Mr Jackson would have drowned. For the moment, and it is with some reluctance, I am going to accept your version of events.'

'Well. Thank you.,' said Katie in a mollified tone.

'So, as you now know what happened today, have you any thoughts on who might wish do Mr Jackson harm?'

'No. I do not know enough about Mr Jackson. I have never met any of his friends or family. And I know nothing about his occupation.'

'Very well.' Carter stood up to indicate the interview was at an end. 'As I have accepted your story, this house is now a crime scene. I am sending in a forensic team who will be with you shortly. Try not to touch anything that your kidnappers may have handled, or used. Most importantly, we shall be looking for fingerprints and material for DNA samples. Also, I shall require you to report to Scotland Yard at nine o'clock tomorrow morning to give a full statement.'

'I will be there,' said Katie as she showed the policemen to the door.

Katie went to the drinks cabinet to pour herself a stiff whisky. The problem with Steven had taken a new twist. With some assistance, he had very nearly succeeded in committing suicide. And clearly his intention was to frame her for his murder. The problem was going to continue and what on earth was she going to do about it?

CHAPTER 17

It was with a strong feeling of *deja vu* that Katie entered the District General Hospital in Eastbourne the next morning. The sister at the reception desk informed her that Steven had recovered well and would be allowed home later that day.

Steven was in a private single room and Katie was quite unprepared for his change in appearance. He was sitting up in bed reading a newspaper and Katie would hardly have recognized him. Steven had become an old man. His hair was turning grey and he had lost a lot of weight, producing sunken cheeks and prominent cheekbones. His unshaven face also had the pallid colour of the permanently unwell.

Steven put down his paper and smiled a welcome, as Katie, grim-faced, pulled up a plastic chair close to the bed.

'Steven, I am very angry.' Katie tried to keep her voice down. 'What the hell do you think you were doing? If you had died, I would have been a murder suspect.'

'You have not complied with my request,' said Steven simply in a matter-of-fact tone. 'I had to take the matter into my own hands.'

'You never expected me to comply with your request,' said Katie sharply. 'And sending me the contents of that plastic carrier bag was ridiculous. All I can say is, that any more episodes like this had better not happen again.'

141

'You do not realize what I have to contend with, do you?' said Steven, now looking at her with an angry expression. 'Every day the same with no hope of a cure. Just imagine, not being able to walk around your own house. Not going to the toilet as and when you please. And never having sex.'

Katie, shocked by this outburst, looked at him and could not find a reply.

'My other problem is that I'm still in love with you. Every morning when I wake up I see your half-naked body. I think about you all the time. Even after what has happened. And then I think about your rejection of me. That I have found so hard to take. That is my torment. And that is why I want to end it all.'

Katie, now very alarmed, stared at him, completely overwhelmed by this second outburst. Eventually she said, 'if you feel that way about me, why did you try and implicate me? If you had succeeded, I would have been a murder suspect.'

'I wanted to involve you. Make you part of my departure. And because I still hold you responsible for my condition.'

Katie stared at him again, trying desperately to find the right words to reply. 'I'm very, very sorry for what happened.' She had totally underestimated Steven's state of mind. By trying to block out all thoughts of Steven since the event, she had not fully thought through Steven's situation and his mindset. 'But I have already told you that I do not feel responsible for your condition. I had to act as I did. I feared for my life. But you have my every sympathy.'

'I just think I deserve some compensation. For what I have to go through. I think you might at least agree to visit me. Perhaps once a week.'

'I do not see the point,' Katie retorted. She had recovered from the trauma of Steven's outbursts and was again thinking rationally. 'What would we talk about? We would only argue.'

142

'Your presence is all that I ask.'

'I'll think about it.' Katie then replaced her chair and left without looking back.

Katie sat in her car in the hospital car park, staring into space, pale and emotionally distressed by the visit. This problem had reached major proportions. She was sure that Steven was going to make another attempt at suicide, implicating her and he might very well succeed. What on earth was the solution?

Inspector Carter was shown into the apartment in Beaufort Gardens by the carer on duty. 'Mr Jackson is feeling very tired. He only came out of hospital yesterday. The doctor says he is only allowed to give a short interview.'

'Fine by me,' said Carter. 'This shouldn't take long.'

Steven was sitting in a chair in his sitting room. He was fully dressed with a blanket around his knees, but did not look a well man. Carter took in the opulence of the furniture and fittings, but what took his attention most of all was a large portrait photograph of Katie, in pride of place on the writing desk.

'Please take a seat, inspector,' said Steven. 'And how can I help you?'

'I have the statement you gave to the constable in Eastbourne,' Carter began. 'Have you anything to add?'

'I don't think so,' said Steven, looking at Carter with an unfriendly stare. 'It happened as I said. I was taken out for the day, but was abandoned on the beach.'

'You didn't know your companions?'

'I had never seen them before.'

'I find it odd that you would go off for the day with total strangers,' said Carter, looking at him pointedly.

'I was told that they were sent by Mrs Talbot. I therefore had no suspicions. Especially as they arrived in her car.'

'So tell me exactly what happened.'

'My carers took a telephone call from a person who said she was Mrs Talbot. Mrs Talbot . . ,'

'You mean the person on the telephone?'

'Yes. This person, supposedly Mrs Talbot, said a trip had been arranged to take me to the seaside for the day. Something for which I was very grateful. A young man and a young woman arrived. I was disappointed that Mrs Talbot was not there as well.'

'But they said that Mrs Talbot had sent them?'

'Yes. Anyway, this couple took me to Eastbourne. They were very nice and friendly and had brought a picnic lunch. Towards the end of the afternoon, they said they were going for ice cream, but never returned.'

'Your cries for help went unnoticed?'

'By the time I realized that they were not coming back, the sun was setting and the tide was coming in. Everyone else on the beach had gone.'

'And you had never seen them before and you did not recognize them from photographs we showed you?'

'No. I'm afraid not.'

'How would you describe your relationship with Mrs Talbot?'

'Mrs Talbot is a dear friend. I value her friendship very much.'

'You didn't think of making a phone call to check with Mrs Talbot about the visit?'

'I didn't think it necessary. I didn't want to bother her.'

Carter's body language said that he was not impressed. 'I understand that you met Mrs Talbot through a dating agency. Not very long ago?'

'It must be six months, or longer. My life changed when I met Mrs Talbot.'

'OK,' said Carter, with a frown. 'So have you any idea who would wish to do you harm?'

'No, inspector. I am a very ordinary and uninteresting person. A far as I am aware, I have no enemies.'

'You work in the City of London, I understand?'

'I am a ship broker and I have several interests in commercial property.'

'No controversial deals recently? Anything that might bring some animosity?'

'Things have been very quiet since the last banking crisis.'

Cater consulted his notebook. 'I see that you came to England from Germany in 1990. What was your occupation before that?'

'I was an accountant with an engineering company in Leipzig, East Germany.' Steven paused. 'I do not see that these personal details are relevant, inspector.'

'I'm sorry, but I am just trying to find any possible reason why you should have been targeted.'

'I am also at a loss, inspector. As I say, I am a very ordinary person. But I shall be on my guard from now on,'

'Do that,' said Carter, getting up to go, as the carer came into the room and held the door open. 'And please inform me if anything else comes to mind.'

#

Katie took a taxi to New Scotland Yard police station. She had taken a dislike to both the detectives, but she could not really say why. She told herself that they were only doing their job. Carter was tall and overweight and Evans was short and overweight and she had nicknamed them Tweedledum and Tweedledee. Maybe this dislike was because of their appearance; their pasty complexions and their ill-fitting suits, together with drab shirts with badly-ironed collars. But it was probably because of their officious and unfriendly attitude.

'Thank you for coming in again to help with our enquiries, Mrs Talbot,' said DS Evans. 'If you sit here in front of the computer, I will firstly show you our enhanced images of the couple in your car at Eastbourne.'

Katie looked at the images. The woman did bear some resemblance to herself, as she was of the same build, but the enhanced image showed the face of someone much younger.

'I'm sorry.' said Katie. 'I have never seen either of these people before.' She turned to look at Evans. 'And it proves that I was not in Eastbourne that afternoon.'

'It certainly does,' Evans agreed. 'But it was only immediately after the event that we suspected you might have been there. Now, let's move on. These are photographs of known criminals who we know have done your sort of kidnap routine before.'

Again, Katie could not make any identification. 'What is your opinion, sergeant?' Katie sat back in her chair. 'These two people who kidnapped me. Have you known of similar cases?'

146

'No personal experience,' said Evans. 'But I know there is, what you might call an 'agency' that will supply people for situations such as yours. More than one, in fact. Minor crime, if you like. Confidence tricksters. Impersonators. But no violence. And no weapons.'

'They did threaten me with a gun,' Katie interrupted.

'Yes. But they wouldn't have used it. But so far all our enquiries have come to nothing. We have informers in these agencies, but nobody seems to know anything.'

'So you have absolutely no idea who my kidnappers were?

'No.' Evans was suitably apologetic. 'We did a thorough check on your house. We couldn't identify the fingerprints, of which we had several good examples. We also had DNA samples, which were not on our database. A complete blank.'

Katie had thought of doing some investigation of her own, but it would seem pointless. Steven's escapade must have cost a lot of money. The solution must be to try and persuade Steven not to repeat the performance.

'Well, thank you for your time,' said Evans as he escorted Katie to the door. 'We will be in touch if we need you again.'

#

Inspector Gordon Carter navigated his rental car with some difficulty through the narrow streets of Grimaud. He was spending a weekend visiting a friend in St Tropez with the ulterior motive of a meeting with Inspector Fabre and being given a tour of Steven Jackson's house.

Carter had to stop several times to look at his street map and eventually came to the house at the top of the hill. Inspector Fabre had parked his car in the yard of the house opposite and motioned Carter to do the same.

Fabre was accompanied by a short, swarthy man in blue overalls. 'This is Jacques, a local locksmith' said Fabre after their personal introductions. 'He will unlock the door for us.'

It did not take Jacques very long to find the appropriate key.

'We locked the door when Jackson left for the hospital,' Fabre explained. 'As far as I know, nobody has been in the house since then.'

'It's in very good order,' said Carter, as they looked round the ground floor rooms.

'Mr Jackson had very good taste,' said Fabre. 'Now, let's go upstairs to where the incident happened.'

'These stairs are lethal,' said Carter. 'A tight spiral and virtually no handrail.'

'Indeed,' Fabre agreed. 'I would think that every visitor would get the same impression.'

'So this where he fell.' said Carter.

'You could only see his feet at the first bend of the staircase,' Fabre confirmed. 'She must have given him quite a push.'

'She told me that it had been an accident,' said Carter. 'That she was in the bathroom and found him on the stairs. Then you told me what had really happened.'

'At first, she told the paramedics it had been an accident,' said Fabre. 'Then, when I questioned her, she confessed to a fight when he tried to rape her.'

'Do you think,' Carter paused, 'that she might have lain in wait and pushed him when the opportunity arose? That there wasn't a fight? It was all premeditated?'

'Hardly,' said Fabre. 'Jackson confirmed her account of the event. OK, he hadn't recovered consciousness for very long and might have been confused. But he never altered his story. And there was the evidence of the torn clothing.'

'But she could have faked that by herself.'

'Perfectly possible. That had occurred to me also at the time. It was Jackson's confirmation that clinched it.'

'Just a thought.'

#

'So what's the progress on the Jackson case?' asked the chef superintendent as Carter and Evans reported to his office.

'Mrs Talbot came in again,' said Evans. 'But she couldn't identify any of the images I showed her.'

'Gordon, your thoughts?'

'I interviewed Jackson. He confirms that he did not know his companions. He thought Mrs Talbot had organized the trip. Apparently it was arranged on the telephone.'

'Presumably by someone pretending to be Mrs Talbot.'

'This was confirmed by the couple who collected Jackson.' Evans interrupted. 'They told the carers that Mrs Talbot had arranged the trip, using her car.'

'We can't blame the carers then,' said the superintendent. 'It would seem very convincing.'

'I also interviewed Sister Graham, the carer in charge,' said Carter. 'She did not take the telephone call, but she had recently visited Mrs Talbot to ask her to help with Jackson's rehabilitation. Mrs Talbot, apparently, was rather unwilling to help. She was very reluctant to visit Jackson.'

'It sounds like this relationship is somewhat one sided,' said the superintendent.

'Quite,' said Carter 'Sister Graham said she started to have doubts when Jackson did not arrive back at the arranged time of five o'clock. She was about the raise the alarm when she heard that we had found him.'

'Gordon, I understand that Mrs Talbot is an intelligent person. If she had planned to murder Jackson in this way, she would hardly pre-arrange the trip and use her own car.'

'I agree that all the evidence points to a set-up,' said Carter. 'That somebody planned this to implicate Mrs Talbot, knowing of her relationship with Jackson. But I just have this feeling, I don't know why, copper's intuition perhaps, that she had a hand in it. She's clever. That's the whole point. I think it's a sort of double-bluff.'

The superintendent looked at him with scepticism. 'I don't agree with you. I would seriously doubt that Mrs Talbot could contrive such a scheme. And what would be her motive for doing away with Jackson?'

'I don't know,' Carter admitted. 'That is making things difficult. There may be something between them in the past that we don't know about.'

'May I remind you that both of them admit to having only known each other for a short time.'

'OK,' said Carter. 'But if it isn't Mrs Talbot, there is definitely someone else out there trying to kill Jackson. I'm convinced the car bomb was meant for him. Our information is that the IRA was not involved.'

'The analysis of the bomb material showed it was from the Czech Republic,' Evans interrupted. 'It's a new form of semtex. The IRA does not possess this explosive. It's not been seen in this country before.'

'I see,' said the superintendent. 'This is getting more complicated.'

'Whatever, again, I still suspect that Mrs Talbot is somehow involved,' said Carter. 'I have the feeling that she is holding something back. She is not giving me the whole story.'

'She hardly seems the sort of person that would have links with international terrorists,' said the superintendent sarcastically.

'For some reason she wants him dead,' said Carter. 'I'm convinced of it. She was there in France when he had his injury. And it wasn't an accident, as she claimed.'

'But it was self-defence. And Jackson confirmed her story.'

'I still think there's more to it.'

'Well, I don't,' said the superintendent firmly. 'This is all getting too far-fetched.' You have no hard evidence.'

'Then what is your opinion, sir?' asked Carter.

'I think Mrs Talbot is innocent. Someone is out to kill Jackson and you have to find that person before they try again. Or else next time they may succeed.'

'Then what do we do now?' asked Carter. 'I hardly think we can assign Jackson 24 hour protection. We have limited manpower as it is.'

'Or keeping Mrs Talbot under surveillance,' added Evans.

'I agree,' said the superintendent. 'We cannot justify assigning manpower to those duties. My advice is to forget about Mrs Talbot and concentrate on Jackson. There must be something in his past to make him a target.'

#

'Doesn't make sense,' said Carter to Evans later that day. 'I could do with another tea. And you could pop out for a couple of hamburgers.'

'The chief super said the answer is in Jackson's past,' Evans reminded him.

'You interviewed his work colleagues. Any more thoughts?'

'They all said he was very boring. Mostly kept himself to himself.'

'No dodgy dealing?'

'Not as far as I could see from talking to his colleagues.'

'CCTV?'

'We have images of the couple collecting Jackson to take him to the seaside. But we have those already from Eastbourne.'

'And before the car bomb?'

'Jackson's car was parked out of range.'

'So we have to look further back,' said Carter. 'He came from the former East Germany. Maybe the answer lies there.'

'Then how do we find out?'

'I'm going to call the German Embassy,' said Carter. 'See if they might be able to help us.'

#

152

The London Embassy of the Federal Republic of Germany is in a Georgian terrace in Belgrave Square. Inspector Gordon Carter had been given an appointment in response to his request for information.

Carter was escorted to an office on the first floor. The room had a high ceiling with stucco decoration and the walls were hung with several large paintings that looked old and expensive. Suzanne Ebert stood up from behind the huge mahogany desk and came forward to shake Carter by the hand. Carter later described her as the most beautiful woman he had ever seen.

'Do take a seat, inspector. I am Petra Schmidt. I understand you are making enquiries about a man who is originally from the former East German Republic?'

'Yes,' said Carter hesitantly, still in awe of Suzanne, whose blue eyes were looking at him directly, giving him the impression that she was as intelligent as she was beautiful. 'His name is Steven Jackson, but I suspect he has changed his name.'

Suzanne examined the file on her desk. 'Indeed, inspector. You are correct. His name was Stefan Weiss. Might I ask why you are making enquiries about him?'

'We think someone is trying to kill him. There have been two attempts on his life and we do not know the reason why. We are looking into his past to try and find a clue.'

'I see.' Suzanne nodded her head slowly. 'Two attempts?'

'The first was a car bomb and the second was when he was abandoned on the beach in his wheelchair.'

'Abandoned on the beach?'

'Mr Jackson is unfortunately partially paralysed. Two people took him out for a trip to the seaside. They left him to face the incoming tide.'

153

'I see,' said Suzanne with a frown. 'So both attempts were unsuccessful.'

'They were. And we think the person or persons may strike again. We want to try and prevent that.'

'Of course,' said Suzanne. 'And I gather you have interviewed Mr Jackson, but that it did not help?'

'Apparently he lives a very ordinary lifestyle with no obvious enemies. We then thought that there might be something in his past, before he came to England. But he said he was just an ordinary accountant with a company in Leipzig. We thought that he might be hiding something and hoped that you might be able assist us with our enquiries.'

'I'm afraid that I cannot be very much help to you,' said Suzanne, looking at her file. 'Apparently, he was a model citizen. He was a member of the local communist party, but not a very active one. In fact, there is nothing in his past history in East Germany that we know about to suggest that he might be a target. And, of course, this is all quite a long time ago.'

'OK,' said Carter, disappointedly.

'Well, I am sorry that we cannot be more helpful,' said Suzanne, getting to her feet. 'I wish you the best of luck in your investigation. And if we discover anything new, we will let you know.'

Carter made his way back to the station with the image of Suzanne still in his mind. The visit had confirmed that Katie Talbot remained his prime suspect.

CHAPTER 18

'We've got twenty tables. That's very good for a charity event. The hospice will be very pleased.' Katie underlined the number at the top of her notepad. 'Eighty people. Can we cope? That's a lot of sandwiches, scones and jam and cake. Do you think big cakes or cupcakes?'

'Ordinary cakes,' said Hazel. 'Then they can take a big slice or a little slice.'

'The problem is,' said Katie, 'you never know how much people are going to eat.'

'Let's allow one cake for eight people. That's ten cakes.'

'Better make it twelve,' Katie wrote on her pad. 'To be sure.'

'I'll go and make us some tea,' said Hazel. 'And we can make a list of who does what. We may need other helpers, as well as the committee members. Could you clear a space?'

'Do you have to bring work home?' asked Katie, looking at the thick file on the table.

'Sometimes,' said Hazel, wrinkling up her nose. 'Depends.'

'I always think your work is more interesting than mine. Property law can be a bit boring. I think I should have done criminal law.'

'Interesting? Yes, but you do come across some really awful people,' said Hazel. 'That file there. Chap accused of being a hired assassin. Nowhere near enough evidence. A prosecution should never have been brought. He was guilty, I'm sure, but it was impossible to prove it.'

Hazel disappeared into the kitchen as Katie moved the file off the table and then absent-mindedly turned over the front cover. There was a photograph of a man of indeterminate age with a shaven head, a bull-like neck and staring blue eyes. Not the type to meet on a dark night, thought Katie. But then a frightening thought occurred to her. She memorized the man's name and address and closed the file just before Hazel reappeared.

#

That evening Katie sat in front of the television with a TV dinner and a glass of red wine and mulled over the possibility. The thought appalled her. Should she pre-empt the situation, as Steven supposedly wished her to do?

#

Katie woke up in a cold sweat, her heart pounding as she relived the nightmare. She was South, declarer in seven no trumps. Doubled and vulnerable. Hazel tabled the dummy. East/West were Carter and Evans, dressed in blue and yellow striped jumpers with matching caps. 'Revoke! Revoke! Director!' they cried. The cards all stood up and marched off the table. Then the Red Queen with the face of Sister Graham arrived. 'Off with her head!'

There was no way she was going straight back to sleep. Katie pulled on a dressing gown and went downstairs to make a cup of ovaltine. Then she sat on the sofa with a grim expression to think through the process yet again.

Steven was going to make another attempt at suicide, implicating her. By a strange coincidence, she had a possible solution. The hitman was called George Manassero and she had his address. Was this another stupid and reckless idea? She was contemplating an assignation with another violent man. It could go badly wrong and could easily end in another disaster, with her coming off worst this time.

Manassero could accept or decline her offer. If he accepted and was successful, or if he accepted and was unsuccessful, there was no way she could be linked to him. He would not know her name or address or know of how she came to hear of him.

There were risks, of course. If Manassero was caught, she would automatically be in the frame, because of past history, but how could she possibly have links to him? And, out of disguise, she was very doubtful that Manassero could identify her.

Was this logic sound? Was there a flaw she had not thought of? Whatever, she had decided to risk it. These were desperate times. She would approach Manassero. Katie went back to bed, but sleep did not come easily.

#

'Katie, what are you up to?' said Angela, sitting down on the bench beside her. 'This is like one of those spy novels. Or that television programme, Spooks.'

That was, in fact, where Katie had got the idea. Spies always seemed to meet in a park or on the Embankment. She was in Green Park, sporadically feeding the ducks.

'I need to ask you a favour. But I'm only asking if you promise not to question why.'

'OK.' Angela shrugged her shoulders. 'Fire away.'

'Can you let me have two thousand pounds in used notes? I daren't take it out of my bank account here. I'll pay you back by transferring the equivalent from my US bank account into yours.'

Angela looked at her with a frown, her face unusually serious. 'I will. But I don't like the sound of it.'

'This time tomorrow? Here?'

#

Nobody recognised her the last time she wore this outfit. It was a fancy dress ball and she went as Marilyn Monroe. Blonde wig, blue contact lenses, cheek pads, too much make-up, short skirt and stiletto heels. Katie looked at herself in the long mirror and was very pleased with the result. She had found the address in the A-Z and it seemed to be very close to the station Custom House, on the Dockland Light Railway. She would drive to the end of the line at Gallions Reach and take the train back into town.

#

There was plenty of room in the car park. Katie parked the car and sat for a while, looking at her reflection in the rear-view mirror. This really was a crazy idea. If the police picked her up now, in this disguise and carrying a lethal weapon, she might very well get a custodial sentence. But what was the alternative? Waiting for Steven to mount another suicide attempt? Katie steeled herself. She locked the car, bought a ticket and boarded the train, feeling very self-conscious, but being the middle of the afternoon, there were very few other passengers.

Katie alighted at Custom House, crossed the Victoria Dock Road and found the address in a side street. It was, as she suspected, a very run-down block of flats. The building was five storeys high and built of brick with concrete coping stones to the balconies. There were a few ancient cars in the car park in front of the flats and some teenagers of all ages and colours were playing football.

Two of the boys jeered at her as she walked past. 'Lovely arse.' 'How much for a blow job?'

Look like a tart and get treated like a tart, thought Katie as she pressed the bell for the lift. Number 437 was presumably on the fourth floor. The lift cage was all metal with no windows. There was an overpowering smell of beer and stale urine and the walls were completely covered in graffiti. Katie emerged at the end of an open balcony that ran the entire length of the building and that gave access to the individual apartments. She found number 437, the numerals painted in white on a peeling green background and, with a lot of trepidation, she pressed the bell.

George Manassero answered the door. Katie recognized his face from the photograph in Hazel's file. He was dressed in a stained white singlet and jeans and his arms were covered in tattoos.

'Not today, sweetheart. I'm shagged out after last night.'

'I have a job for you, Mr Manassero.' Katie held up the plastic carrier bag.

George looked up and down the balcony to check nobody was watching. 'Come in.'

Katie, with rapidly increasing anxiety, entered the apartment as George closed the door behind her. George then suddenly turned and grabbed her by the throat, ramming her against the wall as he took a hunting knife from his belt and pressed the blade against her neck. 'What's your game, then?'

'Like I said. I have a job for you,' Katie managed to mumble as George's grip tightened.

'Drop your bags and turn around,' said George, releasing her. 'Hands high on the wall. Feet back.'

Katie, shaking all over, did as she was told as George ran his hands roughly over her. Then he emptied the contents of the two bags onto the floor.

'You brought a gun.' George unwrapped the gun and examined it.

'It's for you to do the job,' squeaked Katie, trying to keep the terror out of her voice.

'OK,' said George, apparently satisfied. 'Take a seat. I'll just take care of the dog.'

A vicious-looking black and brown hound was growling and showing its teeth. George grabbed it by its studded collar, dragged it into another room and shut the door.

Katie, now breathing a little easier, looked around the living room, trying not to show her distaste. The atmosphere was no better than in the elevator cage. The stale air was a mixture of sweat, dog, beer and cigarettes. She perched on the edge of a sofa that was strewn with newspapers and assorted items of clothing.

'What is it then?' asked George, sitting in an easy chair, the gun still in his hand.

'I want you to kill someone,' Katie said simply.

George scowled at her. 'How d'you hear about me?'

Katie just shook her head. 'You come well recommended.'

'How do I know you're not a scam?'

'You don't.'

'So tell me what you want.'

'I'm expecting it to be easy. Your target is a man who is partially paralysed. Also, he has expressed a wish to die.' Katie indicated the contents of the carrier bag that were still on the floor. 'You have the gun. There is a also ammunition, keys to the property and a deposit of two thousand pounds.'

160

'I charge more than that,' said George.

'If you are successful, I will pay you another eight thousand pounds. That's all I can afford.'

George looked at her with a frown. 'How do I know you will pay me the rest?'

'You don't. I will come back with the money. There has to be some trust.'

George gave a hollow laugh. 'Trust? In this game?'

'No other way,' said Katie. 'Take it or leave it.'

George looked at the gun. 'Beretta. In good order. But I prefer to use my own.'

'As you wish,' said Katie. 'That gun belongs to your target. You could perhaps make it look like a suicide.'

'What's the address?' asked George, picking up pencil and paper.

Katie gave him the address, which George wrote down painfully slowly in large letters.

'Name?' asked George.

Katie shook her head. 'You don't need to know that.'

'Beaufort Gardens,' said George.

'Knightsbridge,' said Katie.

'Posh,' said George.

'You have the keys,' said Katie. 'Just let yourself in, shoot him and leave.'

'It might not be as simple as that,' said George.

'I'm leaving it with you.' Katie got up to go and scooped up the contents of her handbag, also picking up the carrier bag. It was the only item with her fingerprints. 'I know you can decline and just pocket the money. I'm prepared to take that risk.'

Katie let herself out of the door, leaving George staring at the address with a frown on his face.

#

Over the next two days, George made several visits to Beaufort gardens, by foot and by car. He had noticed that the house had more people coming and going than any of the others, with some of the visitors in nurse's uniform. He waited until it was dusk. As he strolled down the street, a nurse left the building and George decided this was the moment he had been waiting for, He let himself in with the keys and took the stairs.

Steven was watching the television and looked up to see George enter through the front door and point the gun at his chest.

'I've been sent to kill you,' said George, advancing into the room, as Steven sat in his wheelchair and looked at him with a baleful expression, apparently not surprised or perturbed by George's presence.

George did not act as instructed. He wandered around the room, picking up the occasional ornament. 'Some nice stuff you have here. I might take a souvenir or two.'

Steven continued to watch him, saying nothing.

'A lady sent me. She said you wanted to die.'

'Then get it over with,' said Steven, a grim expression on his face.

'A quick exit might just cost you,' said George, sitting in a chair.

'I'm sure you are getting paid,' said Steven.

'I am. But a quality job is very expensive.'

'I can't stop you taking whatever you want,' said Steven.

'I see valuable items,' said George. 'But it's cash I'm interested in.'

'I don't keep any cash,' said Steven.

George got up from is chair and walked round the room, looking behind the pictures. 'Aha. A safe. I thought so. Combination?' He looked enquiringly at Steven.

'I'm not giving it to you,' said Steven.

'I was in Iraq,' said George. 'When the war started. We had to get information. We had lots of different ways to get captives to talk. My favourite was cutting off their fingers, one by one. It was interesting to see how long someone could hold out. We never got onto the other hand.'

Steven, no stranger to methods of torture, looked at George thoughtfully. To Steven, George was an amateur. He was overconfident, thinking that this man in a wheelchair was a pushover.

George took a bush knife from the sheath on his belt and went over to stand in front of Steven, testing the sharpness of the blade on his finger. 'Well?' taunted George. 'What's it going to be?'

'The combination is complicated,' said Steven. 'I would have to do it and I'm not able to stand.'

'Then how do you use the safe?' asked George. 'Come on. You're playing for time. Let's get on with it.'

'I usually ask for the bank to come,' said Steven.

'Bullshit. OK. I've given you a chance. You've asked for it.' George took a roll of duck tape from his pocket. 'We're going to secure your wrists first.' But as he bent forward to attempt to apply the tape, his face registered a look of horror and pain. Steven's stiletto, which had been hidden in the arm of his chair, was razor sharp. It entered George's abdomen just below the sternum, went through his diaphragm and into the heart. George died instantly.

Steven sat looking at the body for quite some time. He then wheeled himself over to the window, where he sat staring into space. It was with a very solemn expression that he retrieved the house keys and the box of ammunition from George's pocket and put them, together with the gun, in the locked drawer of his desk. Then he phoned 999.

#

'So tell me what happened,' said Carter, as Evans prepared to take notes.

'I got a ring on the outside door. The man said he was from Tesco's.'

'Were you expecting a visit?' asked Carter. 'At eight o'clock at night?'

'I get most of my groceries from Tesco's,' said Steven. 'They had made a visit earlier in the day. I presumed this was something they had forgotten.'

'And then you let him into the flat?'

'Of course. I had to take the delivery.'

'And then?'

'He pulled a very big knife. Threatened to cut off my fingers if I didn't give him the combination to the safe. I had to defend myself.'

'And you had never seen him before?'

'No. Was he known to the police?'

'Yes, he was,' said Carter, grimly.

'Inspector, do you think my name is circulating in the underworld? Am I considered an easy target?'

'Mr Jackson, I honestly do not know. I am afraid that, as the law stands, I have no option but to charge you with the murder of George Manassero. You will be required to appear at Bow Street magistrates' court tomorrow morning, when I expect you to be granted bail, pending our further investigations.

Next day the event was headline news. Katie picked up an Evening Standard outside the tube station and with trembling hands read the report on the way home. George had messed up. He had not done as he was told. The escapade had come to nothing. Steven was still alive and he knew who had sent George. What was Steven going to make of it? Should she contact Steven? If she did, what was she going to say? Katie suddenly felt very depressed. There was nothing more she could do and she could only deal with Steven's next move as best as she could.

'That's your's. Big Mac, large fries, large coke.' Evans plonked everything on the desk.

'Your thoughts on George,' said Carter, tucking into his hamburger immediately.

'I don't understand it,' said Evans.

'Neither do I,' said Carter. 'And you did a thorough check on his flat?'

'A few thousand in used notes.'

'What you might expect. Nothing else?'

'Just a piece of paper with Jackson's address.'

'George's handwriting?'

'Yes.'

'And acquaintances? Neighbours? Anybody see George having visitors?'

'No chance. We wouldn't expect to get information like that from the locals,' said Evans. 'I did ask around our informants who knew George. Nothing.'

'George was an Iraq veteran,' mused Carter. 'A marksman and small arms expert. If George was on a contract, he would just go round there and shoot him. What was he doing at Jackson's without a gun?'

'He was being a burglar.'

Carter shook his head. 'It's just not George's m.o. George is a hitman. In and out as fast as he can and collect a fat fee. As little risk as possible.'

'Always a first time.'

'Maybe. But I'm still not convinced.'

'Somebody told him that Jackson was an easy target,' suggested Evans. 'Wealthy man in a wheelchair.'

'I suppose you're right,' Carter sighed.

'So. Nothing to link this business with George and the other incidents against Jackson?'

'I don't see that there can be. George always was a bit of an oddball.'

CHAPTER 19

'This guy Bohnen is gaining ground.' Otto Hauswald handed Marshall a tumbler containing a generous amount of malt whisky. 'You've seen the latest polls?'

'I have.' Marshall was standing in front of the huge picture window overlooking Central Park. It was dusk and the lights were coming on, in and around the park, creating a magical effect. 'These guys were never going to take defeat lying down. They were bound to fight back.'

'Up by 5% in a month.' Otto joined Marshall at the window.

'They can't compete on policy. The majority of the public support your policies, as they did in Thüringen. You are telling the voters what they want to hear. Bohnen is now using the alternative tactic of questioning your suitability to lead the party. There is only one area that he can attack and that is your finances. We have been very careful in concealing our financial transactions.'

'I agree,' said Otto. 'But the rumour must be having some effect.'

'Let's wait for the next polls,' said Marshall. 'Review our strategy then.'

'The evening in Dresden will be crucial,' said Otto thoughtfully, sipping his whisky. 'Ideally we should have a decent lead by then. I'm sure I can get the better of Bohnen in the debate. Miserable little weasel. I will show him up for the intellectual misfit that he really is.'

167

'If we don't have a significant lead by Dresden, we may have to resort to more traditional methods,' said Marshall.

'Last resort.' Otto rubbed his chin thoughtfully. 'We would have to very careful. Absolutely no way anybody could connect it to us.'

'I'm going to Prague next week,' said Marshall. 'I always thought that traditional methods might be required at some point. I'll make some preliminary enquiries.'

#

'Quite satisfactory, don't you think?' said Bill. 'The painting being a fake. Made a hole in Marshall's finances.'

'It crossed my mind that we might have had something to do with it,' said Grant with a smile. 'But then I thought that was a ridiculous idea.'

'Indeed. How could we? So, what did you get out of Marshall?'

'As expected, very little. He assures me that his interest is purely philanthropic. He wants to be involved with his homeland.'

'Huh,' snorted Bill. 'Usual bullshit. And this company?'

'Machine tools.'

'Usual excuse. You must check on that, Grant. You might find a missile factory.'

Grant smiled. 'Hardly. But I'll check.'

'So tell me about this woman. Katie. I understand you get on well?'

'I find her very attractive. I think the feeling might be mutual.'

'I said you might get lucky,' said Bill with a grin.

'What is interesting is that Marshall also seems to have taken a fancy to her. He's offered her a job as a PA.'

'Really? With an ulterior motive? I hope I am not stating the obvious, but is Marshall a romantic competitor?'

'I don't think so,' said Grant with a frown.

'Meaning you hope not?'

'He does have a fiancée.'

'Does that mean anything?'

'I am not sure.'

'You will have to strike first. So what will this job as a PA entail?'

'Apparently it will mean accompanying Marshall on special assignments. To international business meetings and impressing foreign clients.'

'She could be a great asset, then,' said Bill thoughtfully. 'If we have her on board. How would you assess her loyalty?'

'I would imagine that she would be on our side.' Grant was thinking laterally. This was the opportunity he had been waiting for. 'Taking everything into consideration, I think it might be a good idea if I relocate to London.'

'I was going to suggest that myself. I am leaving it to your good judgement whether you reveal to Katie who you work for and whether she will agree to supply us with information.'

#

'So you said you had some exciting news.' said Angela. The two women were having lunch in their usual restaurant. 'Is it anything to do with money?'

'No, it isn't. That incident is closed. We will not mention it again.'

'Then it must be about men.'

'Yes. It is.'

'Oh, good,' said Angela, leaning forward. 'Have you had sex with this Alex guy again?'

'No.' Katie shook her head and frowned. 'I wouldn't mind, though.'

'He hasn't contacted?'

'No.'

'Very disappointing. But you have obviously got someone else in mind.'

'First thing is that I have accepted the job that Marshall, he's the guy who gave the party in New York, offered me. The money is generous and will be very useful. It's going to be sort of part-time. He wants me to accompany him to important international business meetings.'

'Does that mean sex as well?'

'No it doesn't.'

'Are you sure?'

'I have accepted on the basis that the arrangement is purely business.'

'You told him that?' said Angela with a surprised expression. 'He still offered you the job?'

170

'Yes. He did.'

'He's probably the sort of guy who will not take no for an answer. You mark my words.'

'Well I think he will.'

'You obviously don't fancy him then.'

'No. I don't. I can't say why, exactly. Maybe it's just that I prefer someone else.'

'Aha. The other guy at the party. But he lives in the US.'

'That's just it. His company is moving him to London.'

'Is he going to live with you?'

'Angela, we've only had one kiss so far. He's renting a flat in Chelsea.'

'Not far away from you. But I'll bet he will want to move in with you quite soon.'

'We'll just have to see how it goes,' said Katie firmly.

CHAPTER 20

Katie answered the ring on her doorbell.

'Good afternoon, Mrs Talbot,' said a cheery Irish voice. 'Father Brian from the Sacred Heart.'

'Please come in, father.' said Katie, not able to match the bonhomie. She had at first refused to see Father Brian, but his brogue had won her over.

'Very kind of you to see me, to be sure,' said Father Brian, coming into the sitting room and taking off his coat, which he draped over an armchair. His appearance was as Katie had envisaged from the telephone call. Father Brian was certainly in his sixties, with a kindly face, close-cropped grey hair and gold-rimmed spectacles. He was dressed in a dark suit and a clerical collar.

'Please take a seat, father,' said Katie. 'And can I offer you something? Tea?'

'Oh. How kind.' Father Brain rubbed his hands together. 'Perhaps a small whisky?'

'Certainly.' Katie went to the drinks cabinet.

'Thank you very much. Cheers! Now, as I mentioned, I've come to see you about our brother Steven. I have come to ask for your help.'

'Hmm,' said Katie, with a grim expression.

'Steven has made a full confession of his sins and, thanks be to God, has returned to the fold.'

Katie looked at Father Brian in dismay. Here was someone else to whom Steven had confided.

'Steven has received absolution. He has received forgiveness from his sins. Steven is truly sorry for the inconvenience he has caused you recently. He has promised me that that there will be no more such instances.'

Katie looked at Father Brian in astonishment. Was this for real? What had caused the change in Steven's state of mind? Could it be because of the incident with George? And if so, why?

'I wonder if you could find it in your heart to forgive him also?' Father Brian looked at her beseechingly.

Katie was finding it hard to come to terms with this sudden change of events. 'It's not a case of forgiveness.'

'Then you have forgiven Steven for his behaviour?'

'Yes. Yes,' said Katie impatiently. 'It's just that I do not like Steven. Period.'

'Sometimes, especially in my job, we do not have to like someone when we need to help them,' said Father Brian softly. 'It's called charity.'

'Maybe it is,' said Katie. 'I still do not want to help.' Notwithstanding this unexpected change in Steven, she could not see how it would change the relationship.

'A shame,' said Father Brian, rubbing his chin. 'That is disappointing. I was hoping to get you on board.'

Katie did not answer, choosing to look out of the window, rather at Father Brian.

'Steven now has a much more positive attitude,' Father Brian continued. 'He has come to terms with his condition. He wants to live life to the full, despite the problems that he faces every single day. In fact, he is helping to counsel other people with similar disabilities. Our church has a tie-up with the local veterans association.'

'Really?' said Katie, finding all this extra information even more difficult to believe. Could Steven have changed this much?

'Sister Graham at the medical centre and I think it would be further help to Steven if you could pay, well, even just an occasional visit.' Father Brain raised his eyebrows.

'You are the main person in his life. This could be seen as a reward, maybe? Perhaps he has deserved it?'

'Huh,' said Katie, still not wholly convinced.

'Jesus taught us to have compassion for our fellow men. For the afflicted. Those less fortunate than ourselves. Sometimes it is hard to imagine how others have to cope with the enormous problems they have to face in their everyday lives.'

Katie looked at him, a frown still on her face.

'Perhaps just once, then?' suggested Father Brian. 'A trial run. A walk to the park, maybe? Steven enjoys driving his electric buggy to the park.'

'OK. A trial run,' said Katie reluctantly. Father Brian had won her over. Maybe the very occasional visit would be worth it for peace of mind, especially if Steven were no longer going to try and involve her in a suicide attempt.

'Wonderful.' Father Brian beamed. 'Sister Graham will give you a call.'

CHAPTER 21

Bert collected Detlef from the airport. 'Good to see you, Detlef.'

'Sorry I couldn't come sooner,' said Detlef. 'There was a job I had to finish. So, the Stefan has returned.'

'He is back from France. He has had an accident and is paralysed.'

'Does that mean that he can't go out?'

'It's not that bad. It must only be a partial paralysis, because he has an electric buggy that he can drive himself. Does his condition affect your feelings towards him?' Bert took a sideways look at Detlef. 'Should he be granted a stay of execution? Perhaps he has been punished enough?'

'Certainly not,' snarled Detlef. 'He still deserves to die. We will put him out of his misery.'

'OK. So be it,' said Bert with a shrug. 'I have been monitoring his movements since he returned. If he goes out, it is in his buggy. But he is always accompanied.'

'Rules out an attack in the street then,' said Detlef.

'Probably. So I think it will have to be a shooting in his apartment.'

175

'But I don't have a weapon. I couldn't bring my rifle with me.'

'Of course not. Rainer's friend, that's the guy who provided us with the bomb, will be able to let us have a handgun. And it has been made easy for us. Because of Steven's condition, he has several carers coming and going all through the day. It seems they do not all have a key, and so the keys are left under a flowerpot at the front door.'

'Hard to believe,' said Detlef,

'There is a gap between carers in the evening. If we turn up at this time it should be easy. But let's go over there and have a look in daylight.'

#

It was with some trepidation that Katie arrived at the apartment in Beaufort Gardens. She had vowed not to have anything more to do with Steven and here she was about to take him for a walk in the park. There had been no contact since the incident with George and Steven knew that she had sent him. Was it a subject for conversation, or were they going to pretend it had never happened?

Katie was met at the door by sister Graham and another woman carer, who guided Steven out onto the street. Steven looked much improved from when Katie had last seen him in the hospital. His colour was much better, his hair was neatly done and he was smartly dressed.

'How nice to see you,' Steven gave Katie a beaming smile.

Katie could only manage a grimace.

'Steven is very good with his electric buggy,' said Sister Graham. 'But he tends to go too fast. You must remind him. Otherwise it's hard to keep up.'

'Thank you for doing this,' said Steven, as he set off down the street.

'You're welcome,' said Katie through gritted teeth, following and pleased that she had decided on sensible walking shoes.

'So what's all this about?' asked Katie, once they were out of earshot of the carers. 'Why the change of mind?'

'I was on the road to Damascus,' said Steven, stopping his buggy to look at her directly.

'What do you mean?' Katie tried to keep the scepticism out of her voice. 'Did you see a blinding light? Did the Lord appear before you?'

'No.' Steven's face was serious. 'It suddenly came to me. Like one of those cartoon comics when they draw a light bulb to mean somebody has had a sudden realization.'

Katie looked at him with a frown, tapping her foot. 'And what did you realize?'

'I sat looking at the body as I waited for the police. He was stupid. I should have died. After the life I have led, maybe I deserved to die. But I was being given a second chance to make some good in the world. To think of others, rather than just of my own personal misfortune.'

'I'm finding all this very hard to believe,' said Katie.

'I was brought up as a catholic. Even though it was a communist country. My family were very devout. I was less so, but the teaching is always with you.'

Katie just looked at him and nodded her head slowly, finding no reply.

'For the first time I looked at it from your side. I behaved very badly in France and I can understand why you rejected me. You had to do what you did when I attacked you. I'm ashamed of my actions.'

Katie stared at him and could again find no reply.

'I also realized what I had put you through.' Steven reached out and took her hand. 'All the anxiety when I tried to commit suicide and the police involvement. Desperation must have driven you to that course of action. It must have taken a lot of courage to engage that man. I drove you to it, through my own selfishness. I apologize.'

Katie took away her hand and wiped away a tear.

'I just hope that we might be friends from now on.' Steven looked at her beseechingly, as Katie turned away from him.

'Let's move on,' said Katie with a sniff.

As Katie and Steven approached the end of Beaufort Gardens, Detlef and Bert were turning the corner from the Brompton Road, intending to walk the circuit of the cul-de-sac.

'That's the countess,' said Detlef in surprise, putting a hand on Bert's arm and guiding him into the shadow of a parked van. 'On the other side of the street. Going for a walk with Stefan.'

'What do you think she's up to?' said Bert. 'They are supposed to be enemies. Stefan took the family treasures.'

'I don't understand it either,' said Detlef.

'Let's follow them,' said Bert. 'See where they're going.'

#

'We've got two busy roads to cross,' said Steven, 'but there are traffic islands and motorists usually stop for us.'

Katie and Steven continued towards the Brompton Road, the conversation now being very one-sided, with Steven all the while informing Katie about his new-found friends at the Church of the Sacred Heart. They crossed the busy road with difficulty and then, after taking a short-cut along two narrow streets, crossed over Kensington Road and into Hyde Park. Detlef and Bert followed at a safe distance.

Steven was keeping to the paths, as they we more suited to his buggy than the grass, which was very uneven in places. The problem was that these paths were also favoured by the numerous horse-riders.

'I have an idea,' said Bert as they followed along Rotten Row, a long straight path that ran alongside the Serpentine. 'Stefan looks very vulnerable in the midst of all those big horses. If one of them bolted, it might do him a mortal injury. And save us a job.'

Bert took a flick knife from his pocket and the pair took closer order. As two large horses walked close behind the buggy, Bert plunged his knife into the hindquarters of the nearest horse. Complete chaos followed.

The horse whinnied and bucked violently, throwing its rider to the ground, and then bolted, cannoning into the buggy and giving Steven a sharp blow to the head. The buggy, out of control, accelerated to the right, straight for the lake. A horrified Katie ran after the buggy, but was unable to keep up and watched as it ran into the lake and disappeared beneath the surface. Detlef and Bert stole away in the opposite direction as fast as they could.

Katie arrived breathless at the lake and jumped in without hesitation. The water at this bend in the lake was only about three feet deep, but it was enough to cover the buggy lying on its side and Steven still strapped into the seat. Katie managed to reach down and undo the seat belt as two young men jumped in beside her and helped to haul Steven to the bank. Steven coughed and spluttered, and was obviously mildly concussed. But he was alive. The next thing Katie knew was the presence of the paramedics, who took charge, wrapping Steven in foil and blankets and stretchering him off to the ambulance.

#

It was with a strong feeling of despair that Katie entered the Chelsea & Westminster hospital. The receptionist told her that Steven was being kept in for observation and, all being well, could leave the next day.

Steven was sitting up in bed in a private room and greeted Katie with a wide smile.

'Thank you for saving my life,' said Steven, as Katie drew up a chair.

'Sounds very strange, your saying that,' said Katie. 'Seeing that up to now you wanted me to kill you.'

'I could have drowned,' said Steven. 'Maybe it is another omen that I am destined to survive.'

Kate could only look at Steven with a frown. She was still finding it very hard to accept the new Steven.

'What happened to the horse?' asked Steven. 'I am very concerned about the horse. Why did it run off like that?'

'I have no idea,' said Katie. 'Horses can be dangerous animals. They do that sometimes.'

'You will let me know if you get any news about it, won't you?'

'Of course.' Katie looked at him with a frown.

'You will visit me again, won't you?' said Steven beseechingly. 'Another walk. Away from the horses next time?'

'OK Maybe.' Katie looked at him thoughtfully, as she got up to go. Could this change of attitude extend to Steven telling her of his life history before he came to England? And perhaps clues as to the whereabouts of the treasures? Any probing would have to very delicately done. 'I'll be in touch.'

#

180

Katie returned from the hospital to find Carter and Evans on her doorstep. Her opinion of the two men had not improved with time.

'Come in, gentlemen.' With a resigned expression, Katie ushered them into her living room.

'Mrs Talbot,' said Carter in a voice of exasperation, 'this seems to be yet again an attempt on the life of Mr Steven Jackson. With you involved. I would like your version of the event.'

'I thought you had come to commend me on saving Mr Jackson's life,' said Katie with as much sarcasm as she could muster.

'I understand there were several people there to help,' said Carter ungraciously. 'I will receive a full report in due time. So, tell me what happened.'

Katie gave them the story of the afternoon, ending by saying, 'the horse behind us bolted. That's what caused the accident. And I mean,' she looked at Carter with an angry expression, 'an accident.'

'Were you aware that the horse had suffered a severe injury, caused maliciously by a passer-by and that's what caused the horse to bolt?'

'No. I wasn't,' said Katie, shocked and surprised. This possibility had never occurred to her.

'You didn't notice anybody near you in the park acting suspiciously?'

'No. I didn't. Everything happened behind us.'

'Quite,' said Carter. 'I am just wondering if you might have had an accomplice in this affair.'

"I most certainly did not,' said Katie angrily. 'It took me completely by surprise. And I am very disappointed in your attitude, inspector. You seem convinced that I am responsible for Mr Jackson's misfortunes.'

'Mrs Talbot, it is my job to ask these awkward questions. I am totally perplexed by this whole affair. My file on Mr Jackson is growing thicker by the day and you feature in most of it.'

'Inspector, I can assure you that I mean Mr Jackson no harm. After these unfortunate events you seem to automatically assume that I am the one who wants to kill him.'

'OK.' said Carter with a sigh. 'But I am asking you one more time if you have any information that may help me with my enquiries. And I remind you that withholding this information is a criminal offence.'

'Inspector, I am as mystified as you are.'

CHAPTER 22

'Mr Maxwell, sir,' said the butler.

'Marshall. Good to see you.' Alex examined his hand to check if it was paint-free, before offering it to Marshall. 'Father's away in Dresden. Another rally.'

'Yes. I know.' Marshall sat down on the chair that was used by the models. 'Alex, I am not best pleased, as you would imagine. In fact, I am very angry.'

'I've had it in the neck from father already,' said Alex, with a shrug. 'I'm sorry. How was I to know?'

'Otto and I knew straight away it had it be one of yours,' said Marshall. 'Why on earth didn't you tell us that you had made a copy?' Marshall looked at Alex in exasperation. 'And when did you do it?'

'I did it between commissions,' Alex explained nonchalantly. 'As an exercise. Ages ago. Before father took it to New York. It took me over a year.'

'I'm not surprised,' said Marshall.

'It was brilliant, though, wasn't it?' said Alex, with a broad grin. 'Fooled everybody.'

183

IAN LAURENCE

Alex's cocky attitude often irritated Marshall. 'Alex, I do not understand why you didn't realize what was going on. You sell a copy painting just before the real one goes to auction. Did it not occur to you what might happen?'

'Not for a minute.' Alex's tone had become more serious. 'Did it ever occur to you as to what might happen?'

'No, it didn't' Marshall admitted. 'It was the last thing I expected. But if I had known about your selling the copy, I would have.'

'If the countess hadn't been there,' Alex grinned, 'the sale might have gone through.'

Marshall was not amused. 'Why didn't you examine the back?'

'Never occurred to me. Very clever of the countess to notice.'

'OK,' said Marshall with a sigh. 'So tell me about when you sold it.'

Alex came to sit near him on the chaise-longue. 'Guy turns up. American, speaking bad German.'

'Did he say how he came to know of you?' Marshall interrupted.

'No. I asked, but he just said 'a friend.' I didn't think it important.'

'OK,' said Marshall, disappointed. 'Go on.'

'Guy looks round the studio. Starts picking out paintings. I firstly sell him a landscape for two thousand US. Then a very ordinary still life for one. Then he spots the copy of the Titian.'

'Just takes his eye by chance,' said Marshall.

The irony was not lost on Alex. 'OK. Clever of him, I suppose. He just casually points and says he likes it. Its much more expensive, I said. It took a long time to paint. Fifty.'

184

'He accepted that?'

'Thought about it, then agreed. He had a travelling bag with cash. When he counted out the money, he had more than what he owed. I could have asked for more.'

'The guy was carrying over fifty thousand dollars in cash. Didn't that make you suspicious?'

'No,' Alex smiled. 'Not really. I reckoned he knew that I was expensive and that I always insist on being paid in cash.'

'Well, I don't suppose there is any way we can trace him,' said Marshall resignedly.

'I'd know him if I saw him again,' said Alex. 'Not that I'm likely to.'

'Let me know if you do.' Marshall stood up to go.

'Any more news on what happened to the real Titian?' Alex asked.

'Absolutely nothing. We still have no idea where or how it was substituted, or where it went.' Marshall idly walked round to see what was on Alex's easel. He stopped and looked hard, unable to believe his eyes.

'Gorgeous, isn't she?' said Alex, looking over Marshall's shoulder. 'A natural redhead.'

'But that's . . . .'

'Katie.' Alex finished the sentence. 'She came to look at father's art collection. He wasn't here and so I showed her round. Then she agreed to sit for me.'

'I . . . I I presume you imagined . . . . the rest of her?'

'No,' said Alex, matter of factly. 'I persuaded her to take off her clothes. I am a professional artist, remember.'

'My God,' said Marshall, still staring at the painting. 'What I wouldn't . . .

'Jealousy will get you nowhere,' teased Alex. 'You will have to try harder.'

'Alex, I have to have that painting.'

'It's not finished. There's the background to do. And anyway, it's not for sale.'

'I'm still taking it. I don't care about the background being finished.' Marshall made to take the canvas off the easel.

Alex took his arm in a vice-like grip. 'Marshall. Not for sale. Even for you. I promised Katie that she could have it when it was finished.'

'Alex I always get what I want.' Marshall tried to wrench his arm free.

'Not this time, Marshall. I'm younger and stronger than you.' Alex looked him straight in the eye.

Marshall, breathing hard and red in the face with indignation, stood back from the easel and brushed down the sleeve of his jacket. 'I won't forget this, Alex.' He then turned on his heel and strode out of the studio.

#

'So, Henry, what's the next book about?' Marshall was having dinner that evening with his old school friend Heinrich Katz in the Elephant Hotel.

'The Polish-German border and how it has changed over the last two thousand years,' said Henry. 'One of my pet subjects.'

'One of mine too,' said Marshall, with feeling. 'You know that generations of my family lived not far from Breslau?'

'Ah, you mean Wroclaw,' said Henry, with a grin, knowing that the remark would provoke Marshall.

'Exactly,' said Marshall, unsmiling. 'All ethnic Germans were expelled from that part of Germany after the last war. That's when our family was resettled in Weimar.'

'Hmm. Yes. The Potsdam Conference had an enormous effect on that part of the world,' said Henry.

'What occurred after the war has been greatly overlooked,' said Marshall. 'In fact, I would guess that most people do not know what actually happened. Nor could they imagine the reality. About fourteen million ethnic Germans were expelled from those territories ceded to Poland. Fourteen million! That's an enormous number.'

'And up to two million died in the process,' added Henry.

'The Potsdam Conference reduced the size of Germany by about 25%,' said Marshall, 'compared to the 1937 borders. There were odd bits like Alsace-Lorraine, but most of that land was ceded to Poland. Do you not think that was excessive?'

'With hindsight, maybe,' Henry agreed. 'The problem was that Russia would not give back all of the land it had occupied in the east. At the end of the war, Russia occupied Poland, Czechoslovakia, Hungary, Romania, Bulgaria and the Baltic States. These countries were re-established as separate communist states, except that Russia kept the territory east of the Curzon Line.'

'Henry, tell me about the Curzon Line.'

'After the first world war, in 1919, the Allied Supreme Council sent a note to the Russians, recommending the line of the Polish-Russian border. It was signed by Lord Curzon, the British Foreign Secretary at the time. The problem was that neither side paid much attention to it. The Russian civil war had a big destabilizing effect in the area and all the skirmishing in this border territory resulted in the Polish-Soviet war. This led to the Treaty of Riga in 1921, at the end of this war, which moved the eastern border of Poland some 250 kilometres to the east of the Curzon Line.'

'So what were the criteria for setting this border called the Curzon Line?' asked Marshall. 'Geographical?'

'Much more appropriate that other British attempts to set borders,' said Henry with a dry laugh. 'It ran roughly along the border between Prussia and Russia that was set in 1797. The reason I say it was appropriate is that it was set on ethnic lines, with mostly Poles to the West and a variety of ethnicities to the East, mostly Ukranians.

So this border was set not just by drawing a line on the map, which the British tended to do, particularly in the Middle East. With disastrous consequences.'

'So what you are saying is, at the end of the war, the Russians felt that they were legitimately in the right to occupy this territory, east of the Curzon Line, going back to what was agreed in 1919?'

'Correct. Also, the excuse was that they wanted extra territory as a barrier to further aggression from the West.'

'Huh,' said Marshall. 'And they were allowed to get away with it. The Treaty of Riga was ignored?'

'That is what happened,' Henry agreed. 'Stalin got his way on virtually everything. Ceding all that land in eastern Germany to Poland redressed the balance. And the Oder and Neisse rivers were a convenient border on which to draw the line.'

'Too convenient,' snorted Marshall.

'Don't forget, Marshall,' said Henry quietly, 'rightly or wrongly, this was seen as a punishment for Germany in starting the war.'

'I would still call it excessive,' said Marshall.

'Maybe. Maybe,' sighed Henry.

'And the decisions of the Potsdam Conference were only provisional.'

'Indeed,' said Henry. 'The condition set down by the Potsdam Conference was that the decisions would be finalised when a German Government, and I quote, 'adequate for the purpose was established.' Virtually no progress was made on this until the fall of the Berlin wall. Then both west and east countries were united and, with full sovereignty, the treaty could be signed.'

'Too much was given away,' said Marshall, stabbing angrily at his food. 'It was re-unification at any price. We were far too soft with negotiations on the Final Settlement Treaty.'

'Helmut Kohl saw it as the way to get international agreement for reunification. He was prepared to make as many compromises as necessary. He saw it as a turning point in the history of Germany and an opportunity not to be missed.'

'It all happened too quickly,' said Marshall. 'There was no negotiation, nobody gave a thought to the eastern border. Everybody knew what Kohl's attitude was. It was an easy solution for everybody.'

'It irritates you that your homeland is now part of Poland,' said Henry. 'I can understand that. But I am afraid that nothing can be done about it now.'

'Henry, do you think that if Germany was in a more powerful position, this treaty could be re-negotiated?'

'You mean ceding that territory in Poland back to Germany?'

'Exactly.'

Henry frowned. 'No. I can't. Not now. But what do you mean by a more powerful position? Germany has already the most powerful economy in the European Union. And this union of countries includes Poland. I can hardly imagine a situation where borders could be negotiated. The whole idea of the Union was to prevent this sort of thing.'

'So what if Germany left the EU and was again independent?'

'I do not think that change is a likely possibility.' Henry sniffed and took another sip of his wine.

'I would be inclined to disagree,' said Marshall. 'The NDVP is proposing just this.'

'An independent and powerful Germany would provoke too much opposition from the world in general,' said Henry dismissively. 'It might even start another war.'

'But what if this independent Germany had powerful new allies. Who would back up her claim?'

'Still very unlikely,' said Henry.

'But not impossible?'

'Impossible? Well, of course not. I just cannot see it happening in the immediate future.'

'The world order is about to change. You're the history man, Henry. Nothing stays the same for ever. You know that.'

'You're right, of course,' said Henry with a sigh. 'Alliances come and alliances go. If history is anything to go by, I suppose the break-up of the European Union is bound to happen eventually. European boundaries have changed consistently over the last two thousand years and I expect will continue to do so. It's just a case of when.'

'Exactly,' said Marshall.

CHAPTER 23

'You're still OK about this, Detlef?' Bert enquired anxiously.

'Most definitely.' Detlef's right hand was holding the gun with a silencer in his jacket pocket as they walked down Beaufort Gardens. They were both wearing anoraks with hoods in deference to the possibility of being picked up by a CCTV camera.

'One carer always leaves by eight,' said Bert. 'And the other one never arrives before ten. We have plenty of time.'

Bert took the keys from under the flowerpot and they entered the hallway of the apartment block. 'Good that they have no CCTV in the building,' said Bert. 'Now, up the stairs.'

Outside Steven's door, Bert put his head to the door and listened. 'Not a sound,' he whispered. 'Maybe he's reading. Or in bed.'

Detlef nodded as Bert carefully and soundlessly unlocked the door.

'OK, my friend. Off you go.'

'And if there's a problem outside?'

'I'll ring the doorbell. Now. Watch him carefully. He's an old hand. Just get it over with as quickly as possible. Good luck.'

191

Detlef stole inside the room. The door opened directly into a sitting room and Steven was sitting in front of a desk, engrossed in the screen of his computer.

'*Guten Abend*, Stefan,' said Detlef.

Steven stiffened visibly in his wheelchair. Then he spun it round to face Detlef, his eyes focusing on the gun pointing at his chest.

'*Wer bist du?*' said Steven, in an arrogant tone of voice. He used the 'you familiar', in this case in a derogatory sense.

'You don't recognize me, do you, Stefan?'

'Should I?'

'My name is Detlef Weber.'

'That means nothing to me.'

'I live on the Arnitz estate on Rügen.'

'I spent time there, but still I do not remember you.'

'You would remember my father, Artur Weber. He was in charge of the estate. You tortured and killed him.'

'That side of affairs was nothing to do with me,' said Steven. 'I was the accountant. I did the books.'

'I remember your being there when my father was taken away.'

'Maybe I was,' said Steven. 'But what happened after was nothing to do with me. My brother was in charge of interrogation.'

'I don't believe you,' said Detlef. 'And be that as it may. You and your colleagues are all guilty. The time has come for you to atone for your sins.'

192

'Huh,' said Steven. 'I am not afraid to die. In fact, I welcome it. But not at your hand.'

Steven ducked his head down and abruptly swung his wheel chair back through 180 degrees.

Detlef aimed a shot at the back of the chair, but it was made of metal and the bullet riccoched harmlessly away.

Steven then swung the wheelchair round again. His aim and timing was perfect as the stiletto was right on target for the middle of Detlef's chest, but Detlef had anticipated this and had thrown himself flat on the floor. The stiletto buried itself in the door as Detlef's next shot was also on target. The bullet went straight through the heart and Steven died instantly.

'Well done,' said Bert, as Detlef let him into the room. Bert looked at Steven slumped in his chair and then at the knife stuck in the door. 'He didn't go easily, then. Now, as quick as we can. We want laptop, mobile phone, any notebooks, address books and diaries. And any money, credit cards, small ornaments. It must look like a robbery.'

'There's a safe here,' said Detlef, as the two men methodically ransacked the apartment.

'Forget it,' said Bert. 'We have not time to try and find the combination.'

'And this drawer in the desk is locked.'

'Soon fix that,' said Bert, taking a large screwdriver from his bag. The lock yielded easily.

'A gun and ammunition,' said Detlef. 'That's all.'

'We'll take these as well,' said Bert.

Five minutes later Bert relocked the doors and the two men left the building with Bert carrying the heavy holdall.

#

Katie alighted from the taxi to be again confronted by Carter and Evans.

'We are back again, Mrs Talbot,' said Carter.

'Please come in, inspector,' said Katie, with a resigned expression and a sense of foreboding. It had to be something to do with Steven.

Katie ushered them into her sitting room. 'So. How can I help you, inspector?'

'Could you please tell us your movements this evening?'

'Certainly. I have been at Lady Crossington-Appleby's house in Belgravia all evening. I arrived around 6.30 and left around 11.00. We had an evening of bridge with supper. And I won a prize.' Katie held up a box of chocolates.

Carter looked at her with a frown. 'I am afraid that Mr Steven Jackson was shot and killed in his apartment this evening.'

'Oh my God,' said Katie, sitting down abruptly.

'The apartment was ransacked and items taken,' Carter continued.

'Another burglar,' Katie concluded.

'CCTV shows us two hooded men approaching and leaving the building,' said Carter. 'We shall be endeavouring to identify them. I wonder if you have any idea as to who these men might be?'

'Inspector,' said Katie firmly. 'I had nothing to do with any of the previous incidents and I had nothing to do with this one. I am profoundly shocked by Mr Jackson's death.'

Carter stood up to go. 'This is now a murder enquiry and you will almost certainly be required to answer further questions. In the meantime, I would appreciate any thoughts that might come to you. And may I remind you again that any withholding of information on this matter from the police would be a criminal offence.'

Katie stayed in her chair as the policemen left, staring into space as the news sank in that Steven had finally died. As Inspector Carter had intimated, she was sure it was not just a casual burglary. It looked as if enemies from Steven's past had finally caught up with him.

Steven was dead and she was surprised how sad it made her feel. But, of course, the chance of getting information from Steven as to the location of the treasures had now gone. In fact, both her leads were completely exhausted. Was that the end of the trail, with nothing to show for it?

#

'This is all rather pathetic,' said Bert. 'He was one lonely guy.'

'I feel no remorse,' said Detlef. 'He deserved to die.'

'Disappointing,' Bert continued. 'Computer gives us nothing significant. It does tell us that he was looking at a German website when you disturbed him. The *Frankfurter Allgemeine* newspaper.'

'What about e-mail?' asked Detlef. 'These notebooks and diary are disappointing. All hospital appointments and carer schedules.'

'Right, e-mails. There are virtually no personal e-mails received. The in box is mostly to do with finance. Medical equipment. Some junk. Let's look at sent items'

This address book is pretty empty,' said Detlef. 'There are one or two German addresses and telephone numbers. I don't recognize them.'

'Something to follow up,' said Bert. 'Odd, really. You would think he had some contact with his brother.'

'What about the phone?' Detlef asked.

'Looking at that now. Let's see. Two 0049 calls to Germany in the last two weeks. In fact, it looks like he calls this number every week.' Bert scribbled the number on a pad of paper. 'Might be interesting.'

'Can we find out who he was calling?'

'Sure can.' Bert picked up the telephone to make the request. 'I have useful friends,' he said, in answer to Detlef's unasked question. 'They are going to call me back.'

'It's just about the only lead we've got,' said Detlef. 'Maybe it's a relative he calls. It might even be . . . .'

'It might well be,' Bert agreed.

After only a few minutes, the telephone rang. 'Fine,' said Bert, writing down a name. 'Many thanks.'

'So?' Detlef looked at the pad.

'Otto Hauswald.'

Detlef frowned. 'I think I've heard of him.'

'You probably have. He is the leader of this new German political party. They just won a local election in Thüringen.'

'Why should Stefan be calling him? Unless?'

'Maybe. Maybe. Let's have a look at him.' Bert punched the keys on the computer. 'That's him. Otto Hauswald. Looks older than 52.'

Detlef stared at the photograph on the screen.

'So what do you think?' asked Bert.

196

'Difficult. It's a long time ago. Now he's got white hair. And a beard and moustache. But there definitely is some resemblance. Maybe that is him' Detlef drummed his fingers on the desk in his excitement. 'Maybe Stefan was calling his brother after all.'

'I'm not so sure,' said Bert. 'I don't think we can come to a definite conclusion. I would very much doubt that Otto Hauswald is Oskar Schimonsky.'

'But why not? He's the right sort of age. Why else would Stefan be calling him? On a regular basis? It all fits.'

'Because, well, OK. Maybe you're right. But I'll say this, Detlef. If this really is Oskar Schimonsky and you want to assassinate him, you will have an almost impossible task. This isn't just a lonely guy in an apartment in London. This is a political leader in Germany and an important figure. He is certain to have day and night security. And just think of the consequences politically if you did assassinate him.'

'That would not concern me,' said Detlef. 'After what he and his colleagues did on Rügen, he is not fit to be a political leader.'

'The first thing, Detlef, is to make sure this is who we think it is. A lot of digging and asking around will need to be done. It will take time.'

'I agree that we have to be certain.'

'Absolutely. You go back to Rügen and I'll let you know how I get on.'

CHAPTER 24

The office of Wilkins and Bradbury, solicitors, was in Mayfair and Katie had an appointment at ten o'clock.

'Good morning, MrsTalbot.' David Wilkins ushered Katie into his office. 'I understand that you know what this is about?'

'Yes. I was informed that it concerns the will of Mr Steven Jackson.'

'That is correct. I have Mr Jackson's will here.' Wilkins indicated the document on his desk. 'My secretary and I visited Mr Jackson only two days before he died.' I drafted the will on Mr Jackson's instructions and it was witnessed by my secretary. The will is very brief. Mr Jackson has named you as the sole beneficiary of his estate and also named you as the sole executor.'

Katie was speechless and could only look at Wilkins in disbelief.

'I understand that Mr Jackson's assets were substantial. I have these items to give to you, on Mr Jackson's instructions. The first is this letter.' Wilkins handed Katie a sealed envelope. 'And this package. I have no idea what either of them contain.'

Katie took the items, still lost for words.

'Mrs Talbot, I suggest you take these items and examine them at your leisure. Also I need to remind you of your duties as an executor. Do you know much about Mr Jackson's family?'

'Virtually nothing,' Katie admitted. 'I have to say, Mr Wilkins, that I am astonished that I am Mr Jackson's sole beneficiary. We were never that close.'

'I had guessed as much,' said Wilkins. 'In which case, the will may very well be contested. It is your duty to inform all that might be concerned about Mr Jackson's death. The contents of the will are public knowledge and can be read by any interested party.'

'As far as I know he was never married and did not have any children. But I know that he had at least one brother.'

'May I suggest a death announcement in the English newspapers and also the national German papers. I would be happy to arrange that.'

'Thank you,' said Katie. 'Maybe I will get more information as I look into his affairs.'

'Yes, probably,' Wilkins agreed. 'If you do find anything, please keep me informed. We will continue as normal unless circumstances dictate otherwise. Although you are yourself a lawyer, this is not your field and you will probably need my assistance is preparing probate. So, if that is the case, please give me a call to arrange an appointment.'

\#

Katie took a taxi home, still dumbfounded by the situation. The first thing she did was to open the letter and as she read she became increasingly tearful.

My dearest Katie,

I know that if you are reading this letter I have met my end. Ever since the incident in France, it had been my intention to die as soon as possible, as I had found it very difficult to come to terms with my disability. However, with the help of the Catholic church, I had managed to regain my will to live and be a useful member of the community.

You are the only woman with whom I have truly been in love. Really, from the first time I met you. It is to my eternal chagrin that I did not match up to your expectations. However, I have always held you to have an equal responsibility for my situation, just on account of your being there and for letting me think you loved me as much as I loved you. I have felt it to be grossly unfair that I have had to live in this condition, whilst you have escaped scot-free.

So, in making you the sole benefactor of my estate, I am hoping to ensure that you never do forget me. For even if you sell all my assets, the change in your life-style will always be a reminder of my munificence.

Steven.

The last sentence turned Katie's sadness and feeling of guilt to anger. His munificence, indeed! For Steven's wealth was really hers. The profits from the sale of her family's treasures were returning to the rightful owner.

Katie next turned her attention to the sealed package. There were several items inside and so she went to the kitchen table to lay everything out. The main items were two small cardboard boxes, each labelled with an address. There was one for the apartment in London and another for the house in France.

Katie opened the box for London. Inside was a set of keys (presumably duplicates of the ones she had given to George) and a sheet of paper on which was written the combination of a safe and the name and details of Steven's housekeeper. The box for France contained only a set of keys.

The rest of the contents of the package were several sheets of paper. Katie leafed through them and the more she looked, the more astonished she became. The details of several bank accounts in different countries were listed, but then came a list of securities. At the end was an end-of-year total of the valuation, at which Katie stared in disbelief, for the assets were valued at about thirty million pounds sterling.

CHAPTER 25

'I've spent a lot of time going through the CCTV records,' said Evans. 'This is what I've got.'

'Good,' said Carter. 'Get us some tea and we'll have a look. And what about those chocolate biscuits?'

'Going backwards. This is the evening Jackson was shot. We have two hooded men walking down Beaufort Gardens. One is carrying a bag. There is a parked van in the way, which obscures our view of the entrance to Jackson's apartment, but we get these guys on the way back. The bag looks a lot heavier.'

'These are the guys that shot Jackson, then,' said Carter. 'No doubt of it.'

'We pick them up later in Knightsbridge,' said Evans. 'They have become careless. This shot shows their faces clearly.'

'Well done,' said Carter.

"These two guys are almost certainly the guys we saw in Hyde Park. They are of the same build, but we didn't get facial images then.'

'So are they on our database?'

'No. But computers are a wonderful thing. I asked the computer to compare these facial images with images of passengers arriving at all

London airports over the last two weeks. One of these guys arrived at terminal one, Heathrow, from Berlin the day before the incident in the park.'

'Probably a German,' said Carter excitedly.

'But we can't correlate the images to passenger lists.'

'So we can't positively identify him?'

'No, but the Germans might.' Evans looked at Carter with a grin. 'I'm sure you wouldn't mind another visit to see Frau Schmidt.'

'Hmm. Yes. Rather. She's quite something. Pity you weren't there to see her.'

'Fancy it then?'

'I fantasise about her all the time. Imagine situations when we might be alone together.'

'And having sex?'

'It always ends up having sex.'

'Why not ask her for a date?' Evans still had a grin on his face.

'Well, she's not married. At least, she hasn't got any rings on her fingers.'

'Worth a try then?'

'No.' Carter frowned. 'She's way out of my league. I wouldn't stand a chance.'

'Then would you fancy Mrs Talbot? She's older than you, but she's still rather gorgeous.'

'I've a tip for you, Evans. Never get involved with people you meet in the line of work. Witnesses, suspects, whatever. If you do, you will eventually come a cropper. Remember that.'

#

At the German embassy, Carter was escorted to the same office as before. Suzanne was dressed very conservatively in a trouser suit and a blouse with a roll collar. Carter was still obviously impressed.

'Thank you for seeing me again, Frau Schmidt,' Carter began.

'Thank you for e-mailing us those images, inspector,' said Suzanne, well used to the reaction that she produced in men such as Carter. 'They were associated with the unfortunate Mr Jackson?'

'Yes. We know that one of the suspects arrived from Berlin. That's why we thought he might be German. The other image from CCTV we could not identify, but we thought he might be German also. That's why we thought you might be able to help us.'

'We have compared your images with our database,' Suzanne put on a suitably disappointed expression. 'But I am afraid we have not come up with a match. The man arriving at Heathrow does not, of course, have to be a German.'

'No, of course not,' said Carter. 'It was just a probability.'

'We are, of course, concerned that both these men might be German and are involved in this incident,' Suzanne continued. 'We will be conducting our own investigation.'

'This is a murder enquiry,' said Carter. 'It is very important that we try to find a match. Our next step is to send these images to Interpol. And to our own security services. And to the CIA.'

'Yes. I see,' said Suzanne slowly. 'That would be a good idea. Let us know if you come up with anything. And we will do the same.'

'Thank you,' said Carter, realizing that the interview was at an end.

'I wish you the best of luck,' said Suzanne, shaking hands. 'Let me know if I can be of any further help,'

After Carter had left, Suzanne sat at her desk for some time, deep in thought. Then she asked her secretary to make a telephone call to arrange an appointment.

'I have just found out something interesting,' said Evans as Carter returned. 'I've been to the Wills and Probate office in High Holborn. It might change everything.'

CHAPTER 26

'Thank you for coming into the station, Mrs Talbot.' DS Evans ushered Katie and Phillip Deacon, her solicitor, into the interview room, as Inspector Carter also appeared.

'Please take a seat, Mrs Talbot.' Carter arranged his papers on the table. 'Evans, see about some tea. And maybe some more of those chocolate biscuits.'

Katie sat down with just a little anxiety. She could not be absolutely sure that she was not going to be accused of any wrongdoing. She could not think of any reason why she might be accused, but the recommendation that her solicitor be present was worrying.

'First of all,' said Carter, 'I should like to thank you for coming in to help with our enquiries. And to you, Mr Deacon.'

'I see no need for this interview,' said Katie tetchily. 'As I have told you all I know already.'

'OK.' Carter made space on the table as Evans returned with mugs of tea and a plate of biscuits. 'Then I should like to start at the beginning. Mrs Talbot, how did you know Mr Jackson?'

'A dating agency.' Katie was not pleased to have to go over old ground.

'And you met, how many times?'

206

'Three or four.'

'I'm sorry to have to ask you this, but how intimate was the relationship?'

'Is that information relevant?' Deacon interrupted.

'Certainly it is,' Carter replied. 'Mrs Talbot?'

'Our relationship was only on a casual basis,' said Katie guardedly.

'Really?' said Carter. 'And yet you went to France with Mr Jackson for the weekend. Do you expect us to believe that this was not a more intimate relationship?'

Katie realized that this would seem somewhat strange. 'I was anticipating intimacy,' she said reluctantly.

'But intimacy had not yet occurred?'

'No.'

'So what happened in France?'

Katie realized that she would have to tell the truth this time. Carter must have conferred with the French police. 'We arrived. Mr Jackson showed me over the house. I then realized that I had made a big mistake. I said that I wanted to go home. Mr Jackson then attacked me. I managed to push him down the stairs. It was my only way of defending myself.'

'I am questioning your excuse,' said Carter. 'Could it not have been that you took the opportunity to push Jackson down the stairs. Without provocation?'

'You can make no such inference,' said Deacon.

'It is a plausible supposition,' said Cater smoothly. 'Well, Mrs Talbot?'

'That is a ridiculous suggestion,' said Katie, who had anticipated the question. 'Mr Jackson confirmed my story when he was questioned by Inspector Fabre.'

'Indeed,' said Carter. 'I have his report here. In fact, I have visited the house in Grimaud and conferred with Inspector Fabre. He was also dubious about your story. That you could have fabricated the evidence yourself.'

'Inspector Carter,' said Deacon firmly, 'Mr Jackson confirmed my client's explanation. That is on record. I see no point in questioning this any further.'

'Perhaps Mr Jackson wanted to protect your client from investigation. Because he was madly in love with her? Despite what had happened?'

'After such an injury?' snorted Deacon. 'Inspector, I expect your questioning to be realistic. Not impossible conjecture.'

'Not impossible at all,' countered Carter smoothly. 'Let us continue and you will see where this is leading us.'

Katie's feeling of dread increased. Where, indeed, was Carter's investigation going?

'I have been talking to the carers who looked after Mr Jackson,' Carter continued. 'Mrs Talbot, Sister Graham and Father Brian both say that you told them that you did not like Mr Jackson. In fact, you have also told me that yourself.'

'It was just that I did not see a future for a long term relationship.'

'It does seem to me that the relationship was a little one-sided,' said Carter. 'Sister Graham and Father Brian both told me that Mr Jackson had an obsession about you. And that you resisted all attempts by them to get you to visit Mr Jackson.'

WINDING BACK THE CLOCK

'That is not true,' aid Katie indignantly. 'I had agreed to visit Mr Jackson. We went on the walk to the park.'

'But very reluctantly,' said Carter.

'It was a visit,' Deacon interrupted. 'That speaks for itself.'

'And I was going to make more visits,' Katie added.

'I am now going to summarize the attempts on Mr Jackson's life,' said Carter, unmoved by the repudiations. 'There was firstly the car bomb.'

'That was mistaken identity,' Katie contradicted him. 'The IRA claimed responsibility.'

'We have inside information that the IRA was not involved,' said Carter. 'They were only seeking publicity. We have to assume that the bomb was, indeed, meant for Mr Jackson. The perpetrators did not expect Mr Jackson to be away for so long.'

Katie sat in stunned silence as Carter continued. 'We now come to the incident on the beach. You could not identify your supposed kidnappers when we showed you photographs of known suspects.'

'That doesn't mean that it didn't happen,' said Katie.

'It means that we only have your word that it happened.'

'You accepted my explanation at the time,' Katie retorted.

'I am now moving on,' said Carter, not commenting further. 'We now come to the incident in the park.'

'I jumped in the lake to save him.' Katie was now becoming more and more anxious. Carter was building up circumstantial evidence against her and she had a feeling as it where it was heading.

209

'Perhaps plus points in your favour, knowing that he was going to be shot?' said Carter, raising his eyebrows.

'Inspector, I must protest at this accusation,' said Deacon. 'You have not mentioned the burglar who Mr Jackson was forced to kill in his apartment. Are you accusing my client of this also?'

'I am treating that incident as unrelated,' said Carter.

'Then might I suggest that all these incidents that you have mentioned are not related to each other?'

Carter ignored the remark. 'We have examined CCTV footage in Beaufort Gardens that show what appears to be the same two men present on all the occasions that we have mentioned. I am putting it to you, Mrs Talbot, that they were your accomplices?'

Katie looked at him with a frown. This was the case that Carter had built up against her and which he believed had some substance. Ever since the police had become involved, she had wondered whether at some point she would have to reveal the truth about her relationship with Steven, about her search for the treasures and why she was in Grimaud. The question was, was this the right time to do this? Would it help her case, or hinder it? No, she decided, this was not the time for a confession. She would wait and see what Carter came up with next.

'Inspector,' Deacon said, in as forceful a manner as he could muster, 'all you have tabled is a continuous list of unbelievable circumstantial evidence that would not have a hope of standing up in a court of law.'

'Up to now, I would agree with you,' said Carter, to Deacon's surprise. 'All this circumstantial evidence is useless without a motive, and I could not see a motive. Until,' Carter paused for emphasis, 'I heard of the contents of Mr Jackson's will.'

Katie and Deacon looked at Carter in shocked silence as the implication sank in.

'As I see it,' Carter continued, 'Mrs Talbot, you knew that Mr Jackson was infatuated with you. You knew that he had left you all his money in his will.'

'Absolute nonsense,' Katie exclaimed loudly. She was now really frightened. Carter seemed to be building up to a climax. 'I was as surprised as anybody when I heard the contents of the will. I had no idea he was leaving all his money to me.'

Carter ignored her outburst. 'You then contrived, with the help of others, as yet unknown, to bring about his death.'

Deacon struggled to find a reply. 'Inspector, that is ridiculous'

Katie, in despair, could find nothing to add.

Mrs Katherine Talbot,' Carter gathered his papers together, 'I am charging you with the murder of Mr Steven Jackson. You are not obliged to say anything, but if you do it will be taken down in writing and may be used in evidence.'

It was later that afternoon that Carter reported to the chief superintendent's office.

'Gordon, I understand that you have charged Mrs Talbot for the murder of Steven Jackson?'

'Yes, sir. She will appear at Bow Street magistrate's court in the morning.'

'But you have only circumstantial evidence?'

'Yes,' Carter admitted. 'But I think I have a good case, with a strong motive.'

'I am afraid that I have to disappoint you. I have just had a call from the Home Office. They have informed me that there is to be no more investigation into the murder of Steven Jackson. The case is closed. That decision is final,' the superintendent said firmly as Carter started to protest. 'On the orders of the Home Secretary herself.'

'But why?' said Carter in despair.

'Ours is not to question why,' said the superintendent. 'It must involve the security services. I don't see it either,' he added, before Carter could protest again.

#

Katie had been escorted to the cells in the basement of the police station. Philip Deacon had stayed with her, consoling her and trying to convince her that the case against her would not stand up in court. He had contacted Hazel, who would act as Katie's defence lawyer. Whilst Deacon had been conferring at length with the barrister, Katie was again thinking about whether disclosure of the real reason behind her relationship with Steven would be to her advantage or disadvantage. She would firstly wait and hear Hazel's opinion of the case as it stood.

Katie and Deacon looked up with distaste as Carter entered the room.

'Mrs Talbot,' Carter could not keep the disappointment out of his voice, 'I have been informed that the evidence against you is insufficient. You are free to go and I apologize for the inconvenience.'

#

'I was beginning to get worried,' said Phillip Deacon as he said farewell to Katie on the pavement outside the police station. 'Carter thought he had built up quite a case against you.'

'I was more than worried,' said Katie. 'I'm still in a state of shock. Why the sudden change of heart?'

'I have absolutely no idea,' said Deacon. 'Carter was told by his chief super to drop it. Let's just be thankful.'

Katie made her way home, thinking that the inspector's reasoning had been logical. She had not killed Steven, but who had? And why?

CHAPTER 27

Katie stood outside the address in Beaumont Gardens and looked up at the building with some trepidation, wondering what she was going to find. She had arranged to meet Mrs Porter, the housekeeper, at ten o'clock.

Katie used her set of keys to enter the building and then took the stairs, rather than the elevator. She rang the bell of the apartment and then used her key to open the door. Mrs Porter emerged out of the kitchen to greet her.

'Katherine Talbot,' said Katie, advancing into the room to shake the housekeeper's hand.

'Very sad business, Mrs Talbot,' said Mrs Porter. She was a round, homely person with a mass of fluffy grey hair, dressed in a flowery housecoat and carpet slippers.

'Yes,' said Katie.

'I made everything tidy after the police had finished,' said Mrs Porter. 'They went over everything. They took away the Persian carpet and they haven't returned it yet. The burglars had left a dreadful mess everywhere and having the police rooting around as well didn't help.' Mrs Porter stopped to wipe away a tear. 'Mr Jackson was always so good to me.'

Katie nodded in sympathy. 'Mrs Porter, I am also the sole executor of Mr Jackson's estate, but I know very little of Mr Jackson's family. Did he speak of his family ever?'

'No. Never. And I didn't know of any close friends. He did have the occasional visitor, but they were all colleagues from his place of work.'

'And diaries, address books, that sort of thing?'

'Those were all taken by the burglars. And the computer. And his mobile phone.'

Yes, thought Katie. As she knew, this was no ordinary burglary. Mr Wilkins had explained the duties of an executor. She must check on whether the death had been registered and she would check with the funeral directors that Mrs Porter had mentioned. But how could she communicate with Steven's relatives, or next of kin, if all his personal documents had been stolen?

'Will you be moving into the apartment, ma'am?' Ms Porter enquired.

'No, I certainly will not,' said Katie with feeling. 'The apartment will be sold when everything has been finalized. But I would like you to stay on, Mrs Porter. Come in as required until further notice.'

'Certainly, ma'am.'

'Well, thank you for all that you have done. That will be all for today.'

After Mrs Porter had departed, Katie wandered around the sitting room, which was as she remembered it. Except that on the desk, in pride of place, was a large photograph of herself. It was an enlargement of the photograph that she had supplied originally to the dating agency. Katie looked at it with annoyance, but left it in place.

Katie expected to find the safe behind a picture, as in Grimaud and, sure enough, it was behind a painting next to the desk. Katie took the piece of paper from her handbag and fed in the combination.

The safe contained the same passports that she had seen before, a wallet containing several credit cards and a large amount of notes in pound sterling. There were also some insurance policies and pension details. Even more assets. And the same list of the family treasures from Rügen.

Katie sat down and drummed her fingers on the surface of the desk. Steven was gone and this list was the only remaining clue to the treasures. Katie looked at the many initials. OH. Otto Hauswald. She was not going to get any information from him. And confronting him with the list would be a waste of time. ND occurred frequently. She had not come across anyone with those initials.

Otto Hauswald had to be the key. She thought back about her conversations with Alex about the family history. From Breslau to Weimar, with a spell in Naumburg. Where Otto had been a clergyman. N could be for Naumburg. Of course, ND. *Naumburger Dom*. Naumburg cathedral. ND was not a person, but a place. And Naumburg cathedral was famous for the statue of Queen Uta.

#

'Nice restaurant,' said Grant, looking round.

'There are lots of good restaurants close to the house,' said Katie. 'But I think this is my favourite.'

'French restaurants are always my favourites.'

They had already given their order in the bar and the waiter brought their first course. Moules mariniere for Grant and goat's cheese salad for Katie. The sommelier poured out two glasses of Sancerre.

'I'm so pleased that your office located you to London,' said Katie, with a mischievous smile. 'What a stroke of luck.'

'I did press hard for it.' Grant returned the smile.

'So where will you be working?'

'From home at first. We have an office here and I may find space there later. We have branches all over Europe. So I will be doing some travelling.'

'So how is your new home?'

'A furnished apartment in Chelsea,' said Grant. 'Could not be better.'

'I'm sorry I could not be at the airport,' said Katie. 'I had an important meeting.'

'No problem. So, tell me about this job with Marshall. I find it strange that Elizabeth is not suitable for the role you have been given.'

'Apparently Elizabeth does not like to attend these functions. I think she struggles with the language. She finds small talk difficult. Also she does not speak German. And I know more about business and commerce than she does.'

'So what happens next?'

'My first assignment is very exciting. There is a conference in Rome next week of world industrial leaders. Marshall wants me to be there with him. As well as meetings, there will be a fashion show, and a formal dinner. I am taking two days off to complete my wardrobe.'

'I am beginning to get jealous,' said Grant.

'You have no need to be,' said Katie, in all seriousness. 'When I accepted the job it was on the condition that it was purely a business arrangement.'

'I'm very pleased to hear that,' said Grant.

'I would not say this to Marshall, but it's just that I do not find him particularly attractive. Something about his manner. I would not trust him, however charming he might be.'

'I would agree with you,' said Grant. 'I do not wish to cast aspersions on your employer, but my dealings with Marshall over the years have shown him to be a very devious character.'

'We are both destined to remain his enemy,' smiled Katie.

Grant decided that this was not the time to recruit Katie into the company. A public place was not appropriate. Another opportunity would have to be found. And he had still not decided whether it was the right thing to do. Would Katie think that he had befriended her just to recruit her? And should he risk that? He decided that he had to. Putting the job first should be his priority. Katie would be a great asset and any information with regard to Maxwell could be invaluable. The waiter brought their main course and the conversation moved to trivia about life in London.

'I'm sorry that I cannot invite you in,' said Katie as they arrived back on her doorstep. 'I am going to Germany early tomorrow morning. On business. And only for a day or so. I will see you as soon as I get back.'

Grant put his arms around her and held her close. 'I will keep in touch by phone.' He gave her a long, lingering kiss. 'You take care now.'

CHAPTER 28

Katie alighted from the train at Naumburg. The station had an elevated position on the north side of the town and she was immediately aware of the cathedral, dominating the red roofs of the old buildings surrounding it, the four towers with spires and domes reflecting the late afternoon sunlight. She was early for her appointment and it did not seem so far to walk.

At the cathedral entrance, Katie stated her business and very soon an elderly man dressed in church robes appeared.

'Good afternoon, countess. I am Richard von Weissenfels, dean of the cathedral. I thought it better that we meet after the cathedral has officially closed for the day.'

'Thank you very much for seeing me.' Katie offered her hand.

'I was very intrigued to hear your request,' said the dean, leading the way into the cathedral. 'Fascinated, in fact.'

'It is only a guess. Well, an educated guess. I am convinced that our family treasures were hidden in this cathedral.'

'Hearsay from a friend, you said. I have been here for five years now and I know the cathedral very well. I know of no secret places where your treasures might have been hidden.'

'I admit that it might be a wild goose chase,' said Katie. 'But I just have to check for myself.'

'I gather this is your first visit to the cathedral,' said the dean, stopping in the nave.

'Yes,' said Katie, looking around the huge building with a sense of awe.

'The cathedral dates from 1213. It is a perfect example of Romanesque and early Gothic architecture. What is unusual is that it was built with an altar at both the west and the east. This is the west choir and this,' the dean waved his hand, 'is what the visitors come to see.'

High on the wall of the choir were twelve life-size painted stone statues, the colours now faded with time.

'The statues are of the founders of the cathedral,' explained the dean.

'They are amazingly life-like,' said Katie. 'Who was the sculptor?'

'Surprisingly, nobody knew his real name,' said the dean. 'He was known only as the Meister von Naumburg. As you say, these statues are remarkable in that each statue is a life-like representation of the subject. By that, I mean that not only the body of the statue is a true representation, but also the face of the statue is the face of the subject. Nobody had ever done that before. Previously, statues always had what the sculptor thought as an ideal representation.'

'And this is the queen,' said Katie, looking up at the statue as a shiver ran down her spine.

'Queen Uta. Famous as being the epitome of German beauty in the Middle Ages. Next to her, with the sword and shield, is her husband, Eckkehard.'

Katie stood for a moment in admiration.

'When it was decided to have only one altar in the east of the church, this area was partitioned off and used for storage,' the dean continued. 'The statues stood there down the centuries, more or less forgotten. Then, not very long ago, an architecture student was doing a thesis and 'rediscovered' them. They have been a tourist attraction ever since.'

'My information is that the treasures were hidden near the queen,' said Katie, looking at the wall and the floor. 'There must be a secret entrance somewhere.'

'Well, I do not see any evidence of an entrance here,' said the dean, with a trace of sarcasm.

'Maybe a crypt that has been covered over,' Katie suggested.

'The cathedral does have a crypt,' the dean admitted. 'It is all that remains from the parish church that was originally on this site.'

'Maybe there is another one?' said Katie.

'I doubt it,' said the dean, 'but let's see if we can find anything.'

Katie began tapping on the wall as the dean examined the floor, which was made of large stone slabs.

Ten minutes later, Katie was in despair. No amount of banging and tapping of the floor, or the wall, had produced a result. The dean wandered away along the choir, looking for a possible clue and Katie sat in a pew, feeling more and more disconsolate. It had been a wild goose chase after all.

The setting sun was sending its rays through the windows at the west end of the cathedral, highlighting the statues and producing shadows, emphasizing every discrepancy, nook and cranny. Katie was looking idly at the wall below the queen. One of the stones seemed to be more recessed than the others. Only fractionally. Maybe even only a millimetre. Katie went over to the stone and looked at it more closely.

The stone was about two feet across and at both ends there seemed to be a small area that was more smooth, even slightly worn. Katie put a thumb over each area and pushed hard. Suddenly, to her shock and surprise, a whole section of the wall opened up, to reveal a flight of steps descending into the darkness.

'Good heavens!' exclaimed the dean, as he rushed to her side. 'I had no idea this was here.'

Katie and the dean stood for a moment looking into the space in the wall, dumbfounded at their discovery.

Eventually the dean said, 'We need some light.' He went to a cupboard and came back with a very large rubber torch.

'How very exciting,' said the dean, looking at Katie with a huge smile. 'Let's see what's down here.'

If anything, thought Katie, as she followed the dean down the steps. She feared that any treasures that had been here had long gone.

The steps led to a small, square room and the dean ran the beam of the torch around the walls. The room was empty, except for a wooden chest in one corner.

'There's something here after all,' said Katie, going over to the chest, as the dean followed with the torch. 'I imagined everything would have gone.'

The wooden chest had a shield painted on the lid with a large letter A in the middle. Katie shivered. This was undoubtedly a chest that had been left in the family cellar by her grandparents.

'I'm sure that this belonged to my family,' said Katie with a lump in her throat, wiping away a tear. 'It was taken from our home on Rügen.'

'Let's have a look what's inside,' said the dean, lifting the lid.

All Katie could see was a mass of old newspaper. The dean bent down and lifted out an object and removed the paper, to reveal a metal, dark grey, almost black, jug.

'I would suggest that this is the family silver,' said the dean. 'There must be quite a number of items here.'

Kati was too overcome to reply.

'Let's go and have some tea,' said the dean, putting a friendly arm around her. 'And talk about what to do next.'

#

'So, let's start at the beginning,' said the dean. They were sitting in drawing room of the rectory, an attractive stone house adjacent to the cathedral. The dean's wife had brought tea and homemade cake.

Katie told the dean about the family treasures being looted from the ancestral home.

'I would imagine there was more than just a chest of silver ornaments,' said the dean wryly.

'Yes,' said Katie with a sniff. 'There were paintings and porcelain too, but I'm afraid all that must have been dispersed. It's a long time now. I feel I'm lucky to have found the silver. I don't know why that is still there.'

'I expect it is of relatively little value,' said the dean. 'The price of the metal has been in the doldrums for the last few years. Not really worth the bother of melting it down.'

Katie nodded. 'I suppose it must have some antique value though.'

'Indeed it must. The problem is that I don't think I can just let you take the chest away with you. I shall have to firstly confer with the chapter.'

'Of course, I understand that,' said Katie. 'But perhaps we could get all the silver cleaned. Then we see exactly what we have got.'

'Indeed. I will arrange that,' said the dean. 'Now, countess. I am intrigued as to how you knew of the existence of the crypt and that it was the hiding place for your treasures.'

'I managed to obtain a list compiled by the thieves,' said Katie. 'They had annotated it with a series of letters.'

'And how did you obtain the list?'

'It was found by chance as our housekeeper was cleaning the family home,' said Katie, repeating the excuse that she had given to Grant. She reached in her handbag and gave the list to the dean. 'This is a list of the most important paintings. At first the letters meant nothing to me, but then I realized that ND was not a person, but a place.'

'But that does not tell you about the crypt.'

'No. That was just a guess. There had to be a hiding place somewhere.'

'I suspect that you are not telling me everything,' said the dean with a frown. 'But no matter. I see that the initials OH occur frequently. The name Otto Hauswald comes to mind. He was a curate here some time ago. And he is a well-known art dealer.'

'Yes, I know,' said Katie.

'It looks very much like he was involved,' said the dean. 'He must have known of the secret crypt and that it would have been an ideal place to store your treasures. This saddens me, that a man of the church could be so involved.'

'I have no proof that Otto Hauswald was involved,' said Katie.

'But the circumstantial evidence is overwhelming.'

'There are other initials on the list,' said Katie. 'I have only deciphered ND and probably OH. What intrigues me is TT and VV.'

'I think the initials may go together,' said the dean. 'I am a collector of antique clocks and I have come across a collector by the name of Theodor Thoden van Veltsen. A bit of a mouthful and he is known as TTVV. Sometimes just TV. He is a Dutchman who made a vast amount of money in the oil business. He collects paintings, clocks and snuff boxes. He is probably the initials referred to here.'

'Then it looks as if some of the treasures were sold to him.'

'Indeed it does.'

'Do you know anything about him?'

'I have met him,' said the dean. 'He lives in Monte Carlo and must be around eighty by now. He's not as active a collector as he used to be.'

'I wonder if I might go and see him,' said Katie thoughtfully. 'for information, as much as anything.'

'I am wondering if you might built a case against Hauswald,' said the dean. 'It is obvious to me that he had a part in the theft of your treasures. He knew of the crypt and could have retained a means of access to the cathedral. Easy to come and go under cover of darkness.'

'But very difficult to prove,' said Katie.

'Yes, I suppose so,' sighed the dean. 'I suggest you try and see TV. He might confess to buying items from Hauswald. He might also confess to knowing that they were stolen. That would be good first step.'

'Do you have an address,' Katie asked. 'Or a telephone number.'

'I'm sorry. I don't.' Then the dean added with a smile. 'Hauswald would.'

'I think I know how I could find out,' said Katie.

\#

The first telephone call that Katie made on the train back to Berlin was to Weimar.

'Katie. Now nice to hear from you. Where are you?'

'On a train. Alex, can you do me a favour?'

'Of course.

'I need the address and telephone number of an art dealer. Theodor Thoden van Velzen. He lives in Monte Carlo. Do you know him?'

'Old TV, you mean.' said Alex. 'Not seen him for ages. It will be in the study. I am on my way. Why do you want it?'

'He may have bought some of the family paintings.'

'Got it here,' said Alex. 'Ready?'

Katie wrote down the address and telephone number.

'He's not as active a collector as he used to be,' said Alex. 'Keeps himself to himself. I don't think he sees many visitors.'

'Thanks. I'll give him a call anyway. One can but try.'

'When are you going to come and see me again,' said Alex. 'Your painting is just about finished.'

'Oh. Well. Soon then.'

'Better be quick. Marshall tried to steal it.'

'What!' Katie exploded. 'Marshall has seen the painting?'

'Yes. He liked it.'

'How embarrassing.'

'Nothing to be embarrassed about. Just try to keep Marshall at arm's length.'

#

Katie's next call was to the number in Monte Carlo. To her surprise. Mr Thoden van Velzen agreed to see her on the following afternoon. She somehow had the feeling that he had been expecting her call. Katie had already ascertained that Lufthansa had a flight from Berlin Tegel to Nice Cote d'azur at ten o'clock the next day and she was able to book a seat online.

#

Katie was feeling very uncomfortable as the aeroplane banked over the Mediterranean on its way in to land. The hills behind Nice were in full sun and Katie was sure she could make out the Clinique St George. And she imagined that every time she came to the south of France in the future the memories would haunt her for the entire stay.

The helicopter took her to Fontvielle and from there a taxi brought her to the Avenue Princess Grace, having dropped off her luggage at the Hotel de Paris. TV (as Katie now mentally called him) lived in a modern tower block right on the sea front.

The uniformed porter in the lobby telephoned to make sure she was expected and then escorted her to the elevator, which needed a special key for the porter to send her up to the twelfth floor.

The elevator door opened directly into a large elegant drawing room, where a tall man, dressed in a yellow polo shirt and matching slacks, held out his hand to greet her. TV looked well-preserved for his eighty years with a tanned, almost unlined face and twinkling pale blue eyes.

'Thank you for agreeing to see me, Mr Thoden van Velzen,' said Katie.

'The pleasure is all mine, countess. Please call me TV.' He laughed. 'Everyone else does. First of all, you must look at the view.'

Floor to ceiling windows made up one wall of the room and one window had been slid back to allow access to the balcony that ran the entire width of the apartment. TV led the way on to the terrace and an uninterrupted view of the Mediterranean.

'What a wonderful view,' Katie exclaimed.

'And it will remain so,' said TV. 'There is no right of light in Monaco. But nobody is going to build in front of here. We overlook the Princess Grace memorial garden and just to our right is the conference centre.'

'I came to see your art collection,' said Katie as they re-entered the drawing room.

'but there are no paintings here.'

'Certainly not,' said TV. 'This room faces south and the light is far too strong. I have in here my collection of clocks and snuff boxes. My art collection is in the rooms at the back, which face north.'

TV led the way out of the drawing room. 'I have three rooms at the back that are supposed to be bedrooms. But I have no children and very few visitors, so these rooms are put to better use.'

'I recognise the Manet,' exclaimed Katie, as soon as she walked through the door into the next room.

'Indeed,' said TV with a smile. 'And I know it used to belong to your family.'

Katie turned towards him. 'And you bought it from Otto Hauswald?'

'Indeed I did.'

'Knowing it was stolen?' said Katie indignantly, scarcely able to believe such an outright confession.

'Certainly,' said TV. 'In fact, I bought six paintings from Hauswald that I knew used to belong to your family. I will show them to you. Save your indignation.' TV held up a hand to silence her. 'I will show you the rest of my collection and then we will talk.'

Katie and TV then passed through the other rooms as TV pointed out the other five paintings and commented on his collection in general. All the time Katie was experiencing a variety of emotions; pleasure and excitement at seeing the family paintings and annoyance that they did not belong to her.

'Now, countess, we will sit on the terrace and have a glass of champagne.'

TV went into the kitchen and then joined Katie on the terrace. 'Cheers,' said TV, taking a seat opposite her.

Katie managed a half-hearted reply, waiting to hear what TV was going to offer as an explanation.

'Since the dawn of civilisation, works of art have travelled around the world,' TV began, taking a sip of his champagne. 'Either by sale or pillage. A prime example being the Elgin Marbles, which, in my opinion, will never be returned to Greece. It was always so and always will be. Therefore my conscience is clear. I know that much of my collection has been acquired, how can you say, privately, but I have no intention of relinquishing any of it.'

Katie's expression said that she disapproved.

'I wasn't there, but I followed what went on in New York with the Titian,' said TV, with a grin. 'I was very amused. The history of that painting is another prime example of what we have been discussing. And still no sign of it?'

'No.' Katie shook her head.

'But you were contesting the ownership.'

'Yes, I was. But after a prime witness died, I had very little to back up my case.'

'I would suggest that would be the situation regarding your family's paintings that are here. With no clear evidence of ownership you could never successfully claim them back through the courts.'

'I might be inclined to try,' said Katie, not at all mollified.

'There is really no need to do that. I am making you a concession. I am only concerned with the collection whilst I am alive. I have no heirs and in my will I am bequeathing the items in my collection as I see fit. If I know of the original owners, I will return the works to them. If not, then they go to the gallery or museum of my choice. After I die, you will have your paintings back.'

Katie could not manage a reply, so unexpected was TV's statement.

'You can rest assured that your paintings are safe,' TV continued. 'One of the reasons I live here is that there is virtually no crime in Monaco. If a felony is committed, the perpetrators are caught within, on average, two minutes.'

Katie was still unable to reply, so surprised was she at the outcome of her visit.

'So, countess, what do think of my proposal?'

Eventually, Katie said, 'I suppose I must thank you for your grand gesture.'

'But you are still at odds with how I have acquired my collection?'

'Candidly. Yes.'

'Then that is something we both have to live with.'

#

Later that evening, Katie sat at her window that overlooked the yacht basin and beyond it the open sea. A lone sailboat was tacking towards the coast, hoping to make landfall before darkness. The remains of the room service meal from the grill room and an empty bottle of wine had been discarded and Katie was in a sleepy and reflective mood.

Her quest had finally come to an end. She knew who had stolen the treasures and where they had gone. She had retrieved the family silver, but that was all. If TV kept his word, she would at least recover some of the paintings. And through Steven's will, she had some of the proceeds. All in all, if she were honest, she had achieved far more than she could ever have dared hope.

Her telephone rang. Grant wanted to know if she was OK. Maybe it was a good time to start afresh.

CHAPTER 29

'Suzie, darling, will you please sit still.' said Alex in an exasperated voice, peering over the top of the easel.

'I get so uncomfortable sitting in this position' Suzanne complained. 'Why can't I sit like the model in that painting over there?'

'You know why. I want you with your legs crossed.'

'You've just got a thing about pubic hair.'

'All I can say is that, in my opinion, you would look better with it.'

'And what would I look like wearing a bikini? They are cut so small these days I would look ridiculous. Anyway, shaving pubic hair is very trendy now. Especially in America.'

'Yes,' Alex sighed. 'I see your point.'

'So did Marshall come to Weimar just to give you a dressing down over the painting?'

'No. I think the main thing he came for was to visit his factory.'

'But it's only a very small affair,' said Suzanne, hoping for more information.

232

'He's bought a big plot of land next to it. He's got plans for an expansion. Said he's going to branch out.'

'Branch out into what?'

'I don't know. He didn't say. Suzie, legs crossed again, please.'

'So I suppose Marshall just came for the day.'

'No. He stayed one night at the Elephant. Met someone for dinner.'

'So when is Marshall coming back?'

'No idea. But he will be coming back for grandmother's birthday party.'

'Yes. Of course,' said Suzanne thoughtfully. 'Is it going to be a big affair?'

'No. Mainly family. She's not got many friends now. But I suppose father will invite some of his cronies.'

'Something to look forward to,' said Suzanne.

'I've had enough of this,' said Alex, putting down his brush. 'Let's do something else.'

Suzanne entered the Hotel Elephant and asked the receptionist if she could see the manager. She represented a tour company and had had a complaint from a customer. The receptionist disappeared and then came back to invite Suzanne to the manager's office.

As the door closed behind her, Suzanne showed her identification. 'BfV,' was all she needed to say.

The manager's expression changed from one of benign co-operation to one of fear and apprehension. Suzanne thought he was probably old enough to remember the days of the STASI. 'Please take a seat,' he stammered. 'What can I do for you?'

'Not a problem with you or the hotel,' Suzanne assured him. 'May I remind you that this conversation is entirely confidential.'

'Of course,' said the manager, obviously relieved.

'I believe Mr Maxwell stayed with you recently?'

'Yes, he did,' said the manager. 'I always greet him personally.'

'And I believe he dined that evening? With a guest?'

'I believe so,' agreed the manager.

'I should like to speak to the person who served him at dinner,' said Suzanne.

'Certainly.' The manager left the room to reappear shortly with a young woman dressed in her waitress uniform. 'This is Brigitte,' said the manager. 'She served Mr Maxwell on that evening.'

'Hello, Brigitte. I am Suzanne.' Suzanne smiled at the girl, hoping to put her at her ease. 'You remember serving Mr Maxwell?'

'Yes. Of course. He always gives his server . . . ,' Brigitte stopped and looked sideways at the manager.

'And Mr Maxwell had a guest?' said Suzanne quickly, to save Brigitte any more explanation.

Brigitte nodded.

'Can you describe him, please?'

234

WINDING BACK THE CLOCK

'I remember him because he was shabbily dressed,' said Brigitte. 'Not immaculate, like Mr Maxwell. Old. Grey hair. Funny old-fashioned glasses.'

'And did you manage to overhear any of the conversation?'

'I remember because they were talking history,' said Brigitte. 'I thought that a bit odd. I expected them to be talking business.'

'What do you mean by history?' asked Suzanne.

'I didn't hear everything, of course, because I came and went. But at first they were talking about the Treaty of Potsdam. And Poland. We did that at school.'

'OK.' Suzanne frowned. 'And later?'

'I didn't hear much later. But they did mention the Oder-Neisse line.'

'Anything else about the conversation you remember?'

'No.'

'Well, thank you, Brigitte. You have been most helpful. May I remind you not to mention this conversation to anyone else.'

Suzanne bade the manager farewell and left the hotel with a grim expression. Marshall and his friend had been discussing the borders.

CHAPTER 30

'So I was right?' said Detlef.

'We had to be doubly sure,' said Rainer. 'That was very important.' The two men were seated in a corner of Marco's bar, each with a litre of Kindl. 'The point is, do you really want to go ahead with this. Isn't one brother enough?'

'I have to. Stefan said to me that he only did the books and his brother was responsible.'

'Did you believe him?'

'No. At the time, I didn't believe him, but on thinking about it, maybe he was telling the truth.'

'So Oskar may have been the one who killed your father?'

'Yes.' Detlef looked at him defiantly. 'I'm sure of it. Maybe not personally, but he was in charge.'

'OK.' Rainer looked at him thoughtfully. 'You know all about Otto Hauswald, as he is now called?'

'I've been doing lots of research on the internet. And reading papers and magazines.'

'Very good. But it is bound to be difficult,' said Rainer. 'You will have to go down to Weimar, where Hauswald lives, and get the lie of the land. See if you can think of an opportunity. I am always here for advice and discussion.' Rainer passed Detlef a piece of paper. 'We do have a mutual friend who lives in Weimar. Anya Detterer. Schneider, that was. You remember her?' Rainer had a smile on his face.

'Not likely to forget her. We were engaged to be married.'

'Anya is sympathetic to your cause and is willing to help.'

'It will be nice to see her again.'

'So what happened to the relationship?'

'It was the DDR. Anya didn't want to live on Rügen. The back of beyond, as she called it. We parted friends.'

'But you kept in touch?'

'At first, but then she met someone else and the correspondence dried up. I haven't communicated for years.'

'She married and you didn't?'

Detlef paused as the memories came flooding back. Blonde hair, long legs and celibate cuddles in the Olympic village. 'I never found anyone to replace her.'

'You may be able to carry on where you left off. She's a widow. Her husband died a year or so back.'

'I doubt it,' said Detlef gloomily.

Detlef need not have worried. He recognized Anya immediately. The tallest woman on the platform; blonde hair now going grey, but still the same smiling face and twinkling eyes.

Anya gave him a hug and kisses on both cheeks. 'Detlef, you haven't changed a bit. It's not fair.'

'Neither have you.'

'Oh yes I have. Lines and bags under the eyes. Grey hair. Bit of a tum. You've none of that and you're not even overweight.'

'I try and keep fit,' was all Detlef could find to reply.

'You pull your suitcase and I'll carry your laptop,' said Anya, leading the way out of the station and towards a very old Volkswagen beetle.

'Have you found somewhere for me to stay?' Detlef asked, loading his suitcase with difficulty into the back of the car that was crammed with cardboard boxes and a pair of rubber boots.

'You're staying with me.' Anya managed to start the engine at the third attempt.

'Oh, good,' said Detlef. 'I had hoped I might, but I didn't know if you had a spare room.'

'No, I don't have a spare room,' said Anya, flashing him a smile. 'Old times, Detlef.'

#

'I was sorry to hear that you lost your husband,' said Detlef, as Anya put the evening meal on the table.

'Five years ago now. Lung cancer.'

'He was a smoker?'

'Yes. I still do. Not much, but I know I shouldn't.'

'Family?'

'I have two boys. One lives not far from here in Apolda, the other works in Frankfurt, West Germany. And yourself, Detlef. You never married?'

'No. I have had a long standing girl-friend. But it has never been really serious. We both had an elderly mother to care for.'

Anya declined to comment. She had met Detlef's parents once at an athletics meeting in Berlin. Detlef's father had been quiet and unassuming, but his mother had been small and dynamic, overpowering and domineering and this was the main reason Anya had decided not to marry Detlef, even though they had been initially engaged.

'So you want to assassinate Otto Hauswald,' said Anya. 'Because he murdered your father. I have every sympathy. My uncle was interrogated by the STASI. He survived, but his health never really recovered.'

'I'm grateful you've agreed to help.'

'I will do what I can. Rainer said that he will come and join us once we have done an initial assessment. So, have you any idea how you are going to achieve this? Hauswald is quite a celebrity figure, now, you know, and his party is proving to be very successful. He will be well guarded.'

'I've brought my rifle. It's new and I've got a very good laser telescopic sight. I can guarantee a hit at up to 500 metres, which should be enough.'

'Then we have to find an opportunity,' said Anya. 'Hauswald's home is here in Weimar, but he's seldom there. He's campaigning in Saxony, that is the next state election.'

'We shall have to find out his itinerary,' said Detlef. 'See if one of the venues would be suitable.'

'The party office is in the *Markt*. I'll go in tomorrow and see if I can get a programme. And you can go and have a look at his house. There might be an opportunity there.'

'I'll do that, but I would doubt it.'

After a very indifferent movie, dubbed into German, Anya said, 'Bedtime. Give me ten minutes.'

A very apprehensive Detlef stole into the bedroom ten minutes later, self-conscious in his nakedness. The only light came from a small bedside lamp. Anya was sitting up in bed, the duvet up to her neck and smoking a cigarette. Except it didn't smell like a cigarette. Detlef slid in beside her.

'Try it.' Anya passed him the joint.

Detlef hesitantly took a puff, coughed and handed it back.

'OK?' Anya smiled at him.

Detlef only nodded.

'It'll relax you.' Anya snuggled up to him. 'Did you expect this?' Anya giggled. 'Before you came to Weimar? My not having a spare room?'

'Well . . . ,' Detlef stuttered, taking another puff as Anya passed the joint to him again.

'But you imagined it?'

'Yes. Of course.'

'You know, I really fancied you back then. You were so strong and muscular.'

'It was the pills they gave us,' Detlef sniffed. 'We all took them. We cheated.'

'I understand lots of the athletes still do.'

'Some of them will always find a way round the tests,' Detlef agreed.

'There were no contraceptive pills in those days. We had to be so careful. There was no way we could risk getting pregnant.'

'Not a problem now,' Detlef bent down to kiss her tenderly.

'Certainly not.' Anya guided his hand to her left breast and then reached down for him.

#

'I'm getting a bit of an idea about this,' said Anya thoughtfully, leafing through the local newspaper that was spread out on the kitchen table. 'I think we might be able to find a chance for you to get a shot at him.'

'I walked all around his house this morning,' said Detlef, taking another beer from the fridge. 'Very big house, more like a palace. Bought from ill-gotten gains. From selling the treasures from Rügen.' Detlef spat out the words with contempt. 'But I'm afraid there is no chance of getting him at home. Unless we could gain access to a house across the street.'

'The NDVP is pulling out all the stops, targeting the Saxony elections. There are meetings and rallies. They have an ad here. Maybe we could get him at one of those.'

'That's the sort of thing we need,' Detlef agreed. 'We might be able to find a vantage point. Even some distance away.'

'Let's hope so. There's an election rally coming up at the football stadium in Dresden. It says here that all candidates will be there to make an address and answer questions.'

'In a football stadium?'

'Yes. They anticipate a large number of people will want to watch the debate and cheer on their candidate. The stadium was the best place. They couldn't find a hall big enough.'

'Security will be tight,' said Detlef.

'Of course, but I think it's our best chance,' said Anya. 'What we need is tickets for the next time that Dynamo Dresden are playing at home.'

\#

'Funny name for a stadium,' said Detlef. 'Lucky gas?'

'It's the name of the sponsor,' said Anya. 'A gas company. The logo is a chimney sweep. Chimney sweeps are supposed to be lucky.'

'Still don't get it,' said Detlef.

'Holds over 32,000 people,' said Anya. 'And I think it's going to be a capacity crowd today.'

Detlef and Anya were being hustled along with the crowd from the car park to the stadium, a huge concrete and steel edifice. The fans were mostly young men, wearing the shirts of the home team and scarves of red and yellow. But there was a good sprinkling of women and youngsters as well. They were approaching the stadium from the side covered in mirror glass that was reflecting the colours of the crowd and the blue sky, for it was a clear, crisp day.

'Is there going to be trouble?' Detlef wondered, seeing fans wearing the blue and white colours of the away team from Berlin, who were exchanging profanities with the home fans.

'Maybe in the bars later,' said Anya. 'Not at the match. The away fans have their own section and it's an all-seater stadium.'

WINDING BACK THE CLOCK

'There's no cover,' Detlef said into Anya's ear after they had taken their seats, such was the baying of the fans that it made communication very difficult. The stadium resembled a huge saucer, the seats coloured in banks of red and yellow in support of the home team. It was hard to imagine anything more open.

Anya nodded. 'I feel very exposed, just sitting here. We'll have a walk round at half-time.'

Behind their block of seats was a wide concrete walkway that ran around the circumference of the stadium. At the back were stalls selling drinks and food. In the interval, Detlef and Anya wandered round towards the other end of the stadium.

Anya motioned Detlef to a corner where they would not be overheard. 'It's all very, very open. And I expect there will be people on the pitch itself and in the seats.'

'They will have to erect a stage somewhere,' said Detlef. 'Probably at one end or the other.'

'I've just had an idea,' said Anya. 'Let's walk round a bit further.'

At the end of the stadium Anya stopped. 'See that booth up there? They send a live commentary to the local hospitals. That would be a very good vantage point. But it must be a good 200 metres from there to where the target will be. Is that OK?'

'No problem, especially with my equipment,' said Detlef, taking a quick glance upwards. 'But that booth is glassed in. We want something open.'

'I don't mean the booth itself,' said Anya. 'The steps up to it. This show is bound to carry on into darkness and wherever they erect a stage you would be behind all the spectators.'

'So our main problem is getting my rifle into the stadium undetected.'

'I've been thinking about that too,' said Anya. 'In the programme they say they do visitor tours. During the day when there isn't anything else on. There may be very little or no security.'

'So we do a visitor tour and find somewhere to hide the rifle,' said Detlef. 'That must be possible somewhere. I noticed so many doors to dressing rooms and offices. One could probably sneak in undetected.'

'That's it, then,' said Anya. 'Terrific. Now let's go back and enjoy the rest of the game.'

CHAPTER 31

Otto Hauswald and his team of canvassers stopped in the middle of the bridge across the Elbe that connected the square in front of the Semper Oper with the area known as New Town.

'Sabine,' Otto said quietly to his PA, 'go on ahead and find me a couple of suitable interviewees.'

Otto squared up in front of the television camera as the soundman positioned his microphone. 'I remember being on this bridge thirty years ago.' Otto waved a hand as the cameraman panned round for a view of the city. 'Yes, the Oper and the Zwinger and the Albertinum had been restored, but the Frauenkirche was still in ruins and the area in front of us across the bridge was very run down, with cheap shops and neglected apartment blocks thrown up by the DDR and washing strung out everywhere between the windows. Now, the Frauenkirche has been rebuilt and we have shops selling designer goods and smart new apartment blocks, but what do the local citizens think about the present and, more important, about the future? Let's find out.'

Otto and his entourage moved on across the bridge and up the hill to where Sabine, clipboard in hand, was pointing to an old man sitting on a chair outside the barber's shop. His scruffy clothes included a stained sleeveless leather waistcoat and a walking stick was propped up at his side. An ancient Labrador was resting its grey muzzle on his boot.

'This is Hans,' said Sabine. 'He's lived in Dresden all his life.'

245

'Good morning, Hans,' beamed Otto, sitting on an adjacent chair and shaking his hand. 'I'm Otto Hauswald, leader of the NDVP. I hope that you are going to vote for our party in the election.'

'Don't think I'm going to vote at all,' said Hans gruffly. He looked at Otto with a belligerent smile, revealing a dentition with several missing teeth.

'Your vote for us would make a difference,' said Otto. 'Our aim is to make Germany a great country again. And that includes Saxony. Dresden has always had an important place in the history of our country. It has had triumphs, but disasters as well.'

Hans nodded. 'I was only a lad. But I remember the firestorm in 1945.'

'Something one could never forget,' Otto agreed.

'We lived over the hill,' Hans continued. 'So our family survived. But everyone lost friends and relatives.'

'They could never put a figure on the casualties,' said Otto.

'No. Nobody knew how many people were in the city. There were a lot of evacuees from Breslau and people from outside the city had been drafted in to help look after them. It was a catastrophe.'

'Let's hope nothing like that ever happens again,' said Otto. 'So how do you see the future, Hans? What would you expect our party to do for you?'

'I worry about my pension,' said Hans. 'Inflation is going up and my money stays the same.'

'I see your point,' said Otto. 'One of party's aims is to leave the common currency. That would mean a return to the Deutschmark, which would be a very strong currency. Your money would be worth more. In fact, our estimate is that the new mark would be worth twenty per cent more. Isn't that a reason to vote for us?'

Hans thought for a moment. 'I would think it is.'

'Now, Hans, I have another important question for you. First of all, how old are you now?'

'I will be eighty three this year.'

'And so you remember when Germany was Germany. How do you think of yourself now? Are you a German, or a European?'

The camera zoomed in to register Hans's reaction.

'German, of course,' said Hans stoutly.

'Good man,' said Otto, slapping him on the knee. 'Germany for the Germans. How about that?'

'Sounds good to me.'

'Then make sure you do vote for us.'

Otto now addressed himself to the camera. 'Whatever happened to the German identity? We have been swept along by the politicians, thrusting the idea of being European down our throats. Lumping us together with all these inferior people. Is that what we really want?'

Otto and the company now moved further up the hill to where Sabine was standing outside a *Konditori*.

'This is Gisela Meyer,' said Sabine. 'She is 23 and is unemployed.'

Gisela was a tall, gangly girl, with straggly brown hair and a small stud in her nose. She kept looking nervously directly at the camera, despite the director's gesticulations that told her not to.

'Hallo,' said Otto, shaking her by the hand. 'I am Otto Hauswald, leader of the NDVP. So, how long have you been without a job, Gisela?'

'Two years now. Ever since leaving college.'

'And what did you study?'

'History of art and social policy.'

'Hmm. Not exactly ideal to find employment easily,' said Otto.

'The problem is that since 2008 there has been so little new development.' Gisela looked at Otto accusingly, as if it were his fault. 'Companies have closed down and no new ones have been coming in.'

'I understand that,' said Otto. 'In Thüringen, we are developing new industrial estates, for example, the one in Weimar. We would aim to do the same for Saxony. Also we are negotiating with the Disney Corporation for a theme park in south eastern Germany. Both these ventures will bring plenty of jobs and increase the prosperity of the population.'

Gisela sniffed. 'Another problem is that so many of the new jobs that are created are going to the immigrants. What are you going to do about that?'

'I agree with you that has been a problem,' said Otto. 'Our party is committed to restrict immigration. Especially if we leave the European union and we are not obliged to admit workers from other Eu member countries. Not only that, but we will be repatriating all non-German citizens who are not useful members of the community. There will be no benefits for useless hangers-on.'

'That would be very helpful,' said Gisela, her facial expression softening.

'Then we can count on your vote?'

'Yes. If you can keep your promises.'

'We certainly can. Thank you for your support.'

'I've just heard some bad news,' said Sabine. 'I think we 'd better stop this now.'

CHAPTER 32

Detlef had obtained a map of the stadium and was calculating distances and angles, imagining where the stage might be, when Anya arrived in a rush.

'You can forget all that.' She went to the television. 'We're just in time for the news on the hour.'

Detlef and Anya listened to the announcer in shocked silence.

Gerd Bohnen, the leader of the CDU, was this morning assassinated in Marienberg. Herr Bohnen was canvassing door to door when a man ran up to him and stabbed him in the chest. The assailant was then driven away by an accomplice on a motorcycle. Herr Bohnen was pronounced dead at the scene. The police are appealing for witnesses to come forward. A spokesman for the CDU said that the planned debate at the Glucksgas stadium would be cancelled and a similar debate would now take place in a television studio, where maximum security could be guaranteed. He stressed that the CDU would still be contesting the Saxony election as planned.

'So that's that,' said Detlef. 'What do we do now? We have no plan B.'

'We will have to think of one,' said Anya. 'We are not giving up. But I think we are up to needing some help. I'm going to ask Rainer to come and visit.'

#

Rainer arrived from Berlin the following weekend. Anya waited until they had finished their evening meal and had opened a few beers before she said, 'Rainer. Any ideas?'

'I think your idea of a hit in the stadium was a non-starter. Firstly, you had to get a weapon into the stadium without detection from all the security. It might have been impossible to find a secure hiding place for the rifle when you did a visitor tour. And not to mention making a good escape.'

'I knew it was going to be difficult,' said Detlef. 'But I did think we had a chance that it might be successful. And we couldn't think of anything else.'

'OK. So all that is out the window and they are not going to have anything similar in the future. At the moment, I can only think of two alternatives. We examine Hauswald's schedule and pick a spot where Detlef can get a shot at him. He also does the occasional house-to-house, but after Bohnen's assassination, security will be much tighter. There might also be the possibility of a car bomb.'

'I don't particularly want to do a car bomb again,' said Detlef. 'It was a complete failure last time.'

'Now. I have had a very good idea,' said Anya.

'Let's have it, then,' said Rainer.

'I was talking to my son this morning. He lives in Apolda, not far away. He goes around with a group of guys that includes Alex. You know, Otto's son.'

'And?' said Detlef and Rainer together.

'Well, they were all going to a concert in Berlin, but Alex said he couldn't go. The concert is the same evening as his grandmother's birthday party.'

'How does this affect us?' said Rainer.

'The point is that Otto will be there.'

'I see,' said Detlef slowly. 'You mean we might be able to get a shot at him. Knowing that at some point he will be in the street outside.'

'No. Much too risky. I am suggesting we put a bomb in the house.'

'But that would kill the other guests as well,' said Detlef. 'They might have a lot of guests.'

'I know. But some of the guests will be friends of Otto. Probably old colleagues from the STASI. We get them as well.'

'I still don't like it,' said Detlef. 'I think that's going too far.'

'Delef, it's just an idea. I want to get this over. Rainer, what do you think?'

'Bit drastic,' said Rainer. 'Detlef's right. To be sure of being effective, we have to use enough explosive to demolish the house.'

'Like a gas explosion would do,' said Anya. 'That's what everybody would think had happened.'

'Lots of technical difficulties and thoughts of their security,' said Rainer. 'But I agree that it's a possibility. We'll walk down the street tomorrow and take a look at the house.'

#

'Did you see the opportunity that I saw?' said Rainer, as they turned the corner into a narrow alley, having walked past the front of the house without paying it any obvious attention.

'I saw nothing in particular,' said Detef. 'What do you mean?'

'There's a trapdoor in the pavement outside the house. I should have thought of that earlier. All the houses have one. It's for coal to be delivered.'

'But not many houses have coal now,' said Detlef. 'They have gas central heating.'

'Of course. But the trapdoors are still there. Bolted down, of course, but, importantly, still there.'

'I see what you mean,' said Detlef.

'Let's walk past again and have another look.'

'Metal cover,' said Detlef, as they turned the corner at the other end of the street. 'It could be lifted with a crowbar.'

'It could,' Rainer agreed. 'But we would snap the bolts. And cause a lot of noise. Make it obvious somebody had tampered with it. Not such a good idea after all.'

'We will have to break in through a door or a window,' said Detlef.

'The problem is,' said Rainer, 'there has to be no evidence of our entry, which would alert security. Let's walk round the back of the house.'

There was a narrow alley, bordered by a high wall that ran along behind the houses and separated them from the houses in the parallel street.

'No open windows. And no way of climbing up, anyway,' said Detlef, looking up at the house as they strolled past.

'It has to be the roof,' said Rainer. 'This terrace has a parapet all the way along with a pitched roof in the middle. That means that there is a flat bit in between. I bet there is a skylight or something that would allow access. In fact, I can see the top of a window in the roof of each house.'

'Very good idea,' said Detlef sarcastically. 'How do we get up there?'

'Did you notice that the house at the very end of the terrace is empty and up for sale? We break into that house and make our way along the roof.'

'Do you think that will be possible?' Detlef asked. 'At night?'

'It's our only chance. We will have to give it a go.'

#

'Good that there's no CCTV here,' said Rainer.

'I hope nobody looks out of their window,' said Detlef.

'Not at two in the morning,' said Rainer, moving an old dustbin into position. 'Right. Over the wall and have a look at downstairs windows. And we only use a torch if absolutely necessary.'

'I think it's been empty for some time,' said Detlef, as they moved cautiously to the back of the house. 'Everything in this garden is very overgrown.'

'In our favour,' said Rainer. 'Especially if nobody visits between now and the party.'

'How about this window?' said Detlef. 'The kitchen window.'

'Good idea.' Rainer took out a large screwdriver from his toolbag.

The window yielded easily. 'Very little damage. Just a bit of a dent in the woodwork. In we go and up to the roof.'

The house was completely empty of all furnishings and fittings and the men made their way up to the top floor. The floorboards creaked and the sound echoed around the rooms and the stairwell. 'Don't worry,' said Rainer, noticing Detlef walking on tiptoe. 'These walls are so thick, nobody is going to hear.'

'As you expected. A skylight,' said Detlef, as they reached the top of the stairs.

Rainer took out his big screwdriver. 'That was easy. Now, give me a leg up and we'll see what's out here.'

'There's a flat bit, but it's narrow.' Rainer quickly shone his torch along the roof. 'Not much more that a gutter for the rain. But quite wide enough to walk along. The outside wall will be some security, but we will still have to be careful.'

Detlef peered along the gutter. There was no moon, but no cloud either. Starlight and the torch showed a very treacherous walkway. The parapet wall was about knee-high and the gutter about half that.

Detlef and Rainer manoeuvred themselves very slowly along the roof. Each house was delineated by a stone buttress about a metre tall. This meant a climb with no security of the low wall on one side.

Rainer, in the lead, went over first. 'Very careful, Detlef,' he whispered. 'It's a long drop.'

The same manoeuvre had to be undertaken twice more before Rainer signalled to stop.

'Are you sure we've got the right house?' Detlef whispered.

'I've been counting,' said Rainer. 'That really would be funny if we got the wrong house. Do you know, I can lift this skylight. The catch must be broken.'

'And has been for some time,' said Detlef, looking at the rusty fitting.

They dropped down from the skylight, landing on a wooden packing case.

'We're in the attic,' said Rainer. 'Hundreds of years of junk. OK. Down to the cellar. I suggest we leave our shoes here. And no torch.'

'You said that just Otto's mother and carer live here,' whispered Detlef, as they set off down the stairs.

'Right. Old people usually sleep more lightly, so I suggest no talking until we are in the cellar.'

'Unless they take pills,' said Detlef. 'You can tell old people live here. It's got that sort of smell.'

'And very dusty,' said Rainer, pinching his nose as he was about to sneeze.

The two men crept down through the house. There was thick carpet on the stairs and landings, muffling any sound and the atmosphere was heavy and stifling, as if there was never any ventilation.

'At least we know that someone's asleep,' Detlef whispered, as they passed a door, behind which came loud snores.

A few steps later and a loud squawk detonated the silence. Detlef nearly jumped out of his skin. He had trodden on a cat. The silence returned and the two men realized that the snoring had stopped.

'Back up the stairs,' hissed Rainer.

The two men scuttled back towards the attic as the light snapped on. '*Dumme Katz*,' said an old woman's voice. '*Laufst du mal runter. Shoo.*' They then heard the trudge of footsteps as the person went to the bathroom, followed by the expected sounds and then the return of the footsteps. The light went out and the two men heaved a sigh of relief.

'Close call,' whispered Detlef.

'Wait for the snores.'

A few minutes later they could proceed on down the stairs to the ground floor.

'This must lead to the cellar,' said Rainer, opening a door under the stairs.

'And this must be the laundry,' said Detlef, as they arrived at the bottom of the steps.

'Let's look round the rest of the cellar.' Rainer shone his torch around the other rooms.

'Big cellar,' said Detlef.

'Same area as the rest of the house,' Rainer agreed. 'They knew how to build houses in those days. Now. Where to hide the device?'

'I don't see anywhere suitable,' said Detlef. 'Wherever we put it, it would be detected.' He sat on an upturned box. 'Rainer, I'm not so sure we should be doing this.'

'You're not getting cold feet?'

'That old woman upstairs. She has to die. She reminded me of my mother. Do you think we could find another way?'

Rainer pulled up another box to sit beside him. 'Detlef, we have talked this through. This is the best plan that we can come up with.'

'Yes. I know. I'm still very keen to kill Hauswald. I have to avenge the death of my father. But all the guests at the party will die too. There might be as many as fifty. Or even more.'

'Detlef, we are not only avenging the death of your father. We are removing a man who would bring about the downfall of Europe. He might even start another war. We are pre-empting the situation. And

256

in cases like this, there will be casualties. Let's not forget that this is an old person's birthday party. Most of the guests will be of a similar age. It's not as if they are all going to be young people.'

'We are still murdering innocent bystanders,' said Detlef with a sniff. 'People who are in the wrong place at the wrong time.'

'You're right,' Rainer conceded. 'But it's like in a war, there are always civilian casualties. That is the price that sometimes has to be paid. We have to look at the big picture. Look at this moment as if we are looking back in history. What we are doing is pivotal for the peace of the world. You have to look at it like that.'

Detlef sighed. 'Yes. I suppose you're right.'

'We have to be one hundred percent on this, Detlef. There can be no turning back.'

'OK,' said Detlef, taking a deep breath. 'I'm one hundred percent.'

'Good man.' Rainer gave him a slap on the knee. 'Let's get to it. I'm seen an obvious place. The central heating boiler. It's a new one. Very efficient. They give off very little heat themselves. And there is plenty of extra space inside the casing. We can pack the boiler with explosive.'

'Are you sure that would work?' Detlef asked. 'Wouldn't the explosive heat up?'

'No, but we will insulate it, just to be sure.'

The return journey went without mishap, with no cat in evidence.

#

'So will it work?' Anya asked as Rainer explained the plan.

'Of course,' said Rainer. 'I will go back to Berlin and get everything prepared in good time for the party.'

#

'I've been thinking about when this is all over,' said Anya, sitting up in bed and lighting another of her 'cigarettes'.

'Assuming nothing goes wrong and we don't get caught, you mean.' said Detlef.

'Everything will be fine, I'm sure. What would you say if I said that I would like to come back to Rügen with you?'

'That would be wonderful.' Detlef took her hand and squeezed it. 'But you refused my offer last time.'

'I know, but that was a long time ago. Times have changed. I've changed. Older and wiser.'

'You said last time that you would be bored. Living up on the coast, miles from anywhere and nothing to do.'

'But that's what I want now. Going for long walks. Breathing the sea air.'

'Well, I think it's a brilliant idea,' said Detlef, giving her a long kiss.

CHAPTER 33

'It seems to have worked,' said Otto, handing Marshall a tumbler of whisky. 'The latest polls give us a ten per cent lead.'

'I always say that traditional methods are the best,' smiled Marshall. 'One is always so sure of the outcome.'

'Nobody got caught?'

'No. We chose well in waiting until Bohnen was in Marienberg. There are so many unmarked tracks through the Erzgebirge.'

'Well. That's a relief,' said Otto. 'And nothing to link it to us?'

'Of course not,' said Marshall. 'But on reflection, I think you were being a little pessimistic. Especially as Bohnen realized he was getting nowhere investigating your finances. You were always going to get the better of him in a debate.'

'He was a very good and persuasive speaker,' countered Otto. 'He championed the status quo. The majority are always afraid of change. Bohnen was focussing on that fear and it was beginning to make a difference'

'And the new leader?'

'The same message, but not nearly as effective.'

'I sense a real political vacuum in the country,' said Marshall. 'The politicians of all parties have become bogged down with the continuing crises over the currency and the talk of more integration. We must exploit this.'

'I'm sure that the German people are tired and fed up with all the political parties,' said Otto. 'They are all singing from the same hymn sheet and it's the wrong one. There is a feeling of frustration. My interviews with the general public reinforce my belief that our radical policies are hitting the right spot.'

'Good. It will be up to you to take the initiative, Otto.' Marshall pointed a finger at him. 'Especially in the television debate.'

'Don't worry,' said Otto. 'I'm confident.'

'Obviously you are going to propose that Germany leaves the European Union and the common currency,' said Marshall. 'Are you going to suggest a review of the Final Settlement Treaty?'

'With respect to the borders, you mean? I don't know. It depends upon how it goes. It's not part of our official manifesto.'

'I had a chat to Henry Katz recently. The problem was that, at the Cecilienhof, Stalin got all his own way. The British Prime Minister changed half way through, because they had an election.'

'If Churchill had stayed, it might have been different,' Otto interrupted.

'I agree. And Truman was new to the job, because Roosevelt had just died.'

'Stalin had them on toast,' said Otto.

'If Stalin hadn't been allowed to keep all that land east of the Curzon Line, which was really part of Poland, following the Treaty of

Riga, there would have been no need to transfer all that land in eastern Germany to Poland.'

'It was a catastrophe that should never have been allowed to happen,' Otto agreed.

'So I think,' said Marshall, 'that if we form a national Government, we would be justified in reversing that decision. The Potsdam Conference totally ignored the Treaty of Riga, which determined the eastern border of Poland. We could make out a legal argument for putting the Polish borders back to where they were in 1937.'

'And our homeland would be German again,' added Otto.

'It must be our goal,' said Marshall. 'Just think. What if the Schimonsky family estates could be regained?'

'But softly, softly,' said Otto. 'I very much doubt this subject will come up in the debate.'

'We must not be seen as too aggressive. We are not going to suggest sending in troops to back up our claim. Well, certainly not at this stage.'

'Any mention of the military must be avoided,' Otto agreed.

'The loss of the Titian has made a big hole in our budget,' said Marshall.

'There are so many art thieves about,' said Otto with a scowl. 'It happens all the time. They never retrieved those paintings that were stolen from that Paris museum in 2010. In someone's private collection, no doubt.'

'Probably,' said Marshall with a smile.

'And Munch's 'The Scream' is always being stolen.'

'He did paint more than one,' Marshall reminded him.

'Ahrens was right. We should never have sent the Titian to auction. Better to have something, rather than nothing.'

'We need to win Saxony with as many votes as possible,' said Marshall. 'That will give us extra state funding. It won't make up for the loss of the Titian, but it will go some way towards it. The next election in Hesse will be crucial. Win that and we really will be on a roll.'

'I'm planning the campaign already,' nodded Otto.

'Changing the subject,' said Marshall, 'did you see that Stefan has died? Shot by a burglar.'

'Yes, I did,' said Otto.

'Like all big cities, London can be a dangerous place,' said Marshall.

'We never made it up with him,' mused Otto. 'Stupid. That squabbling over money. It must be ten years ago now. And especially as Stefan had more than enough.'

'Too late now,' said Marshall.

'The problem was that he was never one hundred percent with us.'

'He dropped out,' Marshall agreed. 'Lost interest.'

'We could never convince him.'

'He just couldn't see the point of it,' said Marshall. 'It wasn't important to him.'

'Called us fanatics,' said Otto.

'Couldn't see that the cause was just,' Marshall added.

'The thing is, what happens to his estate? It must be considerable. Look at all the money we gave him over the years. And he made a very successful career in London.'

'My information from London is that he lived with a woman partner,' said Marshall. 'He left all his money to her.'

'He wasn't married then?'

'Apparently not.'

'Then should the will be contested?' asked Otto. 'We can't let all that money just disappear.'

'I think contesting the will would be foolish,' said Marshall. 'It would drag up too much history. We would be involved. Identities would have to be revealed. And questions would be asked about how Stefan came by his wealth.'

'I suppose you're right. Shame.'

CHAPTER 34

Steven's funeral took place on a grey October day at the West London crematorium in Kensal Green.

As Katie had expected, the funeral was poorly attended. Katie and Mr Wilkins, the solicitor, occupied the front pew. Behind them sat Mrs Porter and her husband and behind them several carers, including Sister Graham and Father Brian. There was also a smattering of colleagues from the City in dark suits and black ties.

'I've had no result from my announcements,' said Wilkins to Katie as they walked away after the service.

'None from Germany?'

'No. Very strange,' said Wilkins. 'However, we can do nothing more. I am proceeding with probate as you requested, but it will take some time, considering the amount and diversity of Mr Jackson's assets.'

'I realize that,' said Katie. 'I have put the apartment on the market and I suppose I will have to go to France to organize the sale of the house.'

'I am anticipating that a large amount of tax will be due,' said Wilkins apologetically. 'Mr Jackson saw no need to mitigate estate duties.'

Katie had arranged for caterers to provide refreshments back at the apartment in Beaufort Gardens. None of the city colleagues came, but Father Brian and the carers came to partake of tea with sandwiches and cake.

'A very sad business, Mrs Talbot,' said Father Brian. 'An untimely death. When I first met Steven, he was very depressed, but we had really turned things around.'

'Your agreeing to visit was a big turning point,' added Sister Graham. 'That perked him up no end.'

'Gave him something to look forward to,' Father Brian agreed.

'His physical condition improved as well,' said Sister Graham. 'It was mind over matter. I always say that.'

'Mrs Talbot, I was just wondering,' said Father Brian, a little hesitantly, 'Steven had taken a great interest in the local veterans. All those unfortunate boys coming back from Iraq and Afghanistan with terrible injuries.'

'We only hear of the soldiers who died,' interrupted Sister Graham. 'They are the only ones mentioned on the television news. But every day there are casualties. Minor and major injuries. Some of them come back with injuries even worse than Steven's.'

'The reason I mention this,' said Father Brian, 'is that Steven had agreed to help financially. He was going to sponsor our new gymnasium fund. There is so much new technology now to assist these young men to improve their lives. Artificial limbs and equipment to help them walk again. These advances even bring something like normality to their future.'

'It's amazing what can be done now,' Sister Graham interrupted again. 'But it's all very expensive.'

'So we wondered if you would agree to be our sponsor,' said Father Brian. 'Take Steven's place. In his memory. The new gymnasium was to be called the Steven Jackson Gymnasium.'

Father Brian and Sister Graham looked at Katie expectantly, not at all sure of her response.

Katie had realized what was coming right from the beginning of the conversation. The cost of the new gymnasium would be substantial, but ever since she had known of the size of her fortune she had been thinking of which charities she might support. This seemed like a very worthwhile cause.

'I would be very happy to be your sponsor,' said Katie. 'I think it is an excellent idea.'

Father Brian and Sister Graham beamed at her with obvious relief.

'We are most grateful,' said Father Brian. 'I will send you all the details.'

'Thank you very, very much,' added Sister Graham.

The least I can do, thought Katie. All along she had told herself that she could not be held responsible for Steven's plight, but if she needed a salve for her conscience, this was as good as any.

CHAPTER 35

The audience in the television studio was proving to be lively. The assorted guests had been encouraged by the producer, wanting an animated and interactive debate. A well-endowed young lady in a low cut dress sitting on the front row had been persuaded to remove her bra. This gave the producer a shot to cut to at regular intervals, with the intention of keeping the interest of the male viewers.

Otto Hauswald, NDVP, Walter von Ahr, CDU and Franz Koch, SPD, had each given their opening address to some heckling. (The FDP and the Green party had declined to appear on the same platform as Otto and Die Linke was not fielding a candidate). The debate was now thrown open to questions from the floor.

A young man with a beard, dressed in T-shirt and jeans, was the first to put up his hand.

'The question,' the moderator repeated, 'is whether the common currency has a future? Herr von Ahr.'

Von Ahr gave a spirited defence of the Euro, stressing that trade was made easier without restrictions and without foreign currency exchanges. And that it was a stepping-stone to the future. Monetary union would be followed by fiscal and political union. This would mean that Europe would become a much stronger, cohesive and commercial unit. He was followed by Koch, basically re-iterating what von Ahr had said.

267

'And your view, Herr Hauswald?' said the moderator, as Koch sat down to rather muted applause.

'As you would expect from my opening address,' Otto began, 'I take an opposite view. The Euro has been a very costly mistake. I said so right at the beginning and I have been proved right. How can you expect countries with very diverse economies, and I take Germany and Greece as the two extremes, possibly abide by the same rules? The instigators of the euro did not take account of the differences between countries in the north of Europe and those in the south. The people of the Mediterranean countries have a totally different mindset. They think differently. For example, manana is incomprehensible and has no equivalent in German. The governments of these countries have different priorities and their economies function differently. This has led to the history of the euro being a continuous fudge of the rules and regulations. If my party win this election and we succeed nationally in the near future, our first priority would be a return to the Deutschemark. To be renamed the Reichsmark.'

This was greeted with loud applause from the audience and Otto had to pause until it died away.

'Why should we continue to prop up these useless countries,' Otto continued, 'with their corrupt governments, bloated civil service and over-generous welfare systems, whilst we work hard and pay our taxes?'

Otto had to pause again, as the audience broke out in loud applause.

'So, not only am I proposing to leave the common currency, but the European Union itself.' Otto paused again as he was interrupted by applause. 'We do not need all these multifarious countries hanging on to our coat-tails, being joined by ever more of them. If Germany was independent of the Union and could negotiate alliances with other strong emerging economies, and I cite China as an example, Germany would forge ahead and we as a nation would be much more prosperous.'

The audience again applauded, much to the discomfiture of the other candidates.

'We hear so much about the American dream,' Otto continued. 'What about the German dream? We have lost our national identity. We need to give our young people a future to aim for and to be proud of achieving it. Germany for the Germans. Let's make our country great again and be a force to be reckoned with.'

Otto had been unsure as to whether he should introduce his next topic, but the approval of the audience so far convinced him to proceed.

'Having left the European community and all its constraints, I feel that we should be free to redress the last injustice that was imposed upon our country. I refer to the decisions of the Potsdam Conference of 1945, when the size of Germany was reduced by as much as a quarter. Our countrymen were displaced with great loss of life. A tragedy that has almost been forgotten. And what is also forgotten is that Potsdam was only supposed to be a temporary agreement, a fact that was totally ignored in the final settlement treaty of 1990.'

Otto left the podium and went to stand in front of the camera. 'Our leaders failed us in 1990.' He pointed a finger at the television viewers. 'They could only think of reunification. It was reunification at any price.'

Otto now turned back to the audience, who had started to give sporadic applause. 'Just think of what else they did. One for one? An ost-mark for a west-mark? Who ever heard of anything so ridiculous? And I say that as a citizen of the former East Germany. It has crippled us with welfare payments ever since. But the biggest crime in 1990 was the ratification of the decisions of the Potsdam conference. This was done under duress from the other signatories to the agreement; The United States, Great Britain and Russia. They said, in effect, agree to this treaty and we will raise no objection to the reunification of Germany.'

Otto now turned back to address the camera. 'I feel,' he said slowly and deliberately, 'that we would be justified in demanding a review of the final settlement treaty of 1990 and, *ipso facto*, a review of the Potsdam Conference of 1945. We will make out a case that the decisions of the conference were illegal in that they did not respect the Treaty of Riga, which determined the eastern border of Poland. This would have the aim of returning the borders of Poland to where they were in 1937.'

At this point, both von Ahr and Koch attempted to complain and rebuff the argument, but the shouts of approval by the audience made it impossible for them to be heard.

Otto now took centre stage and pointed to the camera and the audience in turn. 'What I say is *Deutschland fur die deutsche Volk!. Ehrmaliges Deutschland fur die deutsche Volk! Deutschland über alles!*' Otto sat down to more rapturous applause.

The moderator eventually restored order and Von Ahr and Koch were able to argue against Otto's speech, but their words were met by almost total silence.

The debate moved on to immigration, another contentious issue between Otto and the other leaders, but Suzanne Ebert had seen enough and changed channel. She could imagine the headlines in the tabloid newspapers the following day. Otto Hauswald had won the debate by a handsome margin and, going by the audience reaction, she could imagine a sizeable majority for the NDVP in the coming election in Saxony.

Chapter 36

Katie had decided to cook. It would be far more intimate if they ate at home. Intimate. Katie chewed over the word as she prepared the vegetables. Now was the time she had to decide. And she was not going to take any notice of the comments and advice of that cynic Angela Johnson that were circulating through her head. Love. Was she in love with Grant? Not head over heels, certainly. But she thought about him often enough. Maybe that was the key factor. She was sure that Grant was in love with her. Every look and gesture said so. Katie frowned and paused in her peeling and chopping. She could do far worse. Another factor was the enormous amount of money that she potentially now possessed. Grant knew nothing of her relationship with Steven and the outcome. Her wealth was not going to influence him, but it might influence other gold-diggers in the future. She had made up her mind. It looked as if sex after dinner was inevitable.

'So how was the business trip to Germany?' Grant asked as he poured out two glasses of champagne from the cooler that he had brought with him.

'As successful as I could have hoped.' Katie wondered if she would ever tell Grant about Steven and the hunt for the rest of the treasures.

'And now you're all set for your trip to Rome next week.'

'A little nervous. I'm not sure what to expect. And I'm not sure what my role is going to be.'

'You will be guided by Marshall. He will tell you what your role is.'

'I got an e-mail from Marshall with the programme.' Katie handed Grant the print-out. 'It will be the reception and the dinner that I will be most involved with.'

'I see what you mean,' Grant perused the list. 'The fashion show won't involve much conversation. And I don't suppose that you will be involved with the seminars.'

'Marshall will be having private one-to-one talks with some of the leaders.' Katie ladled out two bowls of asparagus soup. 'I'm not sure if I will be present or not.'

Grant frowned and pursed his lips. It was no good. The job had to come first.

'Katie, I have a confession to make.'

Katie looked up from her soup. Uh-oh. Grant was going to tell her that he was already married.

'I don't work for an insurance company.' Grant looked at her directly. 'I'm a senior intelligence officer with the CIA. I'm sorry if I have deceived you.'

'Well, that's a relief,' said Katie, looking at him with a smile. 'I thought you were going to tell me that you had a wife after all.'

'I was reluctant to tell you, in case you thought that I was befriending you just because of my job. That is not the case.'

'I believe you,' said Katie, putting her hand over his. 'You needn't have been worried. And thank you for telling me.'

Grant was visibly relieved. It had been the right decision. 'I'm sorry if I have been a bit melodramatic.'

'Don't be. I appreciate your concern.'

'The reason I tell you this now is that something has come up. We are worried about what Marshall is planning. He is closely involved with the political scene in Germany and supports a new radical party. They plan to abandon the euro and leave the European Union. Then they would forge alliances with the new emerging economies.'

'I know that there are so many problems now,' said Katie. 'With the community and with the currency. I suppose one could argue that this scenario might be best for Germany'.

'Maybe,' Grant conceded. This was the point when he would find out whose side Katie was really on. 'But it would alter the whole world order and, in our opinion, would be bad news for the United States.'

'But the USA would still be able to trade with all these countries as before,' retorted Katie. 'We could take out new trade agreements with all of them.'

'I agree,' said Grant. 'The problem is that the balance of power would have shifted. Germany would be a much stronger independent country and would start to show its muscle.'

'You mean it would be more war-like,' said Katie. 'I do not agree. Germany is a peace-loving country. The mentality of the third Reich is a memory.'

'I agree that is how it appears right now,' said Grant. 'But history tells us that things can change. Sometimes, very rapidly.'

'Yes. I suppose so.'

'The problem is that we do not know what Marshall is planning with his company. We know that he intends to expand it. It might even manufacture weapons.'

'That would be worrying,' Katie conceded, as she gathered up the soup bowls. The thought struck her that this was not the conversation she had anticipated for a quiet romantic dinner.

'Grant,' Katie stuck her head round the kitchen door, 'I suspect you have a reason for telling me all this.'

Never underestimate a woman, thought Grant. 'Yes. OK. There is. I am going to ask for your help.'

'I thought so. Would you mind taking this dish? And I am delegating you to carve the roast. I always think it's a man's job. You want me to spy on Marshall?'

'In a nutshell, yes.'

'I'm not sure that Marshall will make me a party to any strategic information. I'm just there to smooth his path.'

'Any little snippet might help. Your intuition would be invaluable. It's very important that we find out the substance of his talks with these foreign leaders.'

'I will do what I can,' said Katie firmly. 'But I am not promising anything.'

'Thank you,' said Grant humbly. He could not have wishing for a more successful outcome.

'The meat looks lovely. Please take the gravy as well.' Katie turned his head to give him a kiss. 'And that's the end of that kind of talk for the evening.'

CHAPTER 37

Katie had not been to Rome before. The taxi deposited her at the Crowne Plaza Hotel, venue for the World Industrial Leaders Forum (WILF). The hotel had been selected as it had facilities for 600 delegates, but would not have been Katie's choice. It was not far from St Peters, but it was not in the centre of ancient Rome, where she would have preferred to be. However, she doubted there would be much time for sight-seeing.

In her room she found a folder from Marshall, containing an up-to-date timetable and saying he would meet her in the cocktail lounge at 6.30. Today was Friday. There would be a fashion show that evening. A full day of presentations on Saturday, to which she need not attend. Good news. She could do some sight-seeing after all. A formal dinner for all delegates on Saturday evening and leave on Sunday. Private talks if delegates wished on Sunday morning. Her flight back was at 5 pm on Sunday. Maybe time to see something else, unless she was required.

#

Suzanne Ebert was modelling for Chanel. The catwalk was brightly lit and the audience mostly in shadow, but she could recognize Marshall Maxwell in the front row, sitting next to an attractive red-headed woman in a blue and gold dress, who looked vaguely familiar.

To add glamour to the occasion, the models had been invited to the champagne reception after the show.

Suzanne had been circulating amongst the delegates, but had been able to notice that Marshall was only concerned with talking to the delegates from countries with emerging economies. The European and American delegates were ignored.

'Good evening, Mr Maxwell.' Suzanne had reached Marshall and Katie. 'I have not had the opportunity to thank you in person for your wonderful party.'

'It was my pleasure, Miss Ebert. May I introduce my PA, Katherine von Arnitz.'

'That's a beautiful outfit,' said Katie, shaking hands. Suzanne was wearing a knee-length white dress with an embroidered jacket.

'Classic Chanel,' said Suzanne. 'My favourite designer.'

'Mine also,' said Katie.

'I'm sure we have met before,' said Suzanne.

'I was also at Marshall's party,' said Katie, 'but unfortunately we were not introduced.'

Marshall moved away to talk to another delegate. 'I've remembered now,' said Suzanne in a low voice. 'I saw your picture recently.' She smirked. 'I thought you looked gorgeous.'

Suzanne minced away, leaving Katie with a face like thunder. 'Condescending bitch,' she muttered under her breath. It was not often that she took an instant dislike to someone. But where had Suzanne seen the painting?

\#

Marshall had reserved a table for two in the hotel restaurant.

'Very good attendance,' said Marshall. 'I have made some useful contacts already.'

'I've noticed there are a lot of Asian delegates,' said Katie.

'Some of them have brought their wives,' said Marshall. 'Which reminds me that I need to ask you a favour. The chairman and the CEO of a Chinese company I am having talks with have brought their wives. I would be grateful if tomorrow you could take them sight-seeing?'

Katie frowned. 'Yes. I suppose so. I was intending to do that myself.'

'Perhaps the open-topped bus tour?' Marshall suggested. 'You can get on and off as you please. It goes to most of the important sites.'

Marshall then enumerated the sites that he thought were the most interesting and Katie was able to chip in with the history that she knew. It was towards the end of the meal that Marshall surprised her.

'I think I ought to tell you that I am splitting with Elizabeth.'

'Oh,' Katie managed. 'I thought you had arranged a wedding day.'

'We had.' Marshall fidgeted with a fork. 'It's . . . Well . . . I've decided that we are not really compatible.'

'Uh huh,' was all that Katie could find to reply.

'She's only 29,' Marshall continued. 'I've been thinking that the age difference is too great. We do not have that much in common. I think I should look for someone a little nearer to my age.' Marshall looked at her as if expecting an opinion.

'Maybe,' said Kate warily, as the alarm bells started to ring.

'I just thought that you ought to know.'

'Yes. Thank you,' said Katie, standing up and collecting her handbag from the floor. 'Well, I think it's time I went to bed.'

'Me too,' said Marshall. 'Busy day tomorrow.' He took Katie's hand and squeezed it. 'Thank you for your company.'

'And thank you for yours,' said Katie sweetly.

On the way back to her room she was already composing her letter of resignation, effective from Sunday. Angela was being proved right once again.

#

Katie met the two Chinese ladies in the lobby at 10 the next morning. They were to be accompanied by an interpreter, who introduced herself as Nadia Wong. Nadia was from San Francisco. She was bilingual in English and Mandarin, but had no Italian. Katie hoped that they would get by with tourist English.

By the time they had visited the Spanish Steps, the Trevi Fountain and the Pantheon, they had all become firm friends. Behind Montecitorio square they found an appropriate restaurant for lunch. Katie was not really a fan of pizza, which was everyone's choice. But when in Rome . . .

Nadia was a brilliant interpreter, which, being bilingual herself, Katie appreciated, as Nadia could translate immediately from one language to the other. This included jokes and small talk and discussion of the sites they had seen, as well as the relevant history. As they were leaving the restaurant, Katie asked the Chinese ladies whether they would rather live in Europe or China.

'We may not have a choice,' Nadia translated for one lady. 'If the company starts a new factory in Germany.'

'Even more likely with the new invention,' said the other lady.

Nadia had translated immediately and the first lady shot a nervous glance at Katie.

'Where to next,' Katie said brightly, giving no indication that the last remark had any significance. Grant was going to be very pleased with her.

#

The conference dinner was for all delegates and their companions. Other notables had been invited and Katie found herself sitting next to the German ambassador. The large table also included the two ladies from the bus tour and their husbands.

'I understand your parents were German aristocrats,' said the ambassador after introductions had been made. 'And that you use your German title.'

'I find that it has some advantages,' said Katie, wondering if the ambassador was going to reproach her. 'But I know that it has had no legal significance since 1919.'

'Quite,' said the ambassador. 'The Weimar Constitution made all Germans equal before the law. You are fortunate that in Germany there is no primogeniture in favour of the male heir, as there is in England.'

'Yes, but I believe the law in England is being changed, to allow females that are the first born to inherit a title. Particularly with the future King William and Queen Katherine in mind.'

'So I hear,' said the ambassador. 'But you were born in America. No titles there.'

'Maybe that is for the best,' said Katie reflectively.

'So where would your loyalties lie?' asked the ambassador. 'Do you consider yourself German or American?'

'I was born in the USA,' said Katie stoutly. Had the ambassador been prompted to ask this question, or was he just making conversation? 'I have always considered myself to be American, through and through.'

The ambassador now changed the subject and Katie was left wondering if this had been the preliminary to trying to recruit her, as Grant had done. And for what reason.

#

As they were leaving the dining room, Marshall drew her to one side.

'Katie, I am having private talks with the Chinese company tomorrow morning. I would like you to be there and take notes.'

'But I don't have any shorthand,' said Katie, somewhat dismayed.

'No need. I will just indicate salient headlines to remind me later.'

'Well. Yes. Of course. I'll be there,' said Katie reluctantly.

'Ten o'clock in the lobby.'

#

At first, Katie found the talks with the Chinese delegates very boring, but she had to keep a level of concentration to take notes. Nadia was again translating and seemed to have no difficulty with the technical jargon. The discussion was on the minutiae of the Chinese taking over an industrial site on the estate in Weimar. However, Katie did learn that the company made vehicles and equipment for the construction industry. Also, that they had recently taken over a company that made light armoured vehicles for the military. Katie put two and two together and tingled with excitement.

The Chinese were on a European tour and at the end of the discussions it was arranged that they would visit Weimar on the Friday of the coming week, before flying home.

'Our wives do hope that your charming assistant will be present,' said the chairman. 'They consider her a firm friend. It would make all the difference to our visit.'

'Katie?' Marshall raised his eyebrows.

'Well,' Katie hesitated. In view of what she had learnt, it might be important that she was there.

'We are delighted,' said the chairman, giving her a beaming smile.

'Yes. All right,' said Katie. Her resignation could wait a week.

#

'I'll book you into the Elephant,' said Marshall as they made their farewells in the hotel lobby later that afternoon. 'And there's a party in the evening. You are invited. Otto's mother is eighty. Should be good fun.'

#

'Nothing special as I've been in the office all day,' Katie apologized as she greeted Grant at the door with a hug and a kiss. 'It's convenience from Marks and Spencer.'

'Whatever,' said Grant. 'But I've brought a bottle of Chablis.'

'That will go nicely, thank you.'

'So how was Rome?'

'Hard on the feet. Did you know that the whole of ancient Rome is cobblestones? And not very even ones, either.'

'Probably hundreds of years old,' said Grant, pouring out two glasses of wine. 'But before you tell me the tourist bits, you'd better tell me what's important.'

'I couldn't tell you on the phone.' Katie then related what the Chinese lady had let slip and what the company manufactured.

'Phew,' Grant whistled. 'This is going to stir things up.'

'But it will never happen.' said Katie. 'A Chinese company making military equipment in Germany would never be allowed. And maybe having a secret weapon.'

'If the NDVP form the next government, it might just happen.'

'Do you need to tell Washington? Right now?'

'No need to panic,' said Grant, looking at his watch. 'Later on will do just fine.'

#

Grant called Bill from the secure telephone in the American Embassy to relate Katie's experiences.

'I don't like the sound of this,' said Bill. 'We can't have a Chinese manufacturer of military equipment in the middle of Germany.'

'It can only happen if the NDVP take over the whole country.'

'So how likely is that?'

'It could happen sooner than we think. There is a programme of state elections, with a national election two years from now. If the NDVP win any more state elections, the momentum might be unstoppable.'

'Grant, get your ass over to Berlin asap and give it straight to this Ebert woman that this has to stop. In the meantime, I will brief the president.'

#

282

The Chancellery informed Grant that Frau Ebert would be away until Friday. It was only because of Grant's insistence and diplomatic threats that the receptionist reluctantly made an appointment for two 'clock on the Friday afternoon. Grant managed to get a BA flight on that day, knowing that Katie was also flying to Germany with Netjets.

#

'So the boss came on to you.' Angela took charge of the wine. 'Didn't I tell you so?'

'You did.'

'And you didn't believe me.'

'I didn't know he was splitting with his fiancee.'

'I bet he had it in mind all along when he first hired you.'

'I took the job because I needed the money.'

'I hope that he took your rejection seriously.'

'I made a very negative response.'

'Sad that men have such an obsession with sex,' said Angela. 'I was at a cocktail party last week. Lots of young men and women. I overheard one couple chatting next to me. He was showing lots of interest in her job and her hobbies, but I could tell that what he was really doing was assessing the size of her tits and how soon she would come to orgasm.'

Katie laughed. 'You couldn't really tell that.'

'Certainly. I'm being serious. It's all this modern attitude. It's destroying what I would call a normal relationship. It was much simpler when there was no sex before marriage.'

'So, I've decided to give in my notice. I have agreed to go to Germany at the weekend and that will be it.'

'I thought you said you needed the money.'

'Not now. That's my main news. I have inherited some money. From a distant relative that I had forgotten about,' Katie hastened to add.

'A lot?'

'Enough that I do not need to work again.'

'My,' Angela said wide-eyed. 'So are you going to retire completely? From the law firm as well?'

'Well,' Katie hesitated, 'it depends.'

'On what? Oh, of course, this Grant guy. How is the romance progressing?'

'Really, very well.'

'So are you in love with him?'

'Yes. Well. Not as much as when I met Nigel, but enough.'

'And he's in love with you?'

'Definitely.'

'I'm very pleased for you. Has he proposed yet?'

'No. But I think he's going to. We have talked about what happens when he moves back to America. He wants me to live with him in Florida.'

'Not in the summer, surely? Far too hot and humid. Bugs.'

'I think if I agreed to it, it would be on the condition that we have somewhere else in the north for the summer. Like Cape Cod.'

'Yes,' Angela agreed. 'A house like the one your parents used to rent in Chatham.'

'Of course,' said Katie. 'You visited. More than once.'

'I would really envy you having that,' said Angela wistfully. 'Wonderful sandy beaches. Watching the fishing boats coming in and buying something for supper.'

'Lots of interesting shops and good restaurants,' Katie added.

'Or you could buy a place at Lake George,' said Angela. 'Where my parents used to rent in the summer.'

'I'll let you know what I decide.'

CHAPTER 38

In the middle of Thursday night, Rainer and Detlef again descended into the cellar of the house in the Schlossgasse. This time without any incidents. Rainer held a small low-powered torch, Just in case the cat got in the way.

'This is the very latest from Russia,' said Rainer, as he dismantled the boiler casing. 'Minimum bulk and maximum explosive power. I have calculated that this amount will demolish the house. Well, the inside of the house. These outside walls are so thick they will still be here hundreds of years from now. But between the floors is only wood.'

'I just hope a security check won't find it,' said Detlef.

'They may have done a first check already,' said Rainer, pleased that Detlef did not seem to be having misgivings. 'Just hold that torch up a bit. If they see nothing has changed, we will probably get away with it. Let's do a time check.'

'Coming up to two,' said Detlef.

'We are timing it to go off at nine o'clock. Nineteen hours from now. Right?'

'Right,' Detlef agreed.

'I'm setting it now. When it gets to two, you push this on-off switch here. OK? You are the guy to remove Oskar Schimonsky from this world.'

Detlef checked his watch and pressed the switch. A green LED light showed the number 19.00.

'We are counting down,' said Rainer. 'Right, I've reassembled everything.' Rainer patted the boiler casing. 'No regrets?' He looked at Detlef's shadow behind the torch.

'No.' Detlef also gave the boiler a pat. 'Justice will be done at last.'

'OK. Let's get out of here.'

#

Later that night, Anya descended to the kitchen to find Rainer sitting at the table reading a book. He had been sleeping on the sofa in the living room.

'You OK?' Anya went to a cupboard and then filled a glass with water.

'Finding it difficult to sleep. Hoping the plan works. What are you taking?'

'Paracetamol. I've got cystitis. We've had sex every single night since he arrived. Sometimes twice if he wakes up. He even got me over the kitchen table the other day. And he's such a big boy. I couldn't believe it when I first saw it.'

'I've always understood that the vagina is a very flexible organ,' Rainer grinned at her. 'Or should I say elastic. And they say that size matters.'

'One can have too much of a good thing.' Anya sat down on the other side of the table. 'I'm looking forward to a rest.'

Rainer put down his book. 'Do you think he's hundred percent?'

'Not sure. Not sure if you convinced him.'

'He seemed to be OK just now. We must not let him out of our sight, now that the bomb is in place. Keep your gun handy and shoot to kill if necessary.'

'You've worked out the dose? It's very critical.'

'Good that you saw him on the bathroom scales the other day. I can gauge the dose very accurately.'

'And how long does it last?'

'It takes effect immediately and I am giving him enough to last two hours.'

'Right,' said Anya. 'That will be eight o'clock for the administration, lasting up to ten o'clock.'

'I've hidden some of the explosive here in the house. An anonymous call to the police will tell them where it is.'

'Do we need any other evidence?'

'No. That will be enough. We do not want it to look like a set-up'

'I'm glad I'm not going to be involved,' said Anya. 'I rented this house with false documents.'

'No way they are going to trace you,' said Rainer. 'And we will leave for Berlin as soon as we have dealt with Detlef.'

'I'm booked on a BA flight to London out of Tegel on Saturday morning.'

'Don't forget to give my regards to Jack and the boys when you get home.'

288

CHAPTER 39

All the leaves are brown and the sky is gray,
I've been for a walk on a winter's day
I'd be safe and warm if I was in LA
California dreamin' on such a winter's day.

Anya turned up her collar and tugged her coat a little tighter, as the words of Mama Cass continued in her head. The chill winds of autumn were blowing the fallen leaves in swirls and eddies about her feet. All the historic buildings were more in evidence, now that the trees were bare, especially the bright pink house of Gertrude von Stein, Goethe's companion, near to which Anya was standing.

California dreaming. Next week she would be back home in Los Angeles. United with her American family. Coming back to Germany after so long had made her realize how much she had changed. It was hard to imagine that she had spent her early life here in the days of the DDR. But duty had caused her to return. Good that it was nearly over. It would be back to the warm. Back to civilisation. Away from this backwater of history. No more lousy television, dubbed movies, unhealthy food and all this bickering about the stupid common currency and the misery that it had brought. And she would be rid of this idiot at her side.

'I'm always in awe when I take a walk through the town,' she said to Detlef. 'It's like a history lesson. We have passed the house where Schiller used to live and then where Goethe lived. Liszt lived in that

289

house over there and behind it is the building where Walter Gropius founded the Bauhaus.'

Detlef was standing by the railing overlooking the river Ilm and beyond it the meadow where Goethe had built his summer residence. He had been in a quiet and reflective mood all day. 'I think we should have all gone back to Berlin,' he muttered.

'We had to stay and see it through,' Anya took hold of his arm and looked at him earnestly. 'You have to be here to fulfil your destiny. You mustn't have any regrets.'

Detlef just nodded, maintaining his glum expression.

'I think it's appropriate that what we are doing is happening in Weimar.' Anya led the way down a steep narrow path that led to a stone bridge over the river. 'This evening will be a momentous occasion. Weimar has always had such an important place in German history.'

Detlef did not reply. He picked up a fallen branch and tossed it into the weir, disturbing a kingfisher, which disappeared in a flash of chestnut and electric blue.

'We *are* doing the right thing.' Anya put her arm round him. 'I'm sure of it.'

'Yes,' Detlef sighed. 'I'm sure too.'

'It was watching that last television debate that convinced me,' said Anya. 'Hauswald was getting more and more strident. He was sounding more and more like Hitler. Those short, clipped sentences. Staring eyes. Whipping up the audience and pointing at the camera.'

'You're right. I thought so too,' nodded Detlef.

'Just imagine,' Anya continued, 'if The NDVP took over the country. Left the European Union. Declared the Potsdam Treaty null and void. Demanded the eastern border to be put back to where it was in 1937.'

'And sent in troops to back it up,' added Detlef.

'And Germany had signed a treaty with the BRIC countries,' said Anya. 'Germany with Brazil, Russia, India and China on one side with Great Britain and the rest of Europe, the USA and Japan on the other. What have we got?'

'Another world war,' said Detlef.

'Correct. That's why we are doing the right thing. It's not just revenge for the murder of your father. We are saving the world. We must have a clear conscience on this.'

'I wonder what will happen now,' said Detlef. 'With the coming election in Saxony?'

'Maybe the NDVP will still do well,' said Anya. 'We need a party like that. To shake up the others. Make everybody think. But then to be realistic. I'm with Hauswald in that the Eurocurrency must be abandoned, but we need a strong united Europe.'

'We are saving the world,' said Detlef, giving Anya a hug and a kiss. 'We are doing the right thing.'

#

It was as Katie had imagined. Her presence at the factory visit and now standing on the edge of this muddy field was a waste of time. Katie and the two wives stood huddled against the wind as Marshall and Nadia and the two Chinese men walked about and discussed their future plans.

Eventually Katie was relieved to see the party returning to the field gate.

'They want to visit Buchenwald,' Marshall said to Katie, in an irritated tone of voice. 'I've tried to put them off. They say it's the last sightseeing on their list.'

Katie shrugged her shoulders and looked at her watch. 'I suppose we've got time.'

It took the minibus a good half hour to wind its way up through the wooded hills north of the town. Katie looked out of the window with disinterest as the occasional squall of rain hit the side of the bus. It was a drab landscape, to match the drab weather. The woods were mostly of deciduous trees, now bare of leaves and the fields looked equally bare having either been newly ploughed or shorn of their crop. Large bales of silage covered in black polythene were everywhere. A side road up an even steeper incline brought them to a clearing and a monument, consisting of a bell tower and eleven bronze statues. The whole party got out and the Chinese took several photographs.

'So how many people died here?' Nadia translated with a look of apology to Marshall.

'Many thousands,' Marshall replied.

'You Germans have a lot to answer for.'

'What you are seeing is not a holocaust memorial,' said Marshall. He had anticipated some sort of comment from the Chinese and was determined not to rise to it. 'We are still a long way from the camp itself. This monument was erected by the Russians as a memorial to the communist resistance fighters incarcerated in the camp. They are the subjects of the bronze statues. Buchenwald was mainly a camp for political prisoners. Jews were only sent here right at the end of the war as the Russians advanced.'

'Then why is the monument here, as you say, a long way from the camp?' asked one of the Chinese men.

'Because there was a tower here already that the Russians demolished,' said Marshall. 'It was dedicated to Bismarck, the founder of the nation. The Russians could not resist making yet another political statement.'

A further kilometre up the road, the bus stopped at the site of the camp itself. Everyone got out to view, what was, in reality, an empty space. An enormous area of gravel and loose stones was enclosed by a wire fence. In one corner were some wooden huts that looked quite new.

'The Russians demolished the camp in 1950,' Marshall explained. 'They just left the fence and a couple of watchtowers.'

'*Arbeit macht frei*" said Nadia, reading the sign over the gate. 'That means 'work sets one free'.'

'Put there for the tourists,' said Marshall. 'It's what they would expect to see. This sign was over the gate at the more well-known concentration camps, such as Auschwitz and Dachau. Originally, the sign over the gate here read '*Jedem das Seine*'. That means 'everyone gets what he deserves.'

'Both very significant,' said one man, nodding slowly.

'We can go and look in the huts,' said Marshall quickly. 'There are some statistics and old photographs.'

Katie stood to one side as the party went through the gate, not wishing to accompany them. She shivered and tightened her scarf against the north wind that was blowing across this desolate place. It was rather frightening, standing alone and being aware of the history. What would it be like at night? She imagined the ghosts of the inmates, all skin and bone, lined up and clamouring along the fence. Katie shivered again. She was suddenly feeling very homesick. Marshall would get her resignation in the morning. It was time to go home. Time to return to America. Time to return to places where she was most comfortable. A future with Grant would be very acceptable. She had more money than she could possibly spend. Perhaps she could start a foundation to help the sick and needy.

Marshall and his entourage now reappeared through the gate.

'It does make one think of the future,' said one man. 'If this could happen again.'

'We were thinking of the new party. The NDVP,' added the other. 'If it came to power, would our investment here be safe?'

'Most certainly,' said Marshall, obviously shocked that the Chinese could have thought of these possibilities. 'The NDVP is a democratic and peace-loving party. Your investment would be perfectly safe.'

'We are very pleased to hear that,' was the response, with a nod and a smile.

'Time to go back,' said Marshall curtly. 'We've all seen enough.'

#

Suzanne appeared to be in a much more serious mood as she escorted Grant to her office.

'We have some important information concerning Maxwell's intentions for his company in Weimar,' said Grant, sitting in the chair in front of Suzanne's desk.

'I'm interested,' said Suzanne.

Grant looked at her with a quizzical and irritated expression. Suzanne, for some strange reason, did not sound at all interested.

'In particular, we understand that Maxwell has been having talks with a Chinese company that has recently taken over another small company that makes military equipment. Also, this company appears to have new innovations.'

294

'And your inference from this?' Suzanne fidgeted with a pencil and seemed reluctant to engage in a discussion.

'Suzanne, I will be quite clear on this. The United States will categorically not allow the manufacture of military equipment in Germany by a foreign company that is not a member of the European Union. Or anywhere else in Europe, come to that.'

'Grant, I understand your concern.' Suzanne seemed to be indifferent to the threats. 'But may I remind you that Germany is a sovereign country and we make the rules.'

'Germany is also a member of NATO,' said Grant, now getting rather annoyed. He had come to give, as he saw it, valuable information and the meeting had deteriorated into point scoring. 'NATO rules forbid this.'

'I agree,' said Suzanne sweetly, in an apparent change of mood. 'I am sorry if I have been contradictory. The only way foreign arms manufacturers could come here is if Germany left the European Union and NATO. And that certainly is not going to happen.'

'Then you had better do something about this NDVP lot,' said Grant. 'And quick. I understand they are certain to win this coming election in Saxony. The momentum must be stopped.'

'I can assure you that we have it in hand,' said Suzanne. 'We have a solution. And it will happen quite soon.'

'And what is that solution?'

'I'm afraid I can't tell you. Just trust me.'

Grant left the Chancellery in a bad mood. Trust me. Huh. As far as he could throw her. It was dusk. A mist was settling across the sward in front of the Reichstag and extending into the Tiergarten. The trees had lost their leaves and stood like ghostly sentinels in the gloom. It seemed like the weather was matching Grant's mood.

Quite soon, indeed. And Suzanne had been so indifferent to his information about Maxwell. Grant stopped and looked back to the Chancellery, where the lights were coming on. He was sure that Suzanne was standing at her window watching him. To see where he was heading. Quite soon. What was happening quite soon? The birthday party. That was happening very soon. Otto and Marshall would be there together. And Katie. Grant turned towards Unter den Linden and started to run.

CHAPTER 40

Marshall and Katie took a taxi to the party. The journey lasted less than a minute, but Katie was wearing high heels and Marshall did not want to wear a coat.

Otto was at the door to greet them and to introduce Katie to his mother. Katie presented her with a small gift of chocolates from Fortnum and Mason. She was mindful of her own mother, who in her later years stated that she only wanted a gift that she could either eat or drink.

Katie turned away to be immediately confronted by Alex, who took her by the hand and led her to an empty corridor, where he hugged her close and gave her a long tongue-searching kiss.

'Where are you staying?' asked Alex, his hands round her bottom, pressing her to him.

'The Elephant.'

'Why not spend the night with me?'

'I couldn't. Marshall will find out.'

'Are you bothered about what Marshall will think?'

'No.' Katie frowned. 'I couldn't care less what Marshall thinks.'

297

'Good girl. I'll see you later then.'

#

Across town, Anya, Detlef and Rainer were eating their evening meal with very little conversation, each one glancing at the kitchen clock at regular intervals. At eight o'clock Rainer gave Anya a knowing look and went into the sitting room.

Anya pulled her chair close to Detlef. 'Still OK?' She took both his hands in hers and held them tight. 'We can leave for Rügen in the morning.'

Detlef looked into her eyes as Rainer silently moved up close behind him. What happened next was Anya's fault and it ruined the plan entirely. Anya 's mistake was that her eyes strayed towards Rainer. Only for a split second, but it was enough. Detlef noticed and swung round to see Rainer about to plunge a hypodermic needle into his shoulder.

With one sweeping motion, Detlef's right arm sent the syringe spinning from Rainer's grasp and then hit him full on the point of his chin, knocking him to the ground. Rainer's head hit the stone floor with a crack, knocking him unconscious. Anya made a dash for her coat, but Detlef stuck out a leg and she tripped, falling in a heap beside Rainer.

'You traitors.' Detlef snarled, aiming a kick at both of them. 'You were setting me up. You were going to drug me and leave me to carry the can. I've had my suspicions for some time.' He looked down at Anya, who looked back at him defiantly. 'That was all rubbish, wasn't it? Saying you wanted to come back to Rügen with me. All that persuasion to keep me here until the bomb went off. I see it all now. This is a political assassination. With me taking the rap.'

Anya suddenly made a dive for the hypodermic, just beyond her reach, but Detlef was there first, putting a heavy boot on her outstretched arm. Anya bit him on the leg, but then Detlef sat down hard on top of her, winding her and probably cracking some ribs. Anya was fit and well trained, but she was no match for Detlef. She fought hard, with punches, scratches and kicks, but Detlef was able to keep her pinned to the floor. He picked up the hypodermic and plunged it into Anya's thigh. Anya gave out a scream, but almost immediately lost consciousness.

Detlef looked down at the two unconscious figures with contempt. He then screwed up the local newspaper and made a bonfire on the wooden table with all the other combustible material that he could find. Then he fetched the box of matches from the stove and set the paper alight. He looked at his watch. Only twenty past eight. He had plenty of time to get to the house and switch off the bomb.

#

It was around eight o'clock when Grant abandoned his rental car in front of the Hotel Elephant. The autobahn had been busy, but Grant had made good use of the stretches with no speed limit. All the way down he had been considering whether to telephone Katie and tell her not to go to the party, but he had reluctantly decided this was not the right thing to do. He would be in big trouble if he jeopardized an intelligence operation for personal reasons. He would just have to try and extract Katie from the party as surreptitiously as possible.

'I should like to speak urgently to the Countess von Arnitz,' Grant said to the receptionist. 'And I mean urgently.'

'The countess left the hotel about a half hour ago. I called a taxi for her myself. Would you like to leave a message?'

'No thank you,' said Grant curtly, turning on his heel. He was astonished to see Suzanne descending the staircase, accompanied by two men.

'Before you ask,' said Suzanne, coming up to him, 'a helicopter is much quicker than a car.'

'Suzanne, what is going on?' Grant asked grimly.

'All in good time,' said Suzanne sweetly.

'It's to do with the birthday party, isn't it. I have to get Katie out of there.' Grant turned and made to go to the front door, but at a signal from Suzanne, her two companions each took a firm grip of Grant's arms.

'What is the meaning of this?' Grant was incandescent.

'Grant, I am putting you under house arrest until the morning.'

'You are not. I will speak to the ambassador. I represent the president of the United States of America. You cannot do this.'

'Oh yes, I can. I have the full authority of the chancellor to do whatever I wish. I am not having you jeopardize this operation.'

'To hell with your operation,' said Grant. 'I have to get Katie out of that house.'

'Grant, as I have said to you before. Sometimes sacrifices have to made for the greater good. I am making one myself.' Suzanne went to speak to the receptionist. 'Take him up to Room 145,' she said to Grant's two captors. 'And use whatever force is necessary.'

A furious Grant was frogmarched to the elevator and along the first floor corridor. Outside room 145 one of the captors loosened his hold on Grant's arm to unlock the door and Grant took his chance. As a young officer in training, he had received commendations for his martial arts skills and they now came into play. In less than a minute both men were rendered unconscious with a series of elbow thrusts, chops and kicks.

Grant then dragged both men into the room, where he tied them up securely with whatever he could find; sheets from the bed and cording sets from the curtains. He then locked the door of the room behind him.

CHAPTER 41

Maybe it was the acrid smell that brought Rainer to his senses. Or maybe he would have come to anyway, as he was only lightly concussed. The kitchen was full of black smoke, with the table well alight. Rainer, coughing and spluttering, made it outside. He did not notice Anya, still unconscious, on the other side of the room. He had to assume that Detlef was on his way to the house in the Schlossgasse to raise the alarm. Maybe Anya was with him, as a hostage. Rainer made sure that his gun was in his jacket pocket. Then he took the car keys, which Anya kept in a dish by the front door. A quick glance at his watch told him it was 8.32. Hopefully he could catch up with Detlef before he got to the bomb.

Just for once, the engine started first time. Rainer drove as fast as he dared, pushing the button on his telephone that would connect him with a number at the Elephant Hotel.

#

Detlef heard the old Volkswagen approaching at speed and squeezed himself into a doorway. He cursed under his breath for being too complacent. Two mistakes. He should have tied up Rainer and taken the car himself. But he was almost there and he had to decide what to do. Whether he should just blunder into the house and go down into the cellar.

301

He saw the car stop at the entrance to Schlossgasse. Detlef edged nearer. Rainer had got out of the car and was talking to a woman, who was pointing down the street. Detlef's heart sank. He might have known that they would have thought of this eventuality. There was no way he would be able to get into that house through the front door, or the back. He would be shot on sight. He looked at his watch. 8.40. Twenty minutes to go. The obvious way into the house had to be the one he was used to. Across the roof. He just hoped he had time before the bomb exploded.

Lucky that the empty house was at the end of the terrace. That meant he could get over the wall at the side of the house without being seen from anyone in the street at the front or in the alley at the back. But to get there meant a detour down another, parallel, street and that took up time.

It was with difficulty that Detlef climbed over the side wall, which was higher than the back wall. A dustbin gave him some assistance to get up, but it was a longer drop down. Dropping down into darkness from any sort of height is dangerous, as the eyes cannot gauge how soon one will hit the ground. Detlef landed awkwardly with a shooting pain in his left ankle. He sat on the ground and cursed. It was either a bad sprain, or he had broken a small bone. When he stood up, he could hardly put any weight on his left foot. He hobbled over to the house as fast as he could.

At the kitchen window he realized that he had no tool to prise open the window. Detlef picked up a big rock from the garden and smashed the glass. Someone might hear, but it didn't matter now. He opened the window catch and climbed in. Now up the stairs to the roof as fast as his ankle would let him.

Several people heard the rock go through the window. One of them was Rainer, who was positioned in the alley outside the back of the house. He was guarding the back whilst Suzanne was guarding the front. Rainer realized immediately what was happening. He dashed down the alley and scrambled over the wall. Then through the open window, just in time to hear Detlef reach the top of the stairs. Rainer raced up the stairs and levered himself through the open skylight. He was in time to see Detlef negotiating the first intervening buttress.

'Detlef. Come back,' he shouted. 'It's too late.'

Detlef disappeared from view and Rainer scrambled along the parapet as fast as he dared. He had no torch, but it was a cloudless night and the starlight gave enough illumination. Rainer mounted the next buttress to see Detlef climbing over the next one. Detlef was obviously not going to stop. Rainer took out his automatic and tried a shot, but he was marginally too late as Detlef disappeared over the top. Rainer traversed the next stretch of parapet dangerously fast. He was gaining distance and would catch Detlef at the next buttress.

Detlef realized that in his disabled state he did not have the time advantage to outrun Rainer. There was only one thing to do. As he dropped down behind the last buttress, he crouched down, knowing that Rainer would come straight over. Sure enough, as Rainer dropped down over the buttress, Detlef grappled with him. Rainer's gun fell onto the parapet and the two men, locked in each other's arms, fell through the skylight into the house. The time was exactly nine o'clock.

#

The service staircase and the back door to the hotel brought Grant to a narrow alley and then back to the main square. He knew from his previous visit that Otto lived in Schlossgasse, diagonally across the square and that his mother lived a few doors away. The location was not hard to spot. Grant walked past Otto's house to see two uniformed security guards stationed at the front door of a house half way along the street.

Grant walked nonchalantly down the street, not giving the guards a sideways glance. But he noticed that the windows were ablaze with light and loud laughter and conversation was coming from the open windows. Grant turned left at the next side street and then turned left again, along a narrow alley with high walls on either side. He could now orienteer his way to where he estimated was the back of the house.

IAN LAURENCE

Grant found a dustbin on which he could climb up and look over the wall. There was an overgrown courtyard garden with tubs and small flower beds. This had to be the house, because there was another uniformed security guard outside the back door. Maybe now was the right time to phone. He could give Katie some pretext that he was outside in the street and could she invite him in. No reply. Either her telephone was switched off, or she did not have it with her. Carry on and hope for the best. One corner of the garden to his left was in darkness and Grant climbed over the wall.

There was no time to lose. He did not know what was going to happen and it could happen at any time soon.

It had to be the standard deception. Grant crept up in the shadow as near as he dared and picked up a stone from the garden. He was about to throw it to create a distraction when the guard was joined by another from inside the house. Grant cursed under his breath. If he tackled both of them, the disturbance could well alert others inside the house. He would sit tight as long as he dared. He looked at is watch. 8.45. His guess was an explosive device of some sort. To go off on the hour? Grant was about to risk tackling both guards when there came the unmistakeable noise of breaking glass. As if a large window had been smashed. The guards advanced towards the noise and Grant wondered if he could now sneak round behind them and into the house without being noticed. Then came the sound of a gunshot from the roof.

That's really torn it, thought Grant. He had absolutely no idea what was going on. One of the guards was speaking into his telephone. And both had drawn their pistols. There was now no way he was going to get into that house unnoticed. But get in there he must.

Grant stood up, put up his hands, and advanced into the light. The astonished guards came towards him, pistols at the ready.

'American,' said Grant. 'CIA. I have my identification. I need to see someone in the house. Urgently.'

One guard advanced towards him as the other kept his gun at the ready.

304

'In my top pocket,' said Grant.

The guard reached inside Grant's jacket, but as he did so a huge explosion blew them all into a heap in the corner of the garden.

Suzanne, standing at the end of Schlossgasse, was expecting something dramatic and that is what happened. At nine o'clock the Meissen bells in the town hall tower started to chime, but were drowned by the most tremendous explosion. She was a good hundred yards from the house, but was blown off her feet. She later compared it to when she had watched the launch of the space shuttle at Cape Canaveral. The force of the blast roared up the house and took the roof clean off the building, which was immediately a tremendous fireball. Flames were coming out of every broken window and a sheet of flame twenty feet high reached into the sky from where the roof had been.

CHAPTER 42

The *Markt* was a hive of activity. Blue and red flashing lights from the emergency services vehicles and arc lamps set up by the police made it as bright as day. Overhead, a searchlight from a helicopter was trained on Schlossgasse, from which smoke was still drifting into the square.

Grant and Suzanne were sitting morosely on a bench at one of the market stalls. Both were looking very much the worse for wear, with their clothes crumpled and torn. Suzanne's face was streaked with soot and Grant had a bandage round his head.

'So did anyone survive?' said Grant eventually.

'Only the security guards, who were outside. And two of them are badly injured.'

'Quite a sacrifice.' Grant looked into the distance. 'Katie and I were going to be married.'

'For both of us.' Suzanne snivelled into a handkerchief. 'Alex and I had plans for the future.'

'You might have let me take Katie out of the house.' Grant turned to look at her. 'I would have been discreet. I wouldn't have interfered.'

'I couldn't jeopardize the operation.' Suzanne said defiantly. 'And I couldn't say anything to Alex. To warn him. He and his father had

306

opposing political views, but Alex would not have wanted his father to be killed.'

'I still think you were misguided. You should have let me save Katie. And I think you could have warned Alex at the last minute.'

'It was just too important. You said yourself that they had to be stopped. And you were right. At any cost.'

'Well,' said Grant shortly. 'You certainly stuck your neck out. The BfV is like the CIA. Political assassination is prohibited. Especially in one's own country. Let's just hope that you did the right thing. And,' Grant paused for emphasis, 'your explanation of a gas leak is accepted.'

'The official explanation will show that a massive build up of gas in the cellar could cause such an explosion.'

'That explanation might be questioned.'

'Maybe. But it will be hard to disprove.'

'It was still a drastic decision.'

'We just couldn't take the risk.' Suzanne looked at him imploringly. 'The risk of Germany starting another war. Otto and Marshall were determined that their homeland should be returned to Germany. They would have sent troops into Poland. We couldn't allow that to happen.'

'Very difficult,' said Grant, now with a condescending expression. 'If the Kaiser and Hitler had been assassinated in time, two world wars might have been prevented. I suppose a sacrifice now may be seen to be worthwhile, to save millions later.'

'That's how we saw it.' Suzanne nodded her head and sniffed into her handkerchief again. 'The basic operation had been planned for months and had to be modified several times. The bomb in the house at the end was my idea. We couldn't think of anything better. Something had to be done before the next state election.'

'So how did it all start?'

'Katie will have told you about her ancestral home and that it was destroyed and the family treasures looted?'

'Of course,' said Grant. 'Including the Titian.'

'The perpetrators were agents of the STASI, led by two brothers, Oskar and Stefan Schimonsky. They executed several estate workers, including the husband of the old retainer, Frau Weber, who was going to testify about the painting.'

'Katie told me that Frau Weber died suddenly,' said Grant. 'Before her testimony could be documented.'

'We believe that Maxwell was responsible for Frau Weber's death.'

'Makes sense,' Grant agreed.

'Frau Weber's son, Detlef, was out for revenge. He got to know the identity of Stefan. He contacted a friend, who happened to be one of our agents. He passed him on to another agent in London, who assisted Detlef to kill Stefan. The agent then managed to convince Detlef that the other brother was Otto Hauswald.'

'Which he wasn't?'

'No. You can guess who was really Oskar Schimonsky?'

'Of course. Marshall Maxwell.'

'We only intended to assist Detlef to kill Otto, but in the end he got Marshall as well.'

'Achieving his objective.'

'We had intended Detlef to be the scapegoat. He died in the explosion as well and so we will have to fall back on the excuse of a gas leak.'

'Maybe a better outcome for you,' said Grant.

'I lost two agents as well,' Suzanne continued. 'One of which I had brought back from America. I shall have to inform their families.'

'Not an easy thing to do. So the leader and the benefactor of the NDVP are gone. Can the party survive?'

'Maybe,' said Suzanne, 'but I do not see them winning any more state elections in the near future. Maybe they will find another leader with the same charisma as Otto. What we have gained is time. The European Union has pursued integration too quickly. There is so much history, so much entrenched ethnicity to be overcome. I would not be surprised if it went the other way.'

'You mean that the European Union might break down?'

'Not in the way the NDVP intended. But I can see a return to basics. Back to what the European Union was originally intended to be. That is, a trading agreement. The next ten years will be very interesting.'

Grant and Suzanne then looked up in utter astonishment to see two figures emerging from the smoke of Schlossgasse.

#

'It's a lovely ring,' said Angela, pouring out the wine. 'I think engagement rings should always be diamonds. So when is the big day?'

'We haven't decided yet. We might even fly to Vegas for a quickie.'

'Make sure you invite me.' Angela sniffed and searched for a handkerchief. 'I shall really miss you.'

Katie reached over and took her hand. 'And I will miss you.'

'So what happened in Germany? It sounds really scary.'

'I had a lucky escape. I was invited to this party. Alex's grandmother. Anyway, Alex was there and said the party was too boring and we could go back to his house, just up the street and finish the painting.'

'Good excuse to have sex, of course,' said Angela. 'Much more interesting.'

'Anyway, a half hour later there was this enormous bang. Most of the windows shattered.'

'Oh my God! That must have been *really* scary.'

'We had no idea what had happened. Our first thought was that a bomb had dropped in the market square. We decided to stay put, in case there was going to be another one. Hunkered down under the duvet.' Katie sighed. 'It was wonderful, all warm and cosy and cuddled up and feeling safe, with that mayhem going on outside.'

'And to have sex again.'

'Er, yes, we did, actually. So, there was such a commotion. Sirens and flashing lights. The windows overlooked the courtyard, so we couldn't see anything in the street. Then Alex thought it might have been a gas leak.'

'Which it was?'

'Apparently. We were frightened that there might be another explosion. After about an hour or so we decided it would be safe to go outside and see what had happened. We were devastated. Alex's grandmother's house was just a smouldering shell.'

'Katie. How awful. You could have been there.'

'Everybody at the party died.'

'My God!' Angela reached over and took Katie's hand. 'Lucky old you.'

'Fate,' said Katie, in a matter of fact tone. 'It's time to move on. I've had enough of Germany. And the rest of Europe, come to that.'

'So when are you going?'

'Soon.'

'And the house?'

'I'm leaving it as a base for the boys. Jonathan finishes university soon and Paul's job in Hong Kong is only temporary.'

'So what's the plan?'

'Grant and I are buying a house in Naples. His apartment is too small.'

'Nice house?'

'It's in Port Royal. There are artificial canals, so we have a boathouse.'

'Can I come and visit?'

'Whenever you like.'

'Ladies and gentlemen, thank you for coming to witness this important day in the history of the Metropolitan Museum of Art. As you may remember, The Death of St Peter Martyr, by Titian, disappeared from an auction house in Manhattan and a copy was substituted. After a tip-off, the original was discovered in a warehouse in the Bronx. The seller of the painting has since died and the court has decided that the rightful owner is the Countess von Arnitz, from whose family home this painting was looted after the second world war.

We are extremely honoured and grateful that the Countess has decided to give the painting to the museum.'

Katie now unveiled the painting to loud applause.

'Very pleased that you could be here, Bill,' said Grant, at the reception later.

'Thank you for coming.'

'You're welcome,' said Bill. 'I wanted to be at the final instalment.'

'I suppose it was your idea?' said Grant with a smile.

'I'm really quite proud of it,' Bill admitted. 'Ever since your original investigation of Maxwell, Grant, we had been keeping an eye on him. Sources told us that he was going to sell the Titian. We suspected he was going to use the funds illegally, although, at the time, we were not sure what for. So we commissioned Alex to do the copy. It took him about a year.'

'But the painting was in Marshall's vault,' said Katie.

'Marshall thought it was,' said Bill. 'He didn't know it was in the studio we had set up for Alex.'

'But if I hadn't noticed it was a fake?'

'Alex was there at the auction. He would have owned up. He would have given the same excuse that he gave to his father and Marshall. That he copied it some time ago when the painting was in Weimar. And then he sold it to an anonymous collector.'

'So, Alex was working for us?' said Grant. 'I had guessed.'

'We recruited him when he was at art school in Baltimore,' said Bill. 'He resented his father's fascist politics. He wanted to try and redress the balance.'

312